Prologue

Have you ever lit a match?

When I was a kid, I used to play this gaı

More like a necessity.

After Mum and Dad had gone to bed, I went downstairs, making sure to wide-step over the creaky floorboard, and into the living room. Then I'd push the armchair over to the shelves at the side of the room, climb on top, and reach to the very top shelf to find the book of matches. They came upstairs with me into my room, where I'd open the window, sit on the windowsill, and light them.

You start by raking the match down the strike paper, listening to the hiss of the head igniting, watching the smoke billowing out of the end like a head of steam. The red melts away into grey patches; leaving tiny drops of liquid before they turn to smoke. There's a flame-within-flame effect of the different layers of heat dancing with each other.

Then the flame trickles down the length of the match, humming as the triangle of fire advances down and delicately consumes the elements in its path.

And me, I'd hold onto that match for as long as I could. Until the flame reached out and touched my fingers. God, it was such a beautiful thing. As elegant and silent as it was destructive and malignant.

I wanted to have that one microsecond of connection with it. Even though it stung like hell.

I'd sit there well into the night, striking a match, watching it ignite, and staring into its heat and light as it made its journey to its demise at the hands of my fingertips- purposeless in power, but with power that was relentless.

A lot of things happened in my childhood, but for some reason, the thing I remember most is sat on that damn windowsill, night after night, playing with fire.

WHO'S GOT A MATCH?

By Kieran J Close

ACT ONE- IGNITION

One

The dialling tone was droning on and on, and my mind was whirring again.

Struggles. That's what was on the brain today. I'd struggled to get out of bed this morning, struggled to make it to work on time, struggled to hit targets set for me.

Life is just one great big struggle for power, I think.

There was a CLICK. I zoned back in.

"Please hold. We will connect you as soon as possible."

Hold music filled my ears again. *Little Lies* by Fleetwood Mac. Great song.

But why do people force themselves through struggles to be powerful?

Human brains, I guess, are designed to reward us when we show power. With a sugar lump of dopamine when we take out a rival. And some people just... I don't know, *enjoy* that power. To them, absolute control is one of the greatest thrills you can get in life. To them, animal instinct isn't to be fought.

Another CLICK. I zoned back in.

"Please hold. We will connect you as soon as possible."

But most people don't get a kick out of that anymore. They get it from Instagram likes or alcohol or gambling.

I don't get those kicks. I don't get many kicks.

Another louder CLICK. White noise. And then;

"Hello?"

"Hi, there," I kept my voice in the back of my throat, as quiet and calm as my anxiety would allow for. "I- I was wondering if I could possibly speak to Rupert Mills?"

"Yes, speaking."

"Aha," My voice jumped a little. You're meant to be a little cheeky with your clients at first, you know, show some personality. Well, that's what the other lads did.

So I continued, fake as fake.

"Of course, I fucking well knew that I was speaking to you already. What am I, stupid? Hahaha!"

The words bounced off the inside of the phone like talking to a stick of rock. No response.

Ah- wait. Introductions.

"Hi- hi Rupert, how you doing? It's Tom Percey calling from Benson and Fletcher. Just wondering, er, Rupert, who your insurance provider is?"

A long and protracted silence followed. It provoked me to keep talking.

"If, er, if you, er, don't mind me asking, that is?"

As you can probably guess from my fractured speech, power eluded me.

A sigh from the other end. "Is this about the Battersea storage facility? Because look, we're all up in arms about it. Now is not the time to be discussing anything. Sorry. Goodbye."

"WAIT-wait…" I blurted out the plea. A red flag on the trading floor.

"I'll, er, cut to the point, Rupert- this IS about the Battersea facility, yes. And I'll be the first to say, I genuinely am really sorry about it."

The word 'genuinely' always seems to work wonders for the others, no matter how insincerely they said it. It annoyed me. It *genuinely* annoyed me.

"You're not sorry at all, you clown," Rupert grunted. "Goodbye."

A click. *The other person has cleared.*

"No joy, eh?" a boorish voice from behind me.

I swivelled in my chair. The voice came from a tall and well-dressed man with a waxed quiff, sunbed tan, tiny green eyes, and a confident smile- a real reality TV star, just waiting to be noticed.

He seemed to be having a more boisterous conversation on the phone.

"Yeah, honestly, mate. Saturday was so loose. Went to Twicky, with the boys, you know? The boys, the lads, the men? Anyway, Jonesy only brought a stripper with us! No mate I know, no honestly, deadly serious, she was butters too mate, what a lad, know what I mean?"

He spoke with the received pronunciation of everyone in the Financial District of London. He was from money, and he knew it- he spoke before he thought, treated people how he liked and found humour in the misery of others.

This was my colleague. His name was Wrighty.

"Yeah, no, swear to god, mate, fully butters. Yeah, anyway- what were we talking about? Oh, yeah, so I can offer you that package for- let's say- twenty-two? And I'll throw in ten years theft and criminal damage. That'd set you back, I don't know- eleven G's? You'll do it? That's my boy, what a boy, what a lad! Legend mate, you won't regret it!"

He caught my eye and gave a wink.

"Yeah mate, I'll transfer you through to accounting, they'll complete everything, go through the T's and C's, blah blah blah. Yeah, you too. Have a good one."

He slammed the phone down, fist-pumping with a dustbin hand. "Rob," he hollered. "Rob!"

Across the room, a man dressed in a bottle green suit with a black tie and maroon brogues scuttled over. Rob always dressed outrageously well, perhaps to cover up the fact that his presence at work could be sometimes unclean.

"Well?" his voice was gentle.

"Got it. twenty-two thousand."

"Good," he said back, and then turned to leave.

No more conversation. None needed. He had a saying for his work interactions- be bright, be brief, be gone. This arrogance was completely in keeping with the way he exaggerated his importance, earned huge amounts of commission, had slept with most male models in London, and loved himself almost as much as Wrighty did.

Sadly, they were both part of my team.

As I picked up my phone to call the next of my leads my klutz hands dropped the phone, and he did a double-take. I sensed danger.

He strode over, dark eyes boring into me. He was short- only around five foot six, but his diminutive stature was more than compensated for by his piercing gaze. He was a good-looking guy, dark-skinned, angular Captain-America jaw, curly black hair. This made him even more intimidating.

He raised a shaped eyebrow. "Tom. How'd you get on with Motterson Scaife?"

My body shifted side to side in the desk chair.

"Erm, well, I spoke to Rupert-"

"Ah, yes, Rupert," Rob's voice gained a line of saccharine sweetness. "Rupert. Lovely chap. So, how much did you get?"

"I- I didn't sell."

"Interesting," he said slowly. "Come and have a quick chat with me outside, yes?"

He spun and left. I grabbed my head in my hands, trying for one damn second to regain a little control, away from all this noise, all these distractions, the bleeps and bloops and clicks and laughs and *oh, mate*'s and all the rest of it. This cacophony of false promises, glib charm, backstabbing.

"Don't worry mate. You'll get it."

His smug drawl pricked at my skin. It was hard not to let a spike of fearful personality come out in times of stress.

"Well, how do you do it?" my weird Northern accent croaked. "Like, how did you learn it? Did you get- like- a qualification, or something?"

Wrighty threw his head back and laughed uproariously, attracting the attention of another identikit teddy boy sat next to him.

"Did you hear that, Smithy? He asked if I had any qualifications! Mate, only qualification I've got is a BTech in fingering birds!"

They both laughed again at an unnecessary volume. My cheeks burned.

"TOM," Rob thundered from the door.

Two

It's funny, isn't it; the British pacing system. The pacing elite can walk at a competitive rate- the rest of us have to settle with the awkward half-jog, our strides too short or our co-ordination too poor or the beginnings of some severe neurological disease weighing down our feet and preventing us from walking alongside powerful.

I was, predictably, the latter, chasing Rob down the corridors of Benson and Fletcher as he stormed to the elevator.

"Rob. Please. Slow down. It's under control."

He wheeled. I braked, hard, tripping over my toes.

"Don't fucking tell me *it's uhnda cuntrowl*," he spat, a feeble impression of my accent. "Fucking Motterson Scaife, what were you *thinking*, it was in the palm of your hand, how did you manage to fuck it up?"

"Well, I…" I paused. "I- he wasn't interested."

I was a red-faced groveller now, to an ivory tower peer.

"Your chat stinks," he spat again. "I remember when we interviewed you. And you were giving me all this bollocks about your forecasting masters and all the rest, how you were some kind of go-getter. You've given us nothing back, Tom. We are losing big important contracts here, and it's because of you. I just don't get it. Wrighty's hitting his targets, isn't he? And the only qualification he's got is-"

"-a BTech in fingering birds. I know."

The pressure increased. Rob stepped forward, perfectly manicured eyebrows stretching up into his crown.

"Listen," his voice the most violent whisper I'd heard in months. "Don't start getting cocky with me, like that. There is no reason why you can't sell. And… if you can't improve, then we can't continue. Simple as that."

Indignation burned inside me.

"I've worked so hard for this," I said quietly. "I deserve a chance."

He studied me- eyes flicking from left, right, down, left, right, down, looking for a notch to crack my wall down. He was good at that.

"I get the impression you just don't know people," he said simply. "You can't talk to people, because you just don't have a clue about them."

In my badly fitting suit, with my hair that never looked cool, and my lack of knowledge of all things London and money and class and all the rest of it, I felt sick with shame. The kind of shame that walls off the world, that mutes you, turns you timid, colours you green with envy when faced with anyone with a shred of courage.

The feeling turned me tiny, and I began shrinking into the floor, my clothes drooping around me, barely big enough to fit over the heel of my shoe, as Rob walked across the lobby to the lift and tapped the elevator button. The chrome doors swung open, and he stepped in.

"So prove me wrong, yeah?"

A laugh thick with scorn followed, and the doors whirred shut.

His timing is just impeccable. Rob had this theatrical movement to him, entering and exiting everywhere he went like a stage to play on. Anyone else would have started the sentence, waited for an age for the elevator to arrive, and got an item of clothing stuck in the door. My clunkiness was so amplified by his Teflon capabilities.

Hot with shame, I slunk back into the trading room, ready to fuck up even more sales.

Three

"I mean, sure it was great. But four hundred euros? For one damn minute? Think about that, man. That must be the most lucrative job going, in the western world, full stop. And I bet she didn't go to... I don't know... business school, or anything, you know what I mean? I bet she doesn't have a masters, man, you know what I mean? I mean, God, think how little time it would take, for that woman to be a millionaire. *Literally* a millionaire! And we're here, slaving away, day in day out...you know what I'm saying? We're in the wrong fuckin' business, man!"

Wrighty was off his face. He'd been drinking since the moment we'd got out of work, and sniffing coke since, well, roughly 1:30 pm. It came as no surprise, then, that he was struggling to retain his composure somewhat.

"See, what they should do, hang on..."- he dug into his pocket, removed a Porsche key, and then began to fumble around in the top pocket of his suit jacket. His professional elegance was diminished; he was a lanky, awkward figure, with limbs that seemed far longer than they should from his slender torso. Eventually, he removed a bag with a scant amount of white powder in it, into which dipped his key and with an unsteady hand raised it towards his face. I watched as the contents disappeared up his nostril.

"What they should do, right," he went on, emboldened by my silence, "Is legalise it. Legalise all sex work, no red tape, nothing. So, people having a hard time, yeah, they come to us men in heat, yeah? Then they go home with a fat wad of cash and buy big fuck off houses in Hampshire. You get what I'm saying? Poverty's down, tourism's up, and every fat cat in the city is happier cos they're getting laid for once. You know what I mean, mate?"

I knew what he meant. He hadn't been in any way vague or cryptic in his plan for laying out a sex-fuelled plutocracy. The slight snigger in his voice said he was joking, but the hard, dead-set eyes said otherwise. Wrighty often said disgusting, shocking things, but recently they'd become more sinister.

"G-great idea, Wrighty," I stammered. "Perhaps forward that one to your, erm, local MP."

We were sat in the rooftop bar of the Mayfair Terrace in London. Wrighty had invited Jonesy for a drink, but he said he couldn't make it, and in need of some numbing agents I'd asked to join him. It was late May, and the sun was just beginning to dip in the sky, colouring the clouds a deep pink. The air was warm, and thick with the sound of a hundred conversations, buzzing away like static. Only a few hundred metres away, we heard Big Ben chime ten o' clock. A waitress stopped by the table.

"Good evening," she said with a rehearsed smile. "Any drinks for the table?"

"Yeah, two margaritas, sweetheart," Wrighty slurred, handing over a couple of twenty-pound notes. "Chop-chop."

The waitress tried and failed to hide her disgust.

"Excuse me?" she said incredulously.

"Sorry," I butted in quickly. "Could I please just have another whiskey?"

The waitress nodded, grimaced, and took her leave. Still smiling, he took out a pack of cigarettes, removed one, and offered the pack to me. "Ciggy?"

"No thanks," I said quickly. "Bad for you."

"The best things in life are bad for you, Tom," he quipped.

As he drew his Zippo lighter, I averted my eyes to the horizon, trying to focus on the colours and sounds as I heard the *clink, clink* of his lighter.

Don't think about it, don't think about it. Don't think about the fire.

"Let's just imagine, say, you bought some... I dunno, FELLA,"- Wrighty seemed to spit the word. "And you only lasted thirty secs before you blew your load in his bumhole. Would you not feel hard done by?" He relaxed back in his seat, seemingly confident in his questionable debating skills, and took a long drag. I winced as the tobacco flared.

"Come on, then," Wrighty beamed. "I'm just asking a simple question."

In my time in London- and the financial sector- I had learned that this method was how the elite got away with saying anything they wanted. Every word was objective. Questions were just questions. If someone else was to take offense, that was their problem. And it was the steadfast knowledge of this that kept characters like Wrighty as slippery as they were.

"Thanks for your interest," I said, trying not to look uncomfortable. "But I can't see myself being in that situation."

"But what if you were?" he continued, an underlying force in his words.

"Well, I..." I choked. "Well, I-"

"Oh, hey, darling? I think those are ours," he waved down the waitress, carrying two extravagant looking drinks. You don't buy a pint in central- you pay twenty pounds each for one measure each of spirit and simple syrup in a glass packed to the eyeballs with crushed ice.

"And what are those, er, flaming drinks? You know, the ones with fire on the top?"

This was bad news.

"Zombies," said the waitress dully.

"Two zombies, then, please," Wrighty peeled off another few twenties from his wallet and handed them over.

"Just another whiskey for me, please." I did *not* want a drink that was on fire.

"Oh, come on," Wrighty spread his arms wide in a weird, pissed-up weather reporter gesticulation. "Why are you such a pussy? Loosen up, it's only a drink. Two zombies, please and thank you."

She nodded and was gone. My fate had been sealed.

"So anyway, yeah," he blathered on, "still not heard anything back from Daniels and Becker, not a fucking thing, mate. Radio silence." He dug into his pocket again, searching for his powder. "That's a big one for me too, BIG commission... could be a full quarter's worth..."

I stopped listening after a sentence or so. I didn't need to. His monologues were only ever to himself, really- *The Wrighty Play*, if you like.

My brain slowly turning to mush through exhaustion and booze, I spotted two drinks were brought on a glass tray over to us.

"Two zombies? Here you go. One moment, please…"

She removed a blowtorch from her immaculately ironed apron and there was a harsh CLICK as she pushed the mechanism in, releasing the gas. The whirr of the butane filled the air, the stench of gas burning the edge of my nostril. Opening my eyes a crack, the passionfruit atop the drink was now alight, stood proud in the evening sepia.

Alcohol burns differently when it's on fire. I think I read somewhere that it's the alcohol vapour that catches alight, not the alcohol- hence that sort of 'floating flame' look. It looked like a ghost flame- translucent in its base, rising in a perfect isosceles triangle, gradually turning more and more opaque as it hits the point. I stared as it fluctuated between big and small, peaks and troughs of energy as it burned off into gas.

"Tom?"

Jerking myself back into the dimension of the living, my comrade was looking at me with mild concern.

"Why you just staring at it?" Wrighty asked quietly, now looking as though he wanted to make a bathroom break from which he'd never return.

"I- I just think it looks cool. I've not had one of these before."

His frosty gaze crystallised for a moment as he searched me. Luckily, it soon melted into relief, and evaporated into laughter.

"You've NEVER had one? Oh, mate, drink it up, yeah, it's so good, yeah?"

And so the slivery flame was begrudgingly blown out, the glass held to my lips.

As I took a swig, I smelled the smoke as it wisped off the top.

Four

I'd started my first fire when I was fifteen years old.

By that point, I'd been playing the match game for quite some time and had been itching to apply this strange chemistry of the elements to something else.

I would go to stay with my Dad on a weekend sometimes, up in Middlesbrough. He had an allotment close to his house, and in the summer, he'd spend half the day there, hacking at weeds that grew around his rhubarb and raspberries. One summer, there grew so many, his compost heap overflowed with them, and he'd nowhere to put the rest.

"Here's an idea," he'd said. "We'll lay them out in the sun, so they can dry out a little. Then tomorrow night, we'll come back here, put them on the paving slabs, and burn them."

I had *never* been more excited. The thrill of igniting the bonfire. The control of the immolation, the catalyst of the destruction. Could barely sleep that night.

But he never did take me.

The next day, I took the dog for a long walk near the river, and when I got back, my dad was nowhere to be seen. He'd left me a note in the kitchen:

Gone to the pub

Chicken dippers in the fridge

Back by tomorrow

Love Dad

Short, sharp, effective. Exactly how I would have written a letter to my own son if I'd abandoned burning dry grass in exchange for sociable drinks with friends.

But the younger me was heartbroken. He didn't dare do anything without daddy. But he really, *really* wanted to have that bonfire.

I remember pacing the living room, neurotic, trying to gather my thoughts- before I eventually grabbed the hob lighter out of a drawer and set off to the allotment on my own.

The sky was a vivid pink that night, just like it was tonight.

"Tom?"

I snapped back, my second drift in just a few minutes. Wrighty was staring at me again.

"Let's go back to mine," he snapped. "Rob will come too. Come on."

He was at it again: God, I hated his unpredictability. The belligerence of drinking and cocaine was making Wrighty unstoppable. And he wanted Rob to attend.

Nah. Fuck that.

A thousand and one refusals swam through my mind, but my tongue froze, and before I knew it, we were leaving; Wrighty already bellowing down the phone excitedly to our colleague.

"Yeah, mate, Amsterdam was so sick," he said. "Got this girl though, yeah, from the district, cost me four hundred euros! For one damn minute! Think about that, man. That must be the most lucrative job going, in the western world, full stop…"

The path wasn't quite wide enough for us both to walk side by side, and as such, I had to trail behind Wrighty by about a foot, as he chose to converse with his other friend instead of me. He went on and on, laughing and laughing down the phone, as I walked silently behind, detached.

"John Wright, you're literally such a whore," Rob was chirping over the other end of the phone, the speakerphone covering his voice in tinfoil. "Mucky. Mucky, mucky, horrible man."

Rob was so different outside of work. For one, he and Wrighty were actually friends. They went for drinks together, went to the races, casinos, tailors. And they spoke with disinhibition on the outside. But oh, no, when in work, you had to be cut from the cloth, you had to be prim and proper…

Yeah. Moments like this tended to bother me. My jaw clenched and unclenched, that quiet anger consuming me, fuelled by whatever trivial event it could get its hands on. They were perfect pretenders. And, if you couldn't pretend, you were run ragged.

I hated how it was better to be fake than real down here. God, I hated it.

Five

A few of the main lines had shut early tonight due to strikes or something, so we ambled back through Limehouse to get the tube back to his.

Picking our way through the five storey Victorian terraces, Wrighty continued to drink copiously from a hip flask in his inside jacket pocket, and occasionally stop to enthusiastically snort another dab of his nose candy. He talked on and on, mainly about money, women, and fucking people over. Ordinary life just didn't have enough shimmer for him to find it interesting, and as such, he took lots of drugs, slept with lots of women, and spent money like water.

"On a scale of strong to smelly," he said loudly, causing a colony of nearby bats to flap away. "How would you rate Big Neil's chat?"

Now *that* is one of the great questions of our time. On a graduated range of values, starting and ending with adjectives that aren't used to describe conversation, how would I measure conversation with Big Neil?

A lot to unpack here. Perhaps Wrighty was too much of an intellectual for me.

"I think," I replied, after a lot of deliberation, "that sometimes he thinks it's strong, when really…it's smelly?"

Wrighty laughed, again so loudly that a fox sprinted out of the undergrowth and across the path. "Strong, strong," he said. "Doesn't have a clue, does he. Remember that other day, his whole sob story about the Montserrat thing? Pongy chat, mate, serious pongy chat, know what I mean?"

And so, he went on, and on, and on, alternating between talking to me at an unnecessary volume and talking on the phone to Rob at an unnecessary volume.

Every single little thing that he said, the volume and slowness of his words, his nastiness, his pomp, grated more and more on me.

And slowly, it began to itch. *Really* itch.

Ah, that bonfire. How it grew and grew and got hot and heavy. Hoo-hah! What a thrill that was.

We cut down a little back road, littered, smashed glass on the floor. Wasn't this a little rough for Limehouse...? People here named their poodles things like Coco Chanel.

On the corner stood the Midspeak Hippodrome, some theatre I'd been dragged to by an old flame to watch some shitty satire about Watergate. It was, like anything else here, full of people who had their work cut out battling to sound like the most knowledgeable person in the room. Its towers and lights looked pompous themselves as we walked down the side of it past a fire escape.

"What's this?" Wrighty paused by the door; it was slightly ajar. He peered at me with his psycho eyes.

I said nothing. Taking this as compliance, he nudged the door and it swung open.

"Oh *dear,*" he muttered, his mock sorrow making me feel sick, "now that is just *careless.*"

He entered. I followed him into a kitchen- a little catering annex of the theatre, presumably. It was cold, dark- a dull shimmer of stainless steel on the sinks and surfaces. It smelt of bleach but there was something else here- a musty smell. A neglected smell.

He walked slowly, the streetlight shining through the door onto his back, as he advanced further and further down his path, away from safety. As he turned to check back, there was a hint of a baleful smile on his face.

No, Wrighty, I wanted to say. No, Wrighty, we're not allowed. We need to get out, now. We can't do this, this is wrong, this is wrong. Stop, Wrighty, please, please stop. The words whizzed around my head like a Scalextric.

He stopped suddenly- mid-stride, head cocked, nose forward like a hunting dog. Turning slowly, he raised a finger to his lips. "Wait here," he mouthed.

I obeyed. My fourth act of silence. I'd chosen the side of the oppressor. My oppressor. And now once again I was complicit, pathetic, spineless, out of control. *Always* out of control.

My finger, which had idly been running along the countertop, mind lost in its own destruction, hit something. Not sharp, but- rough?

I squinted, trying to see into the pitch black. Both hands now, fingertips and palms scanning. One hand hit a circular dial. My eyes adjusted; I could see what it was now. A hob.

Oh. Oh. Uh-oh.

It's a strange thing, going back to an addiction. The rational part of your brain- you know, the part that gets you into work, irons your clothes, and writes *Kind Regards* at the end of every email- it tells you, again and again; no, no, no. Stop. Stop it. This isn't a good idea. You'll regret it. Stop. STOP.

Oh. Oh. Oh yeah.

I had to satiate my curiosity. And my curiosity pushed down on the knob and twisted it counterclockwise. Sure enough, there was a hiss as natural gas escaped out into the room.

A rush hit me, my head span, my heartbeat so fast.

Boomboomboomboomboomboom.

I felt like laughing, it could be my night tonight, it could be my lucky night, oh boy-

-oh, you're going to do it, lad, you're not leaving this room til you-

There was a crash from the corridor Wrighty had come from. And then what sounded like a scream.

Abort, my rational brain said, ABORT.

But now the other part of my brain was speaking. Yes, that old lizard part, that acts impulsively, that shows no rationale, that thrives only on what feels good here and now- it says yes. Oh, go on, why not. You know you want to.

And it's that part of your mind that was controlling my eyes. My limbs. My mouth. My plans. And right now, a plan was forming, so quickly and so perfectly irrational I had simply no power to stop it.

I left the hob on.

The bumps and clangs from the corridor grew louder. A shadowy mass emerged, four-legged, lurching.

"Dude, let me go. Please. Let me go, man…"

The voice didn't belong to Wrighty.

"Mate. Please. I can't breathe."

Six

"Look what I got," Wrighty yelled. He had someone in a chokehold. "Stupid fucking tramp tried to jump me."

He threw the other human to the ground, the pale light just illuminating him. His captive was small, with a beanie hat, a black denim jacket, and combat trousers. He looked haggard, with that blank, desperate stare of someone who'd spent too long without shelter or food.

And he had Chelsea smile scars on his face. Big ones. He clutched tightly to a little glass bottle, half-hidden in his coat pocket. His face was fear.

"Look, man, I'm sorry," he slurred in a thick Northern accent. "Just leave me alone. I'll, I'll…"

"You'll do what?" Wrighty's laugh rasped, steel malice in his throat. "Let me piss on you?"

The man tried to stand. Wrighty gave a wail of rage and indignation, and aimed a punch at the figure, knocking him to the floor.

In his hand, to my horror, there was a blade, a little flick-knife.

"You stay there. You stay there, you pikey, or I'll fucking cut you."

In the shadows of his eyes, I could see a warped thrill- a god complex, a sense of achievement, a grandiose righteousness. With another smirk, he turned and began to fiddle with his trousers.

"Wrighty-" for all I tried to shout, my voice was weak. "Wrighty. Don't-"

He ignored me. His insistent eyes went back to his prey.

A sound of unzipping flies. I heard whimpers from the man.

Do something, Perce, do something-

"Open your mouth, you scruffy little twat," Wrighty hissed. My ache was so awful now, a train ploughing through my mind and bones, but I was powerless, powerless without flame.

The tramp's whimpers amplified. I saw his unwilling mouth open.

DO SOMETHING. DO SOMETHING. DO SOMETHING-

My jaw hung, a screech at the back of my throat-

"POLICE!"

I managed to squeeze out the frog in my throat to rasp an exclamation. Just in time.

And it had the desired effect- a moment of confusion from my colleague allowed my new friend to slip out from his position. But he wasn't quite quick enough.

Wrighty did a double-take, and he aimed another punch at him. Another right hook felled him, and then a flurry of kicks fell upon his body. I heard him exhale with a growl, the Harrow educated twenty-something back to his old animal ways. With a satisfied sigh and an odd smile, he began to piss in the corner of the room.

"Oh Collingwood, is wonderful," he sang, the slapping of his urine against the floor audible. "It's full of beer, tits, and rugby..."

I felt my ache worsen still, pulling at my skin until it was tearing right off the bones.

The man began to stagger towards me, his limbs swaying wildly in the dark. I took a step back, my body tensing up. There was an odour of chemical. The ache worsened even more.

From the smell, it seemed like some kind of cheap white spirit, the strongest and most damaging alcohol a man could buy, one that offered no real enjoyment or disinhibition, just a comfortable distance and numbness from the real world. The kind of thing the homeless of London sometimes drank to gain respite from the cold and discomfort.

Spirits such as these tend to be highly, highly flammable.

Oh, wooowwweeeee. Hoo-hah! It was all coming into place.

I reached into my pocket and let the palm of my shaking hand brush against the strike paper of the book of matches. My ache was crippling now but my mind was illuminated, a thousand thoughts, a million, getting brighter and brighter-

"Wait," my voice came out very softly as the man tried to nudge past me to the exit. I tugged the bottle from his grip and inhaled- it was spirits alright, the gentle acridity seeping into my skull. My ache was so bad now I could feel my skeleton trying to dance its way out of my flesh; I was dissociating hard; everything looked small, I could feel my head swell bigger and bigger and bigger, bigger than the theatre, bigger than fucking London...

"Can I- can I keep this?"

The man looked at me. His face was soft and kind besides the scars, young looking, dark eyebrows and thick hair and stubble and crazy bright blue eyes. Handsome.

"Now," I whispered. "Run."

"What?"

"Run," I said again, simply. I was past the point of no return, numbed by the ache, fizzing with the static of mania, oblivious to everything but the task I had set myself, bloody-minded, flame-bodied…

"Oh, Collingwood is wonderful…."

I reached into my pocket, pulled out a piece of paper I'd written a to-do list on earlier, and scrunched it into the neck of the bottle.

And then I grabbed my book of matches and struck one.

You know, it's funny how some moments pass very slowly indeed.

I held it up to my eyes, just like I used to do at Dad's; transfixed as the red phosphorus oxidised into white phosphorus, and then its beauty as it ignited- its heat so intense for a tiny thing, its power ridiculous for something not alive nor sentient. My excitement was hitting screaming point, I touched the flame to the paper-

At that second, I glanced up. The man was still there. He was watching it too, with the same kind of expression as me.

Just as the paper began to burn, I caught a glimpse of a memo I'd made earlier that day. The memo simply said *Buy Popcorn.*

It flittered, the edges curling and blackening, the bright blue flame pulling in shades of green as it hit the ink. I'd planned to spend tonight watching *Father Ted*- undoubtedly the greatest British sitcom- and eating junk food.

As the final remnants of my handwriting wilted away, I wondered what would have happened if I'd just gone home.

The flame took hold, blaze suddenly accelerating.

"RUN," I said louder, through gritted teeth. The man did not move. He stared at it, god, his eyes were so blue, blue and empty like the sea-

"What are you looking at?" It took all my effort not to scream at him. "Run!"

And then I threw the bottle. Hard as I could, bending my knees, swinging my arm back far as it would go, and catapulting it toward the back of his head. The bottle twisted a few times, the alcohol engulfing the flame, turning it into a cylinder of fire.

"Wrighty," I shouted, albeit weakly. "Watch out."

Wrighty span round, dick in hand. The bottle missed and smashed into the wall beside him.

Now, Molotov cocktails- as my cheaply fashioned version could be called- are a crude yet effective means of ignition. When the bottle smashes, the ensuing cloud of fuel droplets and vapour is ignited by the attached wick- or, in my case, popcorn memo- causing an immediate fireball followed by spreading flames as the remainder of the fuel is consumed.

And that's when the gas ignited. Yes, the gas from the stove. See how it all fell into place, in the end, eh?

The fireball was immediate, its damage swift- the kitchen disappeared into a white heat, bubbles of lava and crinkles of gas popping all around me. It's really happening, it's really happening- I was floating, king of the world, looking down on my own carnage-

"SHIT," I heard Wrighty scream, face on fire. "SHIT!"

Some subconsciousness must have pulled my body out of the exit because I was out in the alley again, lungs on fire, heaving and coughing. The man was still there. He simply looked at the blaze, lost, happy. He welcomed it.

"Mate," I coughed, doubling over, all my energy spent on inhaling the night air. "Mate. Get out of here. Get out of here!"

He stood for a second, a faraway look in his eyes, admiring, reflecting. Then, without a second's notice, he finally took off, dashing down the path, his jacket billowing behind him.

A bawl erupted from the exit. A figure appeared- charred, aghast, melting like a wax model. Wrighty was pulling off his clothes, fast as he could, whilst trying to cup his singed balls, smoke billowing off his thousand-pound suit, now in tatters on the ground.

"WHAT THE FUCK HAPPENED," he screamed at me, "WHAT THE FUCKING HELL HAPPENED?"

I could see the rage in his face as he stood, lit, naked. I raised my arm and pointed at the running man, whose life I was about to ruin. Wrighty's face contorted further.

"THAT FUCKING TRAMP!" he squealed, his voice cracking even more. "THAT FUCKING TRAMP SET ME ON FIRE!"

I could barely hear him now. In the depths of Limehouse, I watched that big, beautiful blaze climb through the building, crackling and swooshing as it grew and grew at an exponential rate.

I had succumbed. I'd lit a match.

Seven

I should probably tell you a little bit more about myself before I go on. I'm a twenty-six-year-old man living in London, although I'm originally from the Tees Valley region. I refer to the area, when anyone asks, as 'up north'- after all, who needed specifics when apparently nothing exists outside of the M20 to Londoners.

My favourite food is the chicken parmo, and my favourite film is *Ferris Bueller's Day Off.* My favourite soft drink is Fanta Fruit Twist. My favourite smell is honey. My favourite band is Fleetwood Mac, and my favourite song by them is *Everywhere*, the fifth track from the 1987 album *Tango in the Night*. It's euphoric, relaxing, super-slick, everything a perfect pop song should be.

But its experimental nature shows a different side of the band. One of them descending into chaos, disarray, addiction, alienation to the confusing world of power ballads and electronic drum sets. And yet it is all heavily glossed over with a golden sheen.

I had been listening to this song on repeat for the last two hours or so. I sat on my balcony, watching out over London. From my 28th floor flat on the Carpenters estate in Stratford, I could just make out a little black plume of smoke over near Limehouse. I'd just been sat watching the unstoppable cyclone of smog, imagining the panic of the emergency services, the horror of bystanders, the struggle to control an element not designed by God to be controlled. The fire had taken such a hold that it had all but destroyed the hippodrome, every little inch of its gold-painted, red-curtained pretentiousness burnt to smithereens.

Oh, and another thing about me; I like to set fires.

My head still felt big. Big from all the thoughts- it needed to swell to accommodate them, I reasoned. The glass in my hand seemed so tiny, the whole balcony pixelated and toy-like. Perspective was dulled- perhaps if I reached out into the distance, I could scoop up the combustion in the palm of my hand. It would be tiny in my grasp, and I would eat the burnt chaos whole, and then swallow it, washing it down with a cool mouthful of fruit twist. And then I'd go about my daily business, belly full of charred antimatter…

My phone buzzed. 'John Wright' appeared on the screen. Tapping the little green circle, I held it to my ear, hand numb.

"Wrighty," I said simply.

"Perce," I heard a croak from the other end of the line. "Percy."

Oh, yes, of course- my name is Thomas Percy. And yes, I hated that surname.

"How are you?" My gaze did not waver from the smoke. I knew exactly how he was- following the incident he'd taken off all his clothes, ran down the street, and leapt into a nearby fountain, screaming and massaging his singed tackle. This was to be an image I'd struggle to forget.

"Sore. They discharged me this morning though. All first-degree burns."

I took a long, slow deep breath in through the nose, and out through the mouth.

"Great."

"How are you?" he said.

I was caught off guard by that. He never asked how I was. The pixels intensified, the thick, black smoke engulfing my vision for a microsecond. Everything went fizzy.

"Couldn't sleep," I replied.

"Me neither. Are you still going to work today?"

"Yeah."

"Okay," he sounded, for a second, like his voice was breaking. "But, uh, listen mate. What are we going to say to people at work?"

I had, luckily, had a full sleepless night to consider this.

"We? You need to stay off."

"I want the money," his voice, shaken with pain, was still firm.

Oh, god. He really was coming in.

"Well…I would rather if we kept it all quiet for now," I said, voice deader than the seats and stalls now destroyed by the blaze. "I still feel a little shaken from it all, truth be told."

I finished my fruit twist and set it down. I hadn't been able to taste it.

"Do you mind, John? Just not saying anything, while the dust settles?"

There was a pause at the end of the line. "Yeah. Yeah, mate. Definitely."

I turned back towards the smoke. "Good," I said. "Thank you, Wrighty."

After the fountain episode, Wrighty had called the police, and we'd duly sat in the back of a van for around an hour whilst they spoke to us. He'd explained hurriedly that he'd been attacked by a fire-wielding rough sleeper, emphatically repeating that he'd 'set me on fucking fire' and showing them his charred dick.

I'd sat and stared, absent-mindedly, into the bright sterile light above me in the van. Luckily for me, my voice was hoarse from the smoke, which seemed to give them the impression of vulnerability. The officers had sat forward, concerned, stern but kind, hanging on my every word.

I told them he'd mugged me, and that I'd heard a smash and saw the fire start. I gave them a description of the poor bloke, probably hiding in a squat somewhere now, not knowing the shit that was coming his way. I allowed myself sniffles, croaks, let my sentences purposefully abate. Shock paralyses the mind- I must be rather good at replicating it.

And that was it. No cross-examination, no arrests, no suspicions. Even though we were, quite literally, at the scene of the crime. As it turns out, being articulate and well-dressed seems to make you semi-invulnerable in the eyes of the law.

Eight

I walked through Maryland's dilapidation. I could smell the smoke and wisps of it flew atop the rooves. Everywhere the sense of panic was cultivating.

Groups gathered outside the front doors, whispers and chatters of the nameless threat, kids pointing, mothers talking amongst each other, frantically checking their phone screens.

I strolled, bag on my back, tie in a double Windsor, breathing the smoke in like it was a bracing sea breeze. I was listening, again, to *Everywhere.*

Wrighty was already at the station. He lived over in Knightsbridge but had asked to meet me at Stratford to get the tube into work. This was weird. I tried for a moment to consider what the incident may have done to him, but, for all my effort, I could not.

From a distance he looked okay, hair slicked back, Oxford shirt squeezed around his broad shoulders. But as I drew closer, he looked fraught. He was red, and I could see plasters on his hands, and a blister under his collar. He did not look up as I approached.

"Hey, buddy," I said. "You ok?"

"The cream isn't working," he scowled. "I've been using these instead."

Opening his briefcase, he showed me a small bottle of aloe vera and a much larger bottle of canola oil. In the warm humidity of the morning, he smelt like a stir-fry. He stood up carefully, wincing as he did so, a shadow of the cocksure misogynist he was less than twelve hours ago.

"Do you think it's, like, done any damage?" he gingerly adjusted his trousers.

"The fire? I guess quite a lot. From what I could see, anyway."

"No, I mean, do you think it's damaged my cock?"

I didn't reply. Mercifully, the tube had arrived.

We sat in silence together. My head still felt big, so big it hurt- still a million conversations in my mind, bustling around like commuters. And every single one getting stuck in the little corridors. They piled up, causing congestion, damage.

We alighted at Canary wharf, dim and melancholy, full of steel. Normally, I'd force myself to stand in the packed-out front of the train with the other psychopaths in three-pieces, as they muttered about getting ready to GO, getting ready to TAKE ON THE DAY, gnashing their teeth in anticipation.

Today, the people were just little shapes. Little plastic spheres and sticks clacking their way towards their next destination. The tube does things to your mind, I think. The claustrophobia of a pressurised tube with a thousand strangers, all thinking their own little weird thoughts.

When you come out of the underground the sunlight is dazzling-the pavement in London is so shiny from the constant wear and tear of soles and souls that the sun bounces right off it. You wince, trying to navigate in between the masses whilst shielding your eyes. This is, again, something you never really get used to. I walked with Wrighty down the path, both our eyes cast down, heading to work. As I glanced sideways to him, he looked composed enough, but his eyes were grey, his brow furrowed, his face as ashen, I assumed, as the remnants of the Midspeak.

Benson and Fletcher was a curious-looking building in the Wharf. It had been built to impress, to stand out amongst the skyscrapers and the iconic architecture of the city. As it was, it looked more like a comprehensive school that had been academized, in the hope that a quasi-futuristic new look would improve grades. It was painted a dazzling, titanium white, with a curved exterior and huge glass panes from top to bottom, with thick black rims.

Rob was waiting outside for us. He was dressed in a bottle green suit with a black tie and maroon brogues. He always dressed outrageously well, perhaps to cover up the fact that his presence at work could be sometimes unclean.

"Alright, lads," he said softly. "Been starting fires in Limehouse, have we?"

My brain fired off currents of electricity in a desperate attempt to think up a story. My teeth ground against each other, my tongue all dry and minging like a snake in my massive alien moon head.

"I, er. No, no we haven't. No. No, no. No, no, no, no. No."

Robs dark eyes bored into me.

"You alright?"

"Yeah, yeah, yeah. Oh, yeah. Definitely. Yeah. All good, yeah."

He shifted his glance to Wrighty. "You okay, John?"

Wrighty appeared to be breathing rather heavily. "Yes, boss. Ready to take on the day."

He tried to stretch his haggard face into a grin, but the effort seemed too much- not a moment after, he turned to his left, crouched down, and began to vomit copiously all over the pavement. Rob stared at him. I could hear him sigh to himself. "What's up with him?"

"He's fine," I said. "Just too many mojitos."

"Huuuuuuuuuurghhh," he retched. "Huuuuuuuuuuuuurrrghhh."

The vomit spilled down the pristine pavement, carving a line between us and him. A particularly violent heave sent specks of spew flying onto Rob's shiny shoes.

"Oh, for fucks sake," Rob's voice raised in pitch to a near squeal as he flicked his foot back, trying to avoid more debris. "These are *Versace*."

We stood for a few moments in silence, watching the king of the shop floor commit dry heave after dry heave, until he simply hunched next to the door, shaking. A few three-pieces walked by us, stepping over the sick, throwing us concerned looks.

"So, erm," Rob made a stab at conversation. "What did you, um....DO last night?"

Nine

"You've seen the news, then?" Rob was not breaking stride. The shop floor was chaos. The buzz in the hive was far louder than normal, the rattle of keyboards almost tuned out by the din of overexcited brokers. The usual clean and conformity of the floor was shot- the pristine blue carpet was torn up by shoes, the gleaming white tiled walkways muddied. The high, white ceilings seemed lower for the cramp. The news reports were drowned out by the din, the message board flicking from number to number at an unprecedented rate.

"Yeah. Hard to miss it."

There was a wide-eyed pandemonium in the air today; every man and woman had a strange smile on their face as they chattered excitedly on the phones. Words like 'opportunity' and 'solution' perpetuated the air as they closed in on their targets with words like birds of prey, bending the invisible client on the other end of the phone.

"Well," he said breathlessly, cutting in and out of the desks, "insurance prices are rocketing. Pinker Graves up one point four," he was saying excitedly. "ONE POINT FOUR! Like, are they serious? One point four, man!"

The world of insurance is strange. When people worry, they spend their cash. They fritter it away on things to keep them safe and secure from the enemy- whatever that is. They buy cold remedies and hand sanitizer to keep the winter viruses at bay. They buy burglar alarms and CCTV to keep the seedy underbelly of the city from disturbing their everyday life. They drink CBD oil to numb the aches, pains, and low mood caused by their stressful, underpaid jobs. Luxuries become necessities when humans are faced with anxiety.

And when insurance companies make a shit ton of money, oh ho… their share prices go up. And when shares shift like that, stockbrokers make cash. Simple as that. The energy suddenly made sense to me.

The money was from chaos.

"But…wait," I said suddenly "Fires happen in London every day. Why the sudden hike?"

Rob raised a carefully shaped eyebrow. "Have you REALLY seen the news?" he said, pulling out his phone. "You've seen the arsonist, right?"

My stomach fell through the floor. They knew it was arson. I held out a quivering hand to receive Rob's phone- there was a news article open on it.

Blaze at Midspeak Hippodrome under investigation

Dozens of firefighters spent hours tackling a fire at the Midspeak Hippodrome theatre at Limehouse, in Central London.

The blaze was first reported to authorities at 00:38 GMT. No fatalities have been reported.

About 70 firefighters and 10 fire engines from the surrounding area brought the fire under control by 07:14, the London Fire Brigade said.

The cause of the fire is being investigated.

"Look, look at this," Rob was at his computer now, frantically trying to plug earphones into his desktop jack. "People are going mad over it."

His PC monitor showed a BBC news stream playing. The tagline at the bottom read;

MIDSPEAK HIPPODROME BLAZE: A TARGETED ATTACK?

I fumbled with the headphones and stuck them in my ears, pressing them in hard so I could hear the news report above the din.

"The reports of a fire at the prominent Midspeak Hippodrome in London is having a profound and sustained effect on members of its community," a serious-looking news reporter was saying. "A long-held and often controversial establishment historically belonging to the Pinks of London, the theatre was a prominent holding point for the Eindhoven meetings, a gathering of some of the world's most powerful and influential individuals, to discuss finance and megatrends. Built in 1709, the Midspeak is a prominent part of the local architecture and has seen many monarchical visitors during its time. Unlike most commercial theatres, it holds a strict members-only policy. But today, this slice of history is, quite literally, up in flames."

The report cut to a grainy CCTV image and my stomach lurched. It was my friend from the other night.

"Police are looking for a white male in his twenties, wearing dark clothing and with distinctive scars on his face, seen leaving the area shortly after the fire was reported. We spoke to the owner of the estate, Miss Lola Pink, who had this to say;"

A voice recording. The tone was plummy behind the crackles and clips of the telephone.

"It would seem that some in this society would seek to hurt those who have done well for themselves," the voice scorned. "I do not doubt in my mind that this was targeted, I do not doubt in my mind that this was a statement against people like myself. It is merely a matter of envy why some people would seek to destroy the wealth of others, and envy is a vice that we should not tolerate."

"BBC news," the reporter rounded off, "London."

The video cut. On to the next news story. Some viral pandemic in Wuhan. I pulled out the earphones; Rob was still talking at me, bubbling with figures and prices and names. The background static of a hundred voices gabbling over money. Shaking, I stood up and looked out at the floor.

So that was it. The super-rich were running scared. They thought it was an attack on them. They wanted to play it safe. They were buying their safety. I mean, it *wasn't* an attack on them, oh God no, but-

This is all you, my real voice said in my head.

Sometimes you forget your real voice.

When you are an adult, and you have to get by in the real world, you get used to putting on voices. Voices of reason, voices of authority, voices of charm. But sometimes you just forget what that real voice sounds like.

The voice that reminds you who you really are.

The shy part of you, the strange part of you, the manic part of you.

The part of you that harbours the darkness and the love of smoke and flame.

And that part of me spoke again;

This is all you. This really is all you, it said.

I felt a rush. Again, I felt big, strong as a gorilla, king of all I surveyed. The chaos was down to me. The hysteria was down to me. The situation was spilling out into the streets of London and the lives of everyone here. And it was me. I did it.

"You better take a seat," Rob was jogging on the spot, swinging his arms around like he was about to tackle a hundred metre sprint. "Market opens in five. Listen," he fixed me with a concerned gaze. "Just…try not to fuck anything up. Okay?"

But my phone had already begun to ring. I took a deep breath, filling my lungs with the bedlam. Picking up the phone with my disordered hands, and opening my disordered mouth, I got ready to feed the beast.

"Hello," my voice sounded different. Calmer, cooler. "Tom Percy, Benson and Fletcher insurance."

"Hi, Tom." An apologetic tone. I recognised the voice. "It's Rupert, returning your call."

"Rupert," I said his name loudly enough for Rob to hear me. "How nice of you to call me back."

Rob froze.

"Yes, I think we got off on the wrong foot yesterday," he said. His voice sounded shaky. "But, in light of, erm, recent- events- are you open to a renegotiation?"

Rupert was in the palm of my hand. *Rupert* was in the palm of my hand.

I let out a theatrical sigh. "Rupert, Rupert, Rupert. Of course, I am. Are you sitting comfortably?"

"Yes." I detected a shuffle.

"Then I'll begin. I know you weren't covered properly. I know you have lost a lot of your assets. I know you're probably kicking yourself for not going with a plan tailored to your needs, to suit everything."

A pause. And then he sighed and said it.

"Well, yes. I suppose you're right."

I allowed myself a little laugh.

"Ah, now I've got you, eh? It's cos I used the rule of three."

A frustrated smirk down the phone. "The rule of... three?"

"Yeah, I learned about it in GCSE English Language. Rule of three. I used three short sentences, one after the other, didn't I? 'I know you're not covered; I know you've lost assets, I know you need a plan'...blah blah blah. Now what that does, Rupert, is make the listener more likely to remember the information conveyed, because having three entities combines both brevity and rhythm whilst having the smallest amount of information to create a pattern."

Deep breath in.

"It makes the speaker appear knowledgeable while being both simple and catchy. The ancient Romans used to have this phrase, *"omne trium perfectum"*. You know what that means?"

A little pause. "Uh. Does it mean...three is perfect?"

"Everything that comes in threes is perfect, that's right, Rupert! You must have studied Latin at school, I suppose? I just looked on Wikipedia, but you know, the point still stands, eh? So anyway, where was I...oh yes."

As if I'd forgotten.

"So, Rupert. What I was going to offer you is our comprehensive package. I believe you were only covered for theft, loss, and liability, tut tut tut! So, what this package offers, Rupert, is theft and loss coverage PLUS any damage, including, but not limited to; explosions, earthquakes, lightning, water, wind, rain, collisions, riots, and FIRE. How's that? And I can give you a premium, Rupert, of-"

I caught Rob's eye. He was slack-jawed, watching in disbelief.

£81,098.68. How does that sound?"

"I- I can't- uh- can you hold?"

"Sure thing, Rupert. Take your time."

The sound of *She Sells Sanctuary* by *The Cult* rattled down the phone. Great, great choice for hold music.

"Eighty-one?!" Rob hissed. "That's fucking way too high, what are you thinking-"

I responded with a smile and a thumbs up. "Don't worry," I mouthed.

"Hello? Hello?" The tinny voice came back out the other end of the phone.

"Hi, Rupert. Any joy?"

I wouldn't have felt joyful if I was shelling out eighty-one grand to a stranger.

"We can do that. Yes."

"Good man. You won't regret it. Now, I'll transfer you through to accounting, they'll take you through the T's and C's, and complete payment, are you OK to do that, Rupert?"

"Yep." He was flat. Defeated. Unhopeful.

"Nice, Rupert. You won't regret it, honestly."

"What was your name again?" a flicker of contempt in old Ruperts' voice.

"It's Tom, mate. Tom Percy."

"Very well. Thanks, Tom."

"Have a good one, Rupert."

Phone back in the receiver. I stared Rob down.

"Good enough?"

He stared at me.

"Well," he said slowly, but not without respect. "You best go and bang it, then."

He was referring to a big gong at the front of the hall- in your stereotypical, broker floor style, a large sale was often denoted with a bang of the gong.

I strode over, a little spring in my step, picked the beater from the ground and walloped it.

A cheer erupted from the crowd. I stood and looked out, smiling, pumping my fist. Rob glared over but nodded an approval. I'd won control. It was mine again.

Ten

"This one's nice," Rob observed. "Michel and Black, crushed velvet, fourteen-carat cuffs. Tu amie, Perce?"

We had ventured to Savile Row after work. After a successful day, Rob liked to buy suits. He already had dozens, but he was insatiable in his appetite for formal wear. And at Driffield and Co., his pick of the exorbitant bunch, his cravings were always satisfied. He was holding a peach-coloured suit jacket up to me with an expectant smile.

"I like the colour," I said. "Striking. Very... striking."

"Yeah, I thought that," he said, eyeing it up in his hands. "I'll try it on. You got it in a thirty-two?" he hollered over to the assistant. "Trousers a twenty-eight short?"

The shop assistant flashed a delighted smile. "Of course. This way, sir." She beckoned him to the fitting area, leaving me and a mute Wrighty to wallow in the absurdly priced suits.

I hadn't seen him talk all day. Since his nausea this morning he'd been staring into the void- unkempt, uneasy, a gaunt, frail man of twenty-eight. I decided to check in.

"You alright, kid?" I offered. "You've been very quiet."

He didn't say anything. His eyes bored into mine, his pupils all wide and his expression vacant. I didn't press any further. Couple cigarettes and a line of coke, and he'd probably be right as rain. Probably.

"Didn't he look like a wrong'un, though?" I heard hushed voices by the till. My ears pricked up and I focused in, flicking aimlessly through the imported silk suits and Egyptian cotton shirts. I shuffled slightly closer to the till keeping my back turned. A man and a woman were talking in clipped, received pronunciation.

"Well," the man said, "They think it was a hate crime, don't they?"

"There'll be more," the woman said. "I'm worried now, honestly. Some mad...arsonist, going around trying to scare people? What if people get hurt?"

"I know. And what if-" the man hushed his voice even more. I strained to listen. "What if- other landmarks go up? It's British culture, isn't it? It's an attack on British culture."

I raised my eyebrows. An attack on British culture. Wow.

"Do you think," the woman said, "Do you think...."

But my eavesdropping was interrupted by a clattering of boots down the corridor. Rob slid onto the shop floor like it was a West End musical with all the decorum of a pilled-up Ibiza club rep.

"Ta-daaa," he yelled- I caught the shop assistant's wince. "How...bloody...nice...is this," he gasped, twirling in front of us, admiring himself in as many nearby mirrors as he could. "I don't want to take it off," he continued, somewhat aggressively, before turning and staring at the nervous-looking man behind the till. "You're not going to make me take it off, are you?"

"No- no, sir," the assistant said quietly. "If you are happy with it, sir, I can take payment now-"

Rob strode over, beaming, and produced a card. "Thanks," he said, the toxic air of superiority seeping from his mouth. "You're too kind, you really are."

I saw him insert his card into the reader and smile before keying in his PIN. I craned my neck to see the numbers on the card machine.

£4,278.00.

The machine beeped and he whipped the card out with panache. Smiling, he turned round to face me.

"Love an impulse purchase," he beamed. I felt my eyelid twitch, and his body became big orange blocks.

After we left, he wanted to go to a bar.

"No, I don't like Hush anymore, it's too touristy. All these Americans see it on TripAdvisor and they just go there, so it's packed to the rafters, and it's just- uhh. I want to go somewhere more *authentic,* you know? Let's go to Morton's, I like it there."

Morton's was a member's only cocktail bar that primarily served bottles of champagne for over a grand. It was authentic, alright. Authentically awful.

"Wrighty, hurry up, will you?"

Wrighty was dawdling behind us, his eyes fixed on the ground, busy shoppers bumping past his shoulders.

Rob groaned. "What's up with him?"

"Busy day, I think," I said quietly. "He's had a busy day."

How he'd survived it, I'd never know. I'd seen him on the phone a couple of times, but he'd been idle, unfocused, preoccupied from prior events.

We waded back through the crowd to him to find he had stopped. His eyes were still glazed over, his jaw shaking.

"Wrighty?" Rob hunched down, trying to get a look in his eyes. "Hey. John. Johnny." He slapped his cheek, but Wrighty did not move. His eyes looked sunken; his expression was shame. He barely acknowledged us. Rob stood back up.

"Well, I don't know what's got into him. Fucking catatonic, isn't he."

He turned back towards me. "Put him in a taxi. Let's go. Come on."

"We were there," Wrighty said suddenly. My stomach twisted.

Rob glanced back. "What?"

"We were there," he said again, becoming surer of himself. "We were there. We were there when the fire started." His voice choked up.

Rob stared in disbelief for a second- I felt my blood pressure rise so much my eyeballs could have popped.

But then Rob laughed.

"God, he really is fucked, isn't he."

We put him in a cab, slammed the door, and walked back down the bustling street, brogues clattering off the stone. As I looked through the cab window to wave Wrighty off, he had a pleading look in his eyes.

Eleven

The night, following that, seemed to advance very naturally. Rob procured cocaine from a local, reputable source. In a flash of uncharacteristic philanthropy, he decided to give a small batch of his wealth to me. And so, like the big men we were, we trawled from cocktail bar to cocktail bar, brushing with silk suit after silk suit, sipping mai thai after mai thai and inhaling key after key. We were truly the kings of Fulham that night, well-heeled and well-spoken, my northern accent only becoming barely noticeable after the fifth drink or so. We were at Morton's now, sat across the table from one of Rob's broker acquaintances- a tall, thick-set man with shoulder-length dark hair and a vivid pink three-piece named Hugo.

"Oh honestly, honestly," Hugo was slurring, slapping Rob on the back as boisterously as he could. "We dropped like twelve grand in Bali. Got this villa, you know, Rock star villa? On the Gili's?"

All the while they talked money, money, money.

"Oh, come on," Rob pushed back enthusiastically. "We're from out that way. Of course I know it."

"Wait," Hugo threw his arms out wide. "You're Sri Lankan?"

Rob's smile faded slightly. "I'm from Singapore," he said, his eyes still hazy with affection. "Close enough, though."

"Anyway, you wouldn't believe where we went, after Graddy," Hugo continued to bawl, his voice rising in pitch and volume, "Dad got us all, literally us ALL, flights to Antigua. All nine of us! Honestly, it's so nice, you wouldn't believe, the water, it's this turquoise blue, you can see turtles-"

"Yeah, yeah, yeah," Rob entertained him further. "I've been there a couple of times. You'll have been on one of those resorts just out of Saint John's, yes? We used to stay on North Beach, it's a little private island just off the north coast…"

This was why they were so addicted to it, so they could somehow win at one of their little private battles, in their little twisted way.

"Where'd you go for your graduation, Perce?" Rob shot. "Benidorm?" they both laughed uproariously. I shook off the sudden pang of shame. He knew my background wasn't ritzy.

"I didn't go anywhere," I pushed back. "You see, my Mummy and Daddy don't talk to me much anymore, and they certainly don't send me any money. So, I moved down here and got a job."

I loved doing that. Playing the indigent card. When I needed a bit of silence. They turned to each other with a look of surprise, and then went back to their drinks.

Satisfied, I nudged Rob and motioned towards the toilets. He followed me.

"My heart's doing triple beats," he was gurgling in the cubicle. "Like, boom-boom-boom, boom-boom-boom, boom-boom-boom. Is that normal?" His head rolled on the joint, his emblazoned torso looking weird and two-dimensional against the lurid lime green walls of the bathroom.

"I dunno. Have a bit more. It might even you out."

"Yeah. Good idea." He was very sloppy now - his movements seemed wholly involuntary, twitching and waving his arms around to steady himself.

I unlocked the toilet door and made my move to leave. I didn't like being in such proximity to him.

"Remember what Wrighty was saying earlier," he mumbled suddenly, spilling coke from his key all over the floor as he waved it around like a torch. "That he was at the fire last night?"

"Yes," I said tightly. "Why?"

"Cos I've been thinking. He probably was. He was so... off today, you know? Anyway, more fool him. I made more money today than I did all quarter."

I was at a crossroads here. Quick, choose a path...

I took a breath.

"We were there."

Rob's face twitched. He turned on the spot. "Wait. You were at the Midspeak?"

I nodded. "Yeah. We both were. We saw the guy start the fire. We're witnesses."

Rob took a deep breath, looked down, and let the breath whistle out his lips. When he turned his head to look back up at me, his eyes glowed with a mix of rage and mirth. I turned back toward the door, feeling the cool metal as I twisted the mechanism.

"So, let me get this straight," Rob muttered as we wandered back to his. We had, like the entitled men that we were, ordered our whiskey on the rocks and promptly left with the glasses, sipping them at a glacial pace as we walked. "You're attacked in some alley. The guy in question has something flammable. He sparks you out, sets...a theatre on fire, and then runs. And that's it?"

"Yeah. He chucks the bottle, I guess everything goes up- then he runs. That's it. He was just some mad tramp, I think. There was no motive. There was no... prejudice, nothing like that. It was random."

God. I lie so easily.

Rob sipped his drink. "You think he'd do it again?"

"I don't know," I said, ever so quietly, "I suppose not."

"Interesting. It's just- hang on-"

He pulled his phone out and snapped it to his ear. "Hello. You alright? What's up?"

He looked concerned.

"We're just walking back towards mine. Why, what's up? You been drinking? Yeah, come and meet us, if you want- oh, alright. See you soon. Bye."

He hung up. "Wrighty," he said simply.

We approached his court, as cold and sterile and lifeless as the machine shops its prefabricated blocks were manufactured in. A newer build designed to give the impression of glamour, its grey walls were lit up with blue lighting. A fountain pissed in the middle. Immaculately trimmed hedges cut patterns in the courtyard.

The old days of showing your wealth through gold-tower, Siberian-tiger-owning decadence weren't so prevalent amongst the young money in London, I'd noticed. They liked white walls, obsessive symmetry, grey fittings, black velvet. Minimalist in that maximalist way, millennials pretending they weren't as tacky as our boomer predecessors. We were, of course, just two-tone.

As we drew closer, I saw a figure looming near the lobby and groaned- it was Wrighty. He began to swagger over, although I did see a slight limp, a microsecond of hesitation in his gait.

"Boys," he said, his translucent confidence almost masking the quiver in his voice. "What's going on?"

"What are you doing here," I said, my translucent calmness almost masking the irritation in my voice. "It's 2 am? We thought you'd gone home, anyway-"

Without a word he grabbed my glass with his bony hand and drank the contents, before dropping it on the floor with a smash. I winced.

"*Wrighty,*" I said through gritted teeth. "Pack it in!"

"Sorry mate, but no one actually likes whiskey," he bellowed, cocksure again, pivoting and wheeling to his imaginary audience. "It's gross, it burns your throat, all it tastes like is petrol. There's literally no flavour there. It's just status, mate, people only drink it for the status, know what I mean?"

I eyed him with suspicion. Was he drunk?

"Wrighty," I said again, "What the hell are you doing here?"

Rob was smelling and sipping his glass again. "Stuff like this, yeah, John. Nice stuff has a lot of flavour to it. Burnt caramel, vanilla, sandalwood..."

"It's a free fucking country," Wrighty said, even louder. "I do what I want, know what I mean?"

My skin crawled when I heard him say that. 'I do what I want'.

"I guess you are joining us, then?" Rob finished his whiskey.

Wrighty gave an overzealous shrug. "I do what I want, mate," he reiterated.

Twelve

Rob made a point of wearing a pocket watch everywhere he went, rather than the standard wristwatch he seemed to assume was for mere proletariats. He would check it at work as he hurried from one meeting to the next- it was, as he told anyone who would listen, eighteen karat gold enamel, and in keeping with everything else he wore, hideously expensive. I could see the time telling half-past three as he racked up another line of cocaine on it, grinning in his pomposity. We were sat on the glass kitchen table, wine glasses out, chardonnay on hand, talking heads coming out the stereo.

"Wrighty," Rob was saying, "Wrighty, Wrighty, Wrighty. You have missed a trick today, pal. Pinker Graves was up one point four."

"One point four?!" his eyes widened. His energy had been terse since he arrived, but it was slowly becoming frustration. His hands clenched and unclenched, the hyper-conscientiousness of his work persona coming back into play. "But that's…nuts! One fire? There must be something up there, mate. Has to be. And you-" I heard him struggle for air as he waved a thick finger at me- "You. Did you sell?"

"Yes," I said, noting his fear. "I did."

"How much?"

I told him.

"Fuck me," he said, crackles of anger creeping into his voice. "Why, why-" his eyes reddened- "Why the hell did I take my head out the game?"

He abruptly stood up and kicked the table leg hard, causing it to shift a few inches and the wine bottles to wobble. I grabbed it quickly as it fell.

"Mate," I said, noticing another, unwanted twang of northern-ness creep back in. "Mate. Calm down. There will be more days like this."

Rob smirked. "It was a one-off. It won't."

When he said that, I felt different again.

I felt like I did when I started the fire.

I felt like I did when I'd looked out on the shop floor.

Uh oh. Hoo-hah....

Demons are called demons for a reason. You become a different person under the influence of them.

And right now, I could feel mine seeping through my skin into my spine, gripping at my central nervous system like skeleton hands.

I felt big again. Big Perce. My eyes felt like golf balls, my mouth like a drawbridge. King of the castle.

"Well," I opened my mouth, my voice sounding booming and haughty and so unrecognisable from the one I was used to hearing. "I wish he'd do it again."

They looked at me in utter confusion. I let the silence ring out. I allowed them a tiny smirk, just a hint of the masterplan.

A look of understanding dawned on Rob's face. He leaned closer.

The demon grew stronger. He knew he was winning- he'd planted the seed. "Imagine if there were more?" I went on softly.

The corners of Rob's mouth twitched as he tried to hide a smile. "Money," he said simply. "A lot of money."

"If... he... sets another fire," I let the demon say through me, "we will have another day like today, won't we?"

Rob laughed. "Yeah," he said, slowly becoming surer of himself. "I suppose it would."

The demon was done. And I had succumbed, the damage let loose, the plan formed. Habits are hard to break, addictions harder, and I was too weak to break mine.

Rob was mine now. I'd played him.

I let the silence hang for a bit whilst I sipped my drink. There was a gentle tremor vibrating through the table- it was Wrighty's leg, bobbing up and down at a frenetic pace. His hand was twitching. He looked a little sick.

"I'm going for a fag," he said, standing up, correcting his posture, and striding towards the back door.

Rob was engrossed in his phone, posturing, and smugly smiling into the front camera, ready to make his Instagram followers jealous.

I left him and walked over the tiled white floor to the French doors leading to the balcony and walked over to Wrighty. He was not smoking.

"Alright, mate?"

He had that same look in his eyes that he did the morning after the fire.

"Alright," he said slowly.

"You alright?"

"Yeah, I'm alright." He paused. "Are you alright?"

"Yeah, I'm alright."

This was about as deep as conversations got with us.

"Listen," he said. "About the other night. Has it been- like- on your mind at all?"

"Not really," I lied.

"No, but,"- I heard, possibly for the first time, some distress creep its way into his voice- "Like, I can't stop *thinking* about it. I mean, every time I'm even just stood talking to someone, it's just there, in the back of my mind, all the heat, all the... mate, do you think,"- his voice began to break. "Do you think he, like, actually wanted to...*hurt* me?"

I recalled the ache that spread through my body as I'd seen him kick that rough sleeper, how intensely it had gripped my bones, how compliant my conscience had been to its will. I remembered the memo that burned in the top of the bottle. Buy popcorn, buy popcorn.

"No," I said, after a little deliberation. "I don't. I think it was completely random, I don't think it was targeted at you in any way. You're overthinking it."

"Thanks, Perce," he said meekly. "Appreciate it."

The overpowering scent of cologne informed me that Rob had joined us on the balcony.

"Chaps," he said. "Not to be rude, but I'm going to have to ask you to fuck off. Have some business to attend to." He had a knowing smile. He must be getting laid tonight.

"Not that Hugo?" I said incredulously.

"Yes," he grinned. "*That* Hugo." He did look very pleased.

Wrighty was still breathing heavily. Looking way down to the concrete below, he nodded and pulled himself away from the balcony edge.

Whisper-whisper, said the demon, as I followed them back to the front door. Everything seemed so much glossier in this bright light, the dazzling gleam of the surface almost making me wince. My vision went fisheye, and my two colleagues seemed small. My evil mouth opened again.

"Chaps," I said, a quick assertion in my voice. They turned, a mild surprise in their eyes.

I filled up my belly with bleach-air, about to make history.

"Just…just think about what I've said, tonight. I am not going to push either of you into anything. I would never do that. But just think about the day we've had, and what I've said to you."

Nervous smiles from both parties. Rob's had more intent. Wrighty appeared to be sweating.

"Perce," he said quickly. "Perce. I-"

"I don't need an answer tonight," I silenced him, holding a finger aloft, politician style, bringing peace to the commons. "All I ask is that you think about it. Goodnight, gents."

When I finally got home and locked the door behind me, a gentle but unmistakable sigh of relief whistled through my teeth. Alone is nice. Alone is good. No mask when alone. Only you. Pretend time off.

All at once, a plan hit me. I'd remembered something, something very crucial. Time for action, time for the charge of the light brigade, no prisoners to be taken; I threw open the cupboard door, rifling through the crisps and pasta and sauce and all the other meaningless shit I stocked my cupboards with.

But then- success- I'd found it.

My hand almost trembling, I removed it from the inner recesses of its containment. A packet of toffee popcorn- grab bag sized. All for me, all for me.

Flicking on the TV and putting on the comedy channel, I wondered of the stress and intense sorrow I'd caused, the worry of so many families, the panic of a city. It must be awful, really, I mused, as I tore open the bag of popcorn and inhaled the sweet, decadent scent. Yes, really awful indeed.

The opening bassline of *Frasier* began to boom out the speakers. My mind switched off, and for the first time in days, I did not think of anything at all.

Thirteen

Now here we go again
You say you want your freedom
Well, who am I to keep you down?

Stevie's lyrics floated over my fragile body. I flitted out of dreams and waking in this state, too tired to think straight, not tired enough to fall back into a healing sleep. My head was bouncing, but paracetamol brought such nausea. Well, nothing to be up for. Through the navy blinds, I caught glimpses of bright light. It must be a beautiful day.

It's only right that you should play the way you feel it
But listen carefully to the sound...

Imagine if there was nothing outside? If life as I knew it existed as a microcosm purely inside the walls of my bedroom, with nothing and no one?

If I was always coming down, unable to keep a train of thought, not hungry and not happy but not too sad either. The light would be dulled by the blinds, comforting, the whirr of the aircon providing that gorgeous, whooshing, shifting sound. The sheets would be clean and warm, cold can of fruit twist in the mini-fridge next to me. No one to speak to, no one to answer to, nothing.

....of your loneliness.

The deep, dark bass of the song seemed to be rattling now, loud and unmelodic, and out of time. What witchcraft was this? With what seemed like an unfair amount of effort I prised open my heavy eyelids, one lagging after the other, limbs stuffed with cotton wool, body rolling round like a squid out of water, looking for the offending noise.

It was, to my considerable distress, my phone; I must have drunkenly set the ringtone as *Dreams* last night. How cruel life could be, lulling me into a false sense of security like that. My head killing, I picked it up and examined the number. It was an 0121 landline. Work? Doctors? Client? Opportunistic Adderall salesman? Better answer.

"Hello?"

"Hi," the voice came back, cool and female. "Can I speak to Thomas Percy, please?"

"Speaking," I grunted. The voice sounded familiar.

"Hi, it's Detective Constable Olyvia Rocca."

Blood turned to ice. The room went sepia. Even the floaters in my vision reassembled themselves to form the words OH NO-

"Hi, Officer," I said quietly. "I'm not in any trouble, am I?"

Pins and needles in my face, cobwebs in my mouth, a python slithering into my eye socket. So full of sheer horror I could burst.

A laugh at the end of the phone. "No, no, not at all. Er, listen, Thomas- we'd like to take another statement if that's alright with you. Are you available?"

The pins and needles did not sting any less. "Sure, of course. When?"

"Are you free today?"

I winced. Too much pain. "Yeah. This afternoon?"

Another laugh. "Have we just got you out of bed, Thomas? It's one-thirty."

"What? Er, no," suddenly awake, I ran to the bathroom, only a t-shirt on, pulling the lever on the shower. "When do you need me there?"

"Any time before four is fine. Can you make it by then?"

"Of course. See you soon."

The phone beeped and then returned to the home screen. I took a moment to breathe, just breathe, like my old therapist used to tell me, noticing everything and anything, enjoying the present for what it is. Thoughts are just like cars on a motorway, she'd say, just passing by. Just let them pass by, Tom.

One of the thoughts that passed through my head was this; The Police wanted to speak to me. They must, in some way, have linked me to the incident. I would be arrested; I would lose everything I'd worked so very hard to accomplish. Now, this thought wasn't so much a car, more a freight train derailed and smashing through the M20 at a perpendicular angle, causing a twenty-car pileup, huge fires, and day-long tailbacks. My breath got caught in my throat, I swallowed- and next thing I knew I was throwing up, the steam from the shower and fever from the vomitus making me sweat and sweat.

Was this worth it? No, I mean, really now, come on. Was this *really* worth it? The undigested pieces of toffee popcorn were staring back up at me, judging me from the bowl. A shadow of my reflection lurked behind them, outlined in stomach acid.

I clambered into the shower, the heat stinging my skin. I tried to focus on the water hitting my skin and racing down my arms, but no. My mind simply would not allow me. Round and round it went, helter-skelter, bouncing from the police to the fire to Mum to the police to Wrighty to the reporter to the fire to the police…

I grabbed my hair, tight, pulling it so it hurt. Forehead on knees, I opened my eyes and watched the stink of the night before pouring down the drain.

Police station coffee was disgusting. It was gritty and muddy with none of the salty, earthy flavour of grit nor mud. Its taste reminded me of when I'd chew pens so much in school that they would eventually burst. The payment for such enthusiastic mouth-work would be a load of black fluid dribbling from my gums, my lip service to education essentially climaxing in a sort of anti-money shot. All the kids would laugh, and I would sulk all day, and eat lunch on my own.

Despite the slight post-trauma, I kept drinking. I had to be alert.

The station reception was surprisingly comfortable and homely. I had always imagined stations to be austere and brutalist, with criminals peering through the bars of the drunk tank at civilians waiting in reception. I was alone, on a comfortable green sofa, trying my best to fend off the hangover. I was tense, though- my eyelid was twitching the way it did in times of stress, immensely annoying and distracting. Just hope it's not a tell.

"Mr. Percy?"

I jolted up, looking towards the big wood panelled door. The woman who'd interviewed me the day of the fire stood there, a concerned, kind look in her eyes. I relaxed a little. "Good morning," I quipped, "or should I say afternoon, maybe?"

She laughed. Good start. Get their guard down. Co-operate.

"Hi, it's Olyvia," she smiled. She was tall- taller than me, though that wasn't too hard- jet black hair in a side fringe, thick glasses covering dark eyes. "Made it down here OK?"

"Yes." I smiled. This was a lie- I'd had to throw up again through the gap in my legs in the public toilet in a local Morrisons. "Fine. Um- shall we?"

That's it, that's it. Appear cool, confident. They needn't suspect a thing. If you're innocent, you have nothing to fear, right?

I felt my eyelid twitch and resisted a sudden and strong urge to punch myself in the face.

Now, that REALLY wouldn't have looked good.

I'd imagined an interview room, like the one you see on the TV, big and imposing, white walls, a large mirror concealing a panel of steely detectives; all of them poised to conduct a very thorough analysis of every single thing I said or did. As it was, there was just a desk with a computer in a little office, and a red armchair in the corner. A few dainty houseplants laid on the windowsill- a mug with *Keep Calm I'm a Super Cool Police Officer* laid on the side.

Keep calm, Percy. Keep calm.

"This is nice," I said. "I'd imagined, oh, I don't know- a big imposing room with white walls, and a large mirror concealing a panel of detectives, haha… you know, poised to conduct a very thorough analysis of every single thing I say or do."

Super Cool Officer Olyvia threw her head back and laughed uproariously. "Oh, God, no! This isn't like the movies, you know." She rummaged around her desk for a notebook as my brain started to play long strains of mysterious violin music to add tension to the scene. Perhaps it just wanted to make it that little bit more *film noir*.

I heard water pour into a mug, and the acrid smell of the instant coffee again. She was filling up her *Keep Calm* cup.

Keep calm, Percy.

"You want coffee?" she said brightly. "It's nice from here."

I threw up in my mouth again and swallowed hard. "No, thank you."

Keep calm, keep calm.

"Okay," she said. "Ready? Shouldn't take long. Just need a few more details from you."

"No problem."

"Great. Okay, I'm just going to dive straight in, then," she flicked frantically through her notes. I got the impression she was not going to dive straight in. "God, I swear I'd put it somewhere. Uhhhh…just give me a minute…how's your day been, anyway?"

"Painful," I answered truthfully, "I have a hangover."

She laughed again as she continued to shuffle. "Big night?"

"Yeah, pretty big." I watched her try folder after folder at a rapid rate, occasionally knocking her *Keep Calm* mug and spilling a little of the contents. Her flappable character should have set me at ease, but it was having the opposite effect; I could feel sweat bead on my forehead.

"Been with the Police long?" I chanced. Worth a try.

"Ummm, no, not really," she said. "I'm on the graduate scheme. Justice Ahead, you heard of it?"

I shook my head.

"It's a fast track thing," she was going through the motions here, deadpan. "Oh, here it is. Am I OK to start the recording?"

"Yeah." Shit- did I hesitate just then?

She clicked her mouse. "Okay. I'm going to bring the recording to a start. My name is DI Olyvia Rocca, the time is quarter past four, the date is May the eleventh, two thousand and nineteen." She took a hurried breath and adjusted her notes. "I'm here with Mr. Thomas Percy, first-line witness, case AEB2716. Thomas, can you state your name and the date please?"

"Thomas Percy. May the eleventh."

"Thanks." More shuffling. "And am I alright to call you Thomas?"

"Tom is fine."

"Okay, Tom. I'm going to ask you some questions regarding the incident on the morning of the ninth. Can you start by describing to me, in your own words, the incident in Limehouse that you witnessed?"

"Yeah, we were walking home from a nightclub, myself and John Wright. And at some point in the journey, we were jumped by this man, I think he'd been sleeping rough in the theatre. And I think- I think my lighter dropped onto the ground, cos he took that, too. Then he did something with it, next thing I know, there's a big fire, and Wrighty- um, John- has been hurt. Then he ran away, and we called you."

I measured my words. Nice and slow, broken, short sentences. Not too hysterical, but not too cold. Just a slightly tortured look.

"Thanks. And can you describe the man?"

"Yeah, he was around my height, so... five-eight, black hair, sort of swarthy, pale skin. Black hair. Looked around, I don't know- mid-twenties. And scars, on his face."

"What kind of scars?"

"Like a Chelsea smile."

"Okay, good," a few more clicks of the mouse. "You say he assaulted you. What did he do?"

"He punched me." God, such a liar.

"Okay, good. With his right or left hand?"

"Left. Left hand," I said. "A good punch, too."

"Can you describe his clothes?"

"I- er-"

My eyes had wandered over to the window. It was a beautiful day, only the chemtrails from planes overhead crisscrossing the brightest blue sky I'd seen in ages. Sun radiated through onto DI Olyvia, heat waves rising from the radiator.

But there was a face in the corner now. One that I recognised. Scars and black hair.

"Tom," Olyvia said again. I blinked- the face was gone. "Tom. Can you describe his clothes?"

"Uh...I...I can't..."

"Sorry, is this too much for you?" a face of genuine concern from across the desk. "We can take a break if you'd like. Um, you want a cup of coffee?"

I looked back at the window. No face.

"NO, um, no-" I steadied my breathing. "No, thank you, Olyvia, I'm fine. I'm just trying to remember."

Oh, but I could remember that face, alright.

"He had very pale eyes, like, big blue eyes. I could see them even in the dark. Real black, thick hair. Quite pale, and a beard. And he had scars-"

"Tom," she laughed. "I asked you about his CLOTHES. You sure you're okay? Here, I'll get you a coffee-"

"No, honestly, it's fine." My head was scrambled. "He had a dark hoodie on, jeans, and converse."

"Right," Olyvia was tapping frantically. "Good. Now, did you catch ANY indication of how the man may have started the fire?"

I looked up to Olyvia. In her place, I saw a man in his mid-twenties, blue eyes, scars on his face-

"UHHH," I recoiled. "Uhhh. Oh, God-"

Don't be sick, don't be sick. Keep Calm.

"Shall we take five?" a note of panic in her voice. Come on, Tom. Control.

"No, no. And, no, I didn't. He had a big bottle of something with him though, and I could smell, like, booze? I'm guessing he lit that."

"Right, right." She said. "And what happened after that?"

"He ran off."

"In what direction?"

"Central."

"Okay, good." I bloody wished she'd stop saying that. Nothing was okay, or good. "Now. Any possible motive?"

Keep calm, Tom.

"No, not really."

"Not an aggravated attack, then, you think?"

To be fair, I had been pretty aggravated that day.

"No. Not really."

"Grand," she tapped a few more notes and then finished with a flourish on her enter key. "I think... I think that will be all. So, I'm going to bring the recording to a close- any questions for me, Tom?"

Why haven't you arrested me yet...?

"No, none."

"Okay," she clicked her mouse a few more times and then relaxed back in her chair. "Okay. Well, that's all from me- you've got my number, yes, the one I called you on? Get in touch if you need to. You know where I am."

Her tone was so warm and genuine. People like that were the salt of the earth, really, that ability to talk to pieces of shit like me as though they were real human beings.

"Thanks, Olyvia." I started towards the door in a hurry, but then stopped myself. Just needed to check something.

"Actually," I said, turning on the heel, "I do have a question."

She looked up with a start, tense, pupils all big like saucers.

"This-" I pointed at the houseplant on the windowsill. "It's a cheeseplant, right?"

"Yes," she said. "Brought it in a few weeks ago."

I walked over to it. "Just that- it looks *great*," I gushed, turning on that plastic enthusiasm, "and I've got one at home, but it's wilting. What do you do, to help it, you know, grow so big?"

Her expression softened. "Oh, right," she smiled. "Well, mine used to wilt too. I watered it loads, then I didn't water it at all, and it just kept wilting and wilting, but then, guess what I used? Tomato plant feed. You can get it in Wilko, it's only a pound, comes in a little sachet, you mix it with water, and you want to just give it a spray every day or two. I just use an old detergent bottle with a spray cap. It's dead easy. You alright, Tom?"

Despite the fantastic botanical advice, I had scarcely been listening. I needed to look out of the window. "Tomato feed, huh?" I leant forward, trying not to make it obvious. "I'll try that, cheers."

"No worries. See you soon."

I left with a head full of sand. Not the hangover, not the interview, not the information overload about how to care for houseplants I had never owned.

When I had looked out the window, there was nobody there. Not because whoever the face had belonged to had run away, but because we were two stories high.

Fourteen

"So yeah, anyway, she says to me, 'you're a sexist pig, I can't believe I slept with you, blah, blah blah', and I'm just like, 'Whatever, you slag!', know what I mean, mate?"

Wrighty's voice could have been coming from anywhere. Sometimes it was trickling out of car windows, sometimes it was gushing up from drains. It reverberated from the buildings, stuck to my clothes, stung my eyes like bits of sand. My hand, grasping my phone to my ear with a white knuckle, felt all weird and plastic and dummy like. Eyes and face twitching and bubbling and boiling, heavy with blood flow. The mask was trying to get out.

"You're sounding chirpier," my voice was descending from the sky. "Feeling better?"

"Oh mate, oh mate. Don't know what you're talking about, mate! Hahahahaha!"

Wrighty's wall was fantastic, his bulk undeniable. He could take a hit again after the minor show of humanity. Wincing as he laughed, I pulled into the corner shop near mine. Needed popcorn.

"Yeah, so, anyway. Me, you, and Rob, King's Head at six, beer, banter, baggies. Know what I mean?"

Sunkissed popcorn comes in three flavours, normally- Original Sweet, Sea Salt, and Butter Toffee, which was my favourite. But this particular corner shop must have had the brand as an approved supplier or something, because there was more here. Aged white Cheddar. Bacon Ranch. Apple Cinnamon. Pumpkin spice. Caramel nut crunch. Prawn Cocktail and Dill. Coffee Liqueur. White Chocolate cream....

"Oi, Perce. You still there?"

I was hurriedly stuffing as many bags as would fit into the basket in a mania of childlike glee, the promise of fantastic flavour filling my frontal lobe as my sweaty, clammy hands grabbed greedily at the goods. Literary devices dictating my actions once again, I staggered slowly to the service serf, seating my stow atop the surface. "Oh, yeah," I muttered, trying to fumble some change out of my wallet, "To be honest, I feel like shit, still. I'm just going home."

"Pussy," the reply came. "I need to talk to you, anyway."

"About what?" I tapped my card on the reader as the assistant stuffed my prize into a plastic bag.

"I went to the police, earlier, for an interview." His jovial tone was cracking.

"Yeah, so did I. I'm just on my way home, now."

"Did they show you the CCTV?"

I'd shit so much today my insides were empty, but that didn't stop my heart falling out my arse.

"No. What did you see?"

"Of the guy. They saw him again."

"Where?"

"Maryland, mate. He got the tube there, after the fire. And then they couldn't trace him after that."

"He got off in Maryland?"

"Yeah. And that's been it."

"They haven't caught him or anything?"

"No, mate, no. So, um, if you see him, give him a left, right, goodnight from me, yeah?" a nervous laugh.

"Yeah. Yeah, sure. Listen, I'll, er, I've gotta go. Talk to you later."

"Keep an eye out, yeah?"

When you think something should be there, it IS there. You can always find trouble if you look for it, apparently. The brain looks for trouble, it's how it keeps us safe. It saved us from the bears and tigers when we were Neanderthals.

And oh boy, did old Mr Mind want to keep me safe right now. Why could I smell smoke everywhere?

I walked home, quicker and quicker, my head so heavy it pulled me off balance, along the queued cars facing me. I chanced a glance- shit, was that him? I stared at the car. Oh my god, oh my fucking god, that's him, that's HIM...

The window of the VW golf wound down to reveal a Middle Eastern man who, categorically, looked nothing like my wanted friend.

"What the fuck are you looking at, creep?" he shouted. He wore a taqiyah and had glasses and a long black beard.

Yeah, definitely wasn't him.

"Eat shit!" he blasted off, leaving me to imagine some more.

At the crossroads, it happened again. There was a woman selling sunglasses by the side of the road. As I walked past, I heard his voice.

"Who's got a match, eh? Who's got a match?"

I span. "Wh-what did you say?"

"I said," she said calmly, "Can I interest you in this array of unisex sunglasses, all official Rai-Ban, no fakes, absolutely?"

As she turned her head, I could have sworn I saw scars on her face. The Chelsea Smile. I leapt back, and almost into the path of an oncoming cyclist. Turning again, I saw the pale blue eyes and thick black hair of the man who I had framed for arson.

"Hey, watch yourself!" the cyclist sped off. Peering after him, I decided that couldn't be the man, either. Arse didn't look right.

I elected to do some breathing exercises outside the apartment complex. The elevator could be a little scary sometimes, all small and mirrored and hard to breathe, so I took some deep ones outside the door. In through the nose, two, three, out through the mouth, two, three. In through the nose, two, three, out through the mouth.

And I kept going, and going, and going, until the sky looked less like the blue ceiling I stared at when I could hear Mum and Brandon fighting downstairs, and more like a vast expanse of nothingness, stretching out into infinity.

It was so big and so blue, and so quiet and still and constant, that after a while I forgot all about me. It took a while, sure. But it did feel nice.

I tried to ration the popcorn, but it didn't work. Down and down they went, mouthful after delicious mouthful. A day of self-imposed starvation was taking its toll and I was on a mission to cram as much sugar and salt into my belly as I could. Popcorn is not the most filling material, as you can imagine, so that and a combination of the delicious flavours just implored me on. The second the last Prawn Cocktail and Dill- probably my favourite of the savoury flavours- was done, and its packaging folded into a neat isosceles triangle, the Bacon Ranch was opened. I chugged them down, pausing only to sip my fruit twist.

A wail of the sirens below made me jump from the delicious preoccupation. There seemed to be a few of them, blues and twos, darting amongst the parked traffic. That's when I smelt smoke.

I swivelled to the west and saw a plume. Not huge, not encompassing, but a definite, definite plume of smoke, around a mile toward the city. The horn of a fire engine cut through the mix.

It smelt- good.

And that wasn't just a pyromaniac talking, no. This smelt like an artisan bakery, notes of muscovado sugar and vanilla and cocoa in amongst the carbon.

I heard a clatter, much nearer, and saw a tile split on the floor, just across the road. Eyes tracing up, I saw him. Just a silhouette, sure. But it was him. I knew. I just knew.

My feckless friend from the park.

He was holding something- a can, maybe, a gallon tank? And he was moving, quite nimbly, across the rooftop, agile in his baggy clothes, deft in his movements. He kept low, darting left until I could just see him stop near a chimney- he raised the can upwards, above his head, and I peered and squinted as hard as I could to get an idea of what he was doing. Sirens continued to circle the area. They were on my street now, two parked kerbside, officers outside on the radio. I could see more blue flashing by the corner- gridlock, a sure trap. He was done.

It was the tiniest glimmer of light in his hand that gave him away. He was lighting a match.

Now he was running back towards me, barely slipping on the tiles as he ran like a cat away from the chimney. Almost immediately smoke trickled from his old spot; I knew what he'd done.

He reached the building edge, directly opposite me.

In the pale light, I could see him now- it was unmistakeably him, the scars on his hard face lit up by the intermittent light of the police cars, boom, boom, boom.

He stood there for a while- a dead end, of course, the way back would soon become unmanageable. He studied the scene, flummoxed, arms spread out like an eagle. Then his chin pulled up and he looked over the street.

Right at me.

Now obviously, I shit myself. For many reasons.

I ducked down behind the balcony barrier, heart racing, palms clammy. Shutting my eyes, I pushed my face against the cold glass, hoping I'd done enough…

…wait. GLASS?!

I opened my eyes, and yes, through the TRANSLUCENT glass- Jesus, Perce, you're such a fool- he was walking on air towards me.

Walking on air? Oh, Jesus, this can't be happening…but then, there he was, cool as a cool cucumber in the chilled section, walking- on air.

Knowing stealth to be futile I stood up, pale in the face, accepting my fate, as his scarred face flashed in the emergency light again, boom, boom, boom. He was walking on a telephone line, tightrope walking, so casually up towards me.

This can't be happening.

Ah, yeah. Of course it can't be happening. I'd had these before- what were they called?

Oh yeah, depressive psychotic episodes. After a low mood, your brain struggles to cope with the flood of chemicals in your brain- so, erm, weird shit happens. Must be imagining it. Must be. Just gotta ride it out.

There was a thud as he arrived on my balcony. Now, he really did stink of smoke- ooooh.

Knees went weak. This is a powerful episode. Mhmmmm.

He studied me for a second with his eyes. Then his scarred mug spread across the lines to a huge, genial, smile.

"Oh," he grinned, that incapacitating familiarity to his voice. "It's you again."

Fifteen

My therapist used to do this exercise with me. "Think of a moment of tension," she'd say softly. "A moment where tension filled up your whole mind and controlled it."

I would bring up the memory of Christmas dinner where I'd forgotten to parboil the potatoes before roasting them. I remembered Mum taking the rap for it. I remembered Brandon's face, glazed red like a gammon.

"Let that tension flow through your body," she'd say. "Embrace it. Let it squeeze your muscles. Let it make your chest tight. Let it make your heart pound. Remember- it's *your* tension. You are going to embrace it. The tension belongs to you, and you only. And your tension cannot hurt you."

I'd sit there in the armchair, shuddering in that cold room with the awful 80's décor, just thinking about that shitty Christmas. She'd let me sit like that for a good few minutes, in silence.

"Now," she'd say. "Think of a moment of relaxation. A moment when your mind and body felt completely and utterly free of pressure, of tension. A moment of calm."

Now, usually, I'd think of that time where I'd gotten stoned, completely on my own, shortly after I'd finished my dissertation. I knew I had nothing to give to anyone, no responsibilities to anything at that time. And I could just switch off. I ate my popcorn- it was limited edition akewell tart, I think, and I drank rum and cherry coke. It was so good. So good.

But in the last few hours, this had changed. My ultimate moment of calm had changed.

I was laid next to him, watching him sleep, black hair tousled, scars dimmed. He breathed through his mouth, slowly, deeply. The man who I'd framed for arson and used the resulting fallout for my gain. Yes, that guy.

Now he was just sleeping under the covers, all content and quiet, spooning the pillow, dribbling on it slightly. He radiated heat, and the smell of smoke, fainter now, seemed to mix into the room like a fragrance. I laid there and just watched him breathe, my mind completely switched off.

He'd made quite an entrance.

"Oh," he'd said. "It's you again," that big grin on his face.

It didn't mimic mine. Unable to speak, I'd pushed myself harder and harder against the glass barrier until its structure was compromised, as his body advanced.

He'd extended an arm to help me up, but somehow this had knocked him off balance, and he'd hit the deck, arms still outstretched, goofy grin still spread across his chops. He laid there, laughing still, gasping and gurgling on the ground. He gurgled and hiccupped, like some big drunk baby, his grin missing teeth, his wispy beard long and ragged. His black coat spread around him like a cape, his too-short cargo pants revealing stick-thin ankles growing from filthy red converses. One of his odd socks had Bart Simpson on it. *'Don't have a cow, man!'*, the sock said.

"How, how did you-"

So many questions. How did you find me? How did you start the fire? How did you evade the police for so long?

"How did… how did you walk on that phone line?" I settled on. Legitimate, I thought.

He belched. There was more than an underlying scent of alcohol on his breath, blending so elegant with the smoke. He laughed again. "Babe," he said. "I've been walkin' for fuckin' yeeeeaaars."

He made eye contact with me, and, it would seem, through me.

I held out a hand and helped him to his feet.

"Do you- do you want a glass of water

Alas, he didn't reply. He made a beeline straight for my cupboard, and with admirable dexterity found my bottle of whiskey, pouring himself a glass.

"Nice stuff, this," he slurred. He had a deep Manchester twang and a booming voice that belied his pixie-like figure. "Got a certain… *je ne sais quoi* to it."

"What…?"

"You know, *je ne sais quoi*," he poured a little more, and swirled the glass, getting a lot of it on the floor. "The French say it, don't they? When they drink wine."

"Erm."

It's a dream, Perce. One of your weird dreams.

"I… don't think so…"

"Where's your mate?" he said suddenly, a little scared. "Is he here?"

"He's… not my mate," I said. "I'm really sorry-"

"Fuck, there's a *bath* in here!" I heard him gasp, looking out of the kitchen and into the hall. He exited, and some ten seconds later I heard the bathroom lock go and the sound of water hitting the ceramic.

He'd spent maybe twenty painstaking minutes in there, during which time I'd checked Facebook, Twitter, Instagram, Pinterest, Tinder, Grindr, Bumble, Hinge, Whatsapp a good three times over. I then tried to nap, realised I was too anxious to nap, made a cup of tea, realised the caffeine in it would keep me awake, threw the tea away, and eaten a bag of popcorn, which to my dismay, I could still not taste.

When sounds of movement emanated from the bathroom I ran back into the corridor, poised with a towel, but he emerged already wearing my bathrobe.

"Love a bath," he grinned. "Shame you couldn't join." He ambled off, back toward the balcony.

"Listen," I said, tension starting to rise in my voice. "Are they looking for you? Was it you who started those fires? What's your name," I let out a hollow laugh. "What's your name?"

He stood, dripping, thinking. He stared into the void for a short while before answering.

"Yes, yes, and... Ziggy," he said, finally. He sat back heavily on the hammock with a sigh, then curled up. He laughed to himself, then fixed his sleepy blue eyes back on me.

"You- you fucked me up," he said simply, without judgement. "You made me like it."

I shivered. "Like what?"

"You know what." He glanced at the blaze. It reflected in his eyes for a second. "It never comes back the same, when it's gone," he said simply. "Ashes to ashes, dust to dust, innit. Doesn't matter what it is. Ends up... ashes."

His head lolled backwards, and his eyes closed. Not too long after, deep, relaxed breathing. Then snores.

Good job he was light. I'd never have been able to carry him otherwise.

I laid him gently in my bed and pulled a cover over him. He stirred, seeming to be in a little pain; faint, effeminate mumbles escaping his lips. He must be having a bad dream. What was he dreaming about?

My phone buzzing pulled me to my senses. Nerves pinging, I checked the screen.

Rob.

"Hello?"

A crackle at the end of the line. "Was it you?"

Blood froze. "No. It wasn't."

"Seemed awful near you." His tone was cool. I felt irritable.

"What is the purpose of this call?"

A laugh. "Well, I just thought I'd check, you know? See if you'd decided to get…lucrative."

Ah. Money. "No, it wasn't me. I can see it from here, though."

"Can you talk?"

Another wary glance at my pal. "I'm turning in now. Tomorrow morning."

"Yes, tomorrow morning, then," his tone curter. "Meet at Petruccio's, in Earl's. Get there for ten, don't be late, now."

His change in tone brought a fizz to my mood. Word vomit spilled out.

"Meet at Petruccio's?" I guffawed down the line. "Get there for ten? What do you think this is, some Mafia film? A crime novel? I'll bloody well let you know when I'm ready, Rob."

There was a pause. "I see," he said drily. "Text me, then." He hung up. I breathed a staggered sigh of relief.

A pop and whistle and I was bathed in darkness. Must be a power cut. I needed a light…treading gently, arms outstretched, I made my way back to the bedroom. Kicking out with my legs to determine the edge of the bed, using my hands to fumble and find my side.

My hand brushed his ankle and he snorted- my heart raced again. He still didn't move. Where was my phone? If only I could get a little light…

Ah- wait. There was a way.

Grabbing the box off the bedside table, I felt my mouth twist into a weird little smile as I withdrew a safety match and lit it. As the flicker lit the room he looked so still- now also an arsonist, one on the run, guilty as sin. How had he come to this?

I felt my fingers burn, and quickly blew the match out. I lit another, and another, just watching, just observing, my divine intervention sleep peacefully next to me. Yes, this is meant to have happened, I thought. He was meant to come to me.

When I woke in the morning, he had gone. I searched high and low before I came to an envelope, just in front of the door. The letter inside, in peculiarly neat writing, said;

Thanks for letting me stay

Love,

Ziggy.

Sixteen

I rang my Mum on the way to the café.

"Hello?"

"Hi, Mum."

"Oh, hello!" She sounded delighted. I hadn't rung her in months. "How are you, darling, are you well, are you keeping safe? What have you been up to? Do you know, we got that curry you like last night, that paneer korma? Lovely isn't it?"

"I'm jealous. All I ate was popcorn yesterday."

"Oh, you don't still eat popcorn, do you? I thought you'd grown out of that! Yes, we got paneer korma, and some saag aloo, and chicken madras, it was delicious! From that Balti House, you know, next to the co-op?"

"Oh yeah, they used to do those shawarma wraps, with the bright green mint sauce-"

"Oh yes, I remember, you had one that time and got it all over the sofa-"

"Yeah."

We both fell silent for a second, in memory of what'd happened *after* I'd spilled the mint sauce all over Brandon's new crushed velvet sofa.

"So," I restarted. "How are things?"

A little pause while she gathered herself.

"We're good. I've been doing... well, not a lot, as usual, I saw your Aunt yesterday, I planted some hydrangeas the other day, and some sweet peas, right at the back, near the compost heap..."

And then she went on and on about nothing.

And god, it was nice.

"So- will you be coming home any time soon?" Her voice became urgent.

I sighed. "No. I don't think I can, can I."

"But- well, I was thinking," the urgency rose. "We could meet, maybe, at Cassiobury Park? We could go for a walk, and get an ice cream, feed the ducks-"

"I don't know, Mum. It'd be weird. It'd feel weird."

"He's mellowed out now, you know," she said. "Brandon."

A swell of anger.

"I can't. Sorry."

There were so many people on the street today. Dodging in and out of me. Everywhere.

"What about my graduation, are you coming to that?"

Ah bollocks. The graduation.

"Yeah. Course. Wouldn't miss it for the world."

"Okay, love," she said finally. "Nice to hear from you. Take care."

"Bye, Mum."

I hung up, looking out on all the people on the street. I felt alone.

Rob was there already when I walked in. His hand tapped on the table, ten to the dozen, the other fluctuating between checking his pocket watch and his chai latte. Dressed in a suit jacket, t-shirt and jeans, his casual appearance belied his frenzied mannerisms.

"Sit down," he said, as I was sitting down. "Got a lot to discuss, me and you."

"I suppose we do."

He smiled, but there was some malice there.

"So. It wasn't you, was it?"

"No. It was not."

"I don't believe you."

"I went straight home last night and ate popcorn all evening," I said dully. "It wasn't me."

"Was a big job though, huh?" his eyes glinted. "*Two* big jobs. How were they executed?"

"I don't know," my voice was heating. "It wasn't me."

"Dude," he leant in, whispering. "You are a fucking *genius, man!*"

I tried to hide my confusion.

"The places that went up," he went on, "were Maik, who make artisan bakery products, and Hilande Threads- they're a sort of new clothing boutique. Very nice stuff, very expensive. Shame it went up, really. They're both private ventures, and they're both set up by...guess who?

"Um..."

He flashed a smile cloaked in avarice.

"*Lola Pink.*"

Still confused, I watched the mettle of his already shallow morals battling with material.

"She's running scared, Perce, her and her pals, they'll buy, buy, buy, like it's nothing to them, see? But think about how far we could push this, Perce, just think, webo cu- sorry, WE COULD BE- really, really rich from this, you know..."

Ever the articulator, he only got his words jumbled up in a thought disorder like that when he was plotting. I shuddered.

"Opportunity," he said, "opportunity, opportunity, opportunity. But we can't stop now. She has to know she's under threat. Then we can hold the cards."

For one of the first times in my life I'd been honest with him. And he hadn't believed me.

"Yes," I said, after a pause. "You're right."

He leered at me, took a sip of chai latte, and then leant further forward.

"So," he went on, "Imagine if the next place to go up was her country club?"

The man on the table next to me was wearing converse. Ziggy wore converse.

Despite the magnitude of the conversation my mind was wandering.

"Oi," Robs tone held impatience. "The country club. Perfect, right?"

It was perfect. I could see it now, all that gold decadence, all that elitism, all that pristinely prepared, immaculately served, pretentious fucking food. Up in flames.

But I couldn't feel it.

I tried to imagine the flames licking the soles of my feet as the world closed in around me, wreathed in red. But it felt like anime, some trite childrens cartoon, with me- some fucking cartoon character- why- why couldn't I feel anything?

"So, erm," Rob drummed his fingers on the table. "I'll just sit here awkwardly, while you think of a response. Feel free to acknowledge or reply to my plans any time soon."

Wait- what had he said? Force a reply, Perce-

"Yeah. Er, well it's good to tie it all together. So, we should all do what's best for us. Good to have a solution." All the snippets and mental notes of vague manager-speak I'd learned through the years.

"What?" an exasperated reply. "Look, erm, yeah. So, if you're up for it." He laughed a little nervously. "Weird, this, isn't it? Like, actually gonna go fucking- start a *fire*-" he shuddered with excitement. "And- oh god, it's just mad, right? Mad that one night, I've been sat in bed just going through my accounts, fucking watching my stocks go down, and I've thought, hm. How can I make a bit more? And an actual, legit thought, that popped into my head, was- 'I'll go and help my friend plan an arson attack!' Haha," his eyes widened, his humourless grin stretched. "But seriously...we should do it soon, if we're gonna do it," his composure returned, smooth as silk. "We need to plan."

"I'll sort it out." I said, staring at the back of my hand. "Just...leave it with me and I'll sort it." The words just dribbled out, my mouth all soapy and full of dishwater, my words slurred and quiet.

Seventeen

A gentle tinkle from the shop floor bell as we walked out. The ground felt spongy, pins and needles fizzed in my feet and hands. Everything sloped off to the side.

"So," I could hear his voice in my ear. "So. Wrighty has been there before, to play golf, he says there's alarms and whatnot, but, I dunno, surely we can get around that, right? People break into banks and get away with it- where are you *going*?!"

You know that painting, where there's a monster chasing a man, and it looks like the monster is huge but it's the same size as the man- there's just no perspective?

That felt like this street right now, everything was slopey and weird and tiny and disorientating.

My skin felt numb, I just wanted to- *scratch* at it, slice at it, just to make sure it was still there- I had to do it now-

"Listen man, if you don't want to do it, I'm gonna find someone else- hey, *listen* to me," I felt a grab at my arm. His face was fierce now, desperate, furious. "Listen. Let me- let me give you a ride home, eh? Come on. Get in. Get in the car."

He pulled me over the cobbles, greedy fingers drilling into my arm. I complied. I saw the indicators on an Audi R8 click over the road. Matt black, convertible. It looked expensive. Dead, though- the other cars shimmered, his was cold, stern, hard in its beauty.

I pulled the handle- a little too sharply, and the door came within an inch of the Corsa next to it. I swear I heard him squeal.

"*Jesus*, Perce," he growled. "Be careful, will you?"

"Don't...worry," I said, still out of it, each word a bench press in effort. "Scratches... add character..."

"Yes, Perce," his exasperated voice boomed from beside me. "But they don't add fucking *value*, do they?"

Now, I'd never been in the car with Rob, but a few things became abundantly clear very quickly. Number one, this was his pride and joy, cleaned to an obsessive degree. I noticed this when I pulled open the glove compartment and saw a hand vac, polish, wet wipes, leather shine, air freshener, and a plethora of business cards from various boutique car valeters.

Number two- and one to which I took a considerable dislike- was that Rob very much wanted to be *seen* in his car. He had the top down and he played his music LOUD.

When I say loud, I mean maximum volume, seat shaking loud, so loud that even if I had shouted at him, he'd have been completely unable to hear me. The noise of the deep house moved through me, ringing in my ears.

I didn't like noises to be too loud. I just- I just didn't.

He glanced at me from time to time, noticing me squirm, a flicker of a smile on his face. He had the power, and despite his feigned altruism, he knew it.

When we finally arrived at my flat, he parked in the courtyard, right outside the building. As he put on the handbrake and the noise finally silenced, I felt no relief, just embarrassment, a million eyes from the opposing tower blocks scoping me out like snipers, revelling in my embarrassment.

"Rob," I said. "You can't park here."

"Where am I supposed to park then? His histrionics had returned.

"There's a car park round the back, I have a pass for it-"

"Fuck that," he advanced towards the lobby. "Let's go and sit on your balcony. It's nice."

Eighteen

I took the top from the whiskey bottle. Hurgh. I remembered it smelling nicer. Maybe Wrighty was right after all, nobody really liked whiskey, maybe I didn't either. No, that was crazy talk, I loved whiskey- didn't I?

I glanced toward the window.

Ziggy was outside.

Wait- what? WHAT THE FUCK?! I leapt, whiskey knocking on the counter, a glass topping over and clacking against the counter.

Rob came out of his phone to eye me suspiciously. "Erm. What are you doing?"

"Sorry, Ziggy. I slipped."

"Ziggy?"

"I- er- Rob."

Come on, Ziggy- no, wait- *Tom*- god, stop flipping out on me, brain, this isn't funny, calm the hell down, come on...

The ice slipped from my hand into the glass and I managed to pour whiskey from the bottle into the glass with my polystyrene hand. Just about.

I glanced at the window again- of course, Ziggy wasn't there. Why on earth would he be there?

Rob raised the glass to his lips, inhaled, and took a long drink. The ice clinked on the glass, and he took a long, satisfied exhale. "It's no Hibiki," he said, "but it's nice."

"It is Hibiki," I said. "The bottle's on the side."

He shrugged. "Whatever. So. Pink."

"Pink?" I had one eye on the window. Just in case.

He groaned. "*Lola Pink,*" he said dangerously. "What is wrong with you? So Wrighty is a member, obviously. He goes there all the time. It's empty on a night, no cash left in the building. And he says the exterior has security, like- you talk into a receiver, then they let you in- but there's not much in the way of it inside. So, if we can, you know, somehow get inside, and stay there til it shuts, then we could- I'm sorry," he cut off abruptly. "Am I being ridiculous? Like, is it a ridiculous idea? I'm not just... being stupid, am I? Am I missing something?"

I looked at him. His voice was still collected, but he had a different look in his eyes now, a student with a keen thirst for knowledge.

"No," I said, checking the window again. "Why would you- why would you think you're being ridiculous?"

"Because," he flashed a taut smile. "You're looking at me, like I'm being ridiculous."

"I'm not looking at you like anything."

"So, you don't think I'm being ridiculous, with this plan that we- literally- burn an associates' property to the ground."

"I- err. No."

"Good," His brow relaxed. "I was a bit worried that it was, you know-ridiculous."

He took another swig, relaxing back in his chair. "But I mean- if we get this, if somehow this works, then- well, imagine it. Imagine how much we could make." His glee was back. "I know it's a bit daft, I know it's a bit crazy, but you know. When you started talking about it, saying that there *could* be more fires, well- you were right. There could."

A *clunk* from the balcony brought me out of the trance. Sounds don't happen by themselves. Even stoic Rob looked a little concerned.

"Mind if I just go- check out there?" I stood up, bringing my whiskey with me.

He shrugged. "No." And then he was back to immersion in his phone, scrolling, tapping, liking.

I pulled open the sliding doors and closed them gently. A quick scan around confirmed there was no one there, but I was in no hurry to return, to sit in that protracted tension with Rob. I paced the balcony, all two by five metres of it, the hammock hidden from the door.

It emitted a decidedly loud creak. It looked weighted down.

It's the blankets, I told myself, it's just the heavy blankets in there.

Rob was still on his phone. A quick check?

I drew closer, holding a trembling hand out, and pulled it down at one edge. As I suspected. Blankets. I took a shuddery breath, steadying my breathing.

"BOO!"

I shit myself. Leapt a foot in the air.

"Arghh! Jesus-"

"Ha, ha ha. Did I scare you? Did you not see me behind the cheeseplant?"

I was bent over double, seeing stars. God, I needed a new heart.

He was stood there, a huge, goofy grin on his face. His dishevelled face and greasy hair remained, but he appeared to be wearing a suit jacket. I resented his handsome untidiness.

"No," I gasped. "I didn't even-"

I stood up, shock leaving my body to accommodate every other possible emotion there was-

"What the hell are you *doing* here?" I squeaked. "Why- what- "

"Ah," he said, "Champion."

He took my whiskey, drank it, and handed me back the glass, giving me a wink. "Yeah, so," he said, taking a step closer. "I was gonna stay in the park again last night. But your bed was *sooo* comfy," he took another step closer. "So I thought-"

A click from the door reminded me we weren't safe.

"*Hide,*" I whispered urgently as the door began to slide open. "Hide! Hide in there!"

A look of resentment passed his eyes, but he obliged, and deftly dived into the hammock, pulling the sheets over him. Rob was already at the doorway.

"What was that noise?" his curiosity was piqued. Did he know?

"Some... big bird swooped down and pecked me," I said shakily. "I'm scared of birds."

"You are?"

"Well, yeah. Cos...they flap around and fly at you, like they don't know what they're doing."

"Hmm." He sipped his whiskey. "Know what I'm scared of, Perce? Moths. No sense of personal space."

We stood there for a moment, staring out at London, in acknowledgement of one another's irrational fears. Rob stared out at the horizon.

"Look at those tower blocks over there," he mused. "I wonder what kind of people live there?"

He pointed at the old council blocks out North. Big brutalist towers, gleaming pink in the evening light.

"Just people, I guess, Rob."

"Little people," he said scathingly. "You know, I went to Trellick Tower once. And the people there, god…" he trailed off, his disgust giving him jaw lock. "They just live like *animals,* you know. Filth, crime, vandalism, prostitution, drugs. It's disgusting. Subhuman."

I retched the whiskey. "What were you doing there, then?"

"Oh, picking up," he said, without a trace of irony in his voice. "But you know, Perce. People like that, all they know is crime. There's nothing else for them. In and out of jail all the time, begging on the streets, and using all their money to pump shit into their veins. I don't pay taxes to…mollycoddle people like that."

"You don't pay your taxes at all, Rob."

"Quite right." He was unmoved. "Listen, though. Imagine if we went there. Talked to a few of them. Said we have a job for one of them."

I felt a chill. Not a good chill, either.

"I- don't think that's a good idea."

He looked affronted. "Why? They won't care. People like that, Perce, they don't care how they make their money. They don't care about how immoral it is. If it's money, they'll take it."

Again, not a trace of irony. Not an inch.

I had another flashback. Not a good one, either.

"No, Rob," I said. "I'll do it. I'll take care of it."

"You?" not an ounce of belief. "How the fuck would you do it?"

"I know how to set fires," I said, sending a chill down my own spine as I said it. "I've done it before."

Once again, Rob searched my face. Frisked it. His eyes examined every corner, from my brow down to my jaw. He missed nothing. He must know I wasn't lying.

And then he threw his head back and laughed, a loud, awful, squawking laugh that made me stare at my shoes.

I hate it when people properly crack up like that. At something serious. It's not a laugh at something you said. It's a laugh at you.

"Alright, Perce," he said, wiping a tear from his eye. "Whatever. Eh, listen, I'm gonna get off, I think. Hahaha." His residual laughter cut me, too. I didn't lose eye contact with my shoes.

He took a step toward the door then stopped. "Oh, yeah," he said. "What about your tramp friend?"

I retched again, swallowing the sick. "What tramp friend?"

My ears focused on the hammock. Don't move, Ziggy. Please don't move.

"The one who torched the Midpoint, you moron," he said. "Why don't we get him to do it?"

I stood frozen to the spot.

"He'd do it, for sure, the peasant," he went on. "Only problem is, if we got him into the group, I think Wrighty would rape him."

I dropped my glass. It shattered on the balcony.

"DON'T SAY THAT," I thundered. "DON'T SAY THAT WORD."

His smile faded but a little. I almost saw humility cross his face- but then, he was such a great actor.

"Sorry," he said, simply. "Sorry mate. Walk me down to my car, yeah?"

As he left, I glanced back at the hammock. It did not move.

Nineteen

We rode the elevator down and crossed the lobby in silence. He walked no more hurriedly than normal but there was just a bit of discomfort in his gait.

I stood at the door as he walked towards his car, still uncovered in the courtyard, the sun beaming down on to it. It had been so hot today, the sky so insanely blue, as if it'd never rain again. Rob trotted towards it. "Beautiful, isn't it?"

"Watch out," I said. "That leather will be hot, after being out in the sun all this time."

He laughed again. He laughed a lot at things that weren't funny. "I admire your caution, Perce," he said. "No, really, I do. Watch out, he says. Watch out."

"I have to ask," I said. The temperature was rising. "But what are you laughing at, just then? Why were you laughing at me?"

"You just make me laugh, Perce. You're just- I dunno," he laughed again. "*Different*, that's all. Watch out! Watch out!" he mocked, trying again to do his northern accent. "That's you, all the time. Watch out!"

I only saw it for a second, but something landed in Rob's car, through the open roof. I heard a glass smash. I grit my teeth.

Rob jumped. "What the- what was that?"

I saw just a flicker of smoke emanate from his car.

"Watch out, Rob," I said, quietly.

The flame in his car began to grow. Slowly, at first, but irreversible, the gorgeous amber flame licking against the matt black of the car.

Rob span round. "Wh-what?" he said dumbly. "What?"

God, I know it sounds bad. But I'd have loved to have seen his face.

"What?" he said again, his voice rising in pitch. "What? What? WHAT?!"

He staggered back, jazz hands frantically waving as he fell backwards onto the stairs, fingertips brushing his temples, head shaking, back curled over double. "NO!"

Now, I'd never actually seen a car on fire before, for all my past. The flame had obviously started in the footwells, and it spread so rapidly through the interior, the flames dark red, rippling like a stream across it in the breeze. There was a *pop* as the window smashed. Black smoke trickled out from under the bonnet, more by more, until it was in flow. It looked so action-movie, so dangerous.

"Call the police, Perce," Rob said weakly. "Call the police!"

The flame in the car grew, and grew, and grew, until it was two metres high, and then- it took hold of the engine.

The explosion is every bit as spectacular as you'd imagine. You got, like, a split second of white, behind the cracks in the doors and the bonnet and boot. Just a split second. Then, this- *force*- propels everything outward. I just can't describe its power, it's so…attractive. Everything just, boom, blows outward, every direction, huge 2-tonne car components chucked around as if the holy spirit was playing softball with them. And yes, there is a mushroom cloud. Ten metres high, black and red, like lava.

Rob screamed. And then he screamed again, bloodcurdling scream after bloodcurdling scream. He leant on the steps, weeping, coughing, covered in ash.

I'd never seen grief run through someone like that.

I turned from the carnage and walked in, ash and bits of debris on my shirt. My face singed from the explosion; my palms numb. The cool metal of my door handle stung as I went back in.

He was there, of course, when I walked back into my flat. Another whiskey in hand, stood in the kitchen.

I made my advance. "Was that you?"

He didn't move but he smiled sheepishly.

"Was that you?" I said again.

He bit his lip. "Well, did you like it?"

"Answer me," a sternness I hadn't realised was there crept into my voice. "Was that you?"

He gulped, and nodded, looking deep into my eyes.

I took a parting look out the balcony window, the air still thick with smoke, Rob's choked screams still in my earshot. Then I looked back at him again.

He had that look about him, glancing from my eyes to my mouth, my eyes to my mouth again.

It was a bad idea to kiss him then. But, as Wrighty always used to say, the best things in life are bad for you.

ACT TWO- DETONATION

One

Picture this. A blistering day in Kent. The M2 carves a scar through its average countryside, with caravan parks and wind turbines dotting the horizon. The heat is dry, and a drought has set in. The river Medway has sunk a few metres in the last week. For the first time in years, a hosepipe ban has been set in Chatham, Gravesend, and its surrounding towns. Crows fly like vultures into the road, pecking at roadkill, sometimes becoming it themselves. A beautiful day. A disgusting day. For most people, probably an ordinary day. A very, very, very, hot day of ordinary-ness.

There's absolutely nothing going on here, is what I'm saying.

Now picture this. A bright green Citroën C1 with its windows down and the tiny boot so packed full of bags there's no view out of the back, snakes its way down the motorway. The heat creates ripples off the road, the air-con making a feeble attempt to lower the baking temperature.

WHY is it SO HOT?!

And finally picture this. A twenty-six-year-old arsonist driving down the motorway with his new-found protégé, about to experience an assault on the senses conducted entirely by himself and his dehydrated, unstable mind.

I'd set off when it was morning, and still cool. Four hours later and an age queuing on the London ring road, the temperature had doubled. With far too little water later, I was still on the motorway.

The smug drawl of the sat-nav began to speak. "At junction 37, take the exit. Then at one thousand feet, at the roundabout, take the-

My attention was drawn suddenly to a cloud in front of me.

Wait- what did the satnav say?

My eyes and mind were beginning to wander. This had been a very, very long drive, and anything to take his mind off the monotony of BBC Radio Kent and the protracted silence of my companion was an enormously welcome distraction. This cloud seemed to emanate a golden glow in the afternoon light, with strata branching off from a thick mass of grey directly in front of me in the sky. It looked like a hand, reaching out to high-five me. A bloody taunt, it was-a huge high five of airborne water to two dehydrated men.

"Take the exit", the sat-nav crooned.

Well, which exit exactly might that be? THERE'S ONLY ABOUT TEN-

The voice in my head grew louder and louder. I gripped the steering wheel harder. I felt my jaw lock.

Taking the first exit, I noticed that the second one had a small sign with *Elmley Golf course* painted onto it.

And now we were on a dual carriageway, with a sign saying *No stopping for 7 miles.*

Ziggy erupted with laughter. "As if you've gone the wrong way. Amazing."

His laughter pounded my ears, my skin.

My brain started to make some irrational connections.

I was out from my seat in the car, all the way up to that cloud I saw earlier, cloud eight, an angry little cloud that always cloud nine-

"Err Tom," a slightly panicky voice. "you wanna slow down?"

I think I'd been involuntarily pushing down on the accelerator more and more, because we were doing over a hundred now. I'd leant forward a lot more. I'd started to sweat.

"Calm down, Tom," Ziggy never seemed to show an ounce of anger. He put a hand on my leg. "What's stress going to do to help you?"

I imagined striking him full force. My shoulder seemed to lunge forward, as if I'd thrown a punch; I felt a sudden, wild urge to crash, to purposefully crash the car, just to teach myself a damn lesson for letting myself feel one damn thing at all-

-the car was travelling so, so fast now, hitting a kerb before hurtling through the air and bursting into flames and then-

"In a quarter of a mile, turn right onto Cornborough road"

Woah there, Perce.

How long have I been out? Could've been seconds, could've been hours. That was an ugly thought. Come on Perce. Keep it together.

We had stopped at a red light. I glanced at Zig, suddenly ashamed.

He laughed again, but the tone was more subdued. He went back to staring at his converses.

Two

I could smell cut grass as I approached the gate of Lola Pink's country club. It was a big sandstone building, glass and metal and beige, angles perfect, some *grand-designs* looking thing. Futuristic, it looked like it'd been cut up out of 2050 New York and plonked into the English Countryside. I could see Jags, Aston Martins, Porsches dotted in the heaving car park.

A broad security guard stopped us at the gate.

"Can I help?" his tone was calm. I fumbled on my key fob for my pass.

"Yeah. It's Phil Hartley. I'm from Chloro-Phil Greenkeeping."

He took my pass- a feebly cut-and-pasted rendition of a driving license with a backdrop of grass- and gave it the once over. He stared and stared; the fake ID reflected in his sunglasses. Eventually, he handed me it back.

"Great name for a business," he said. "really like that."

"Thanks," I said encouragingly. "It's a combination of my first name- Phil- and the word chlorophyll, which is-"

"I know what chlorophyll is," he said dully. "Off you go."

Ziggy laughed again as I drove in. "Check you out, trying to school the security guard. He sure told you, didn't he? Definitely did his A Level Biology."

"Evidently," I replied quietly. "Now let's not speak to anyone else for the rest of the day."

He looked embarrassed. He hated it when I did that, shot down his jokes with seriousness. That was Ziggy's thing, humour, humour in unlikely places. He'd told me that it comes from living in hostels, and on the street and whatnot. Humour was his thing. Granted, I'd only known him a few days. But I really *knew* him now. I really really did. Really.

It had taken one night to pull together a cover. A pass, khaki overalls, a hurriedly sold car on Gumtree. One night. Amazing what you can do when you put your mind to it, eh?

I called Wrighty. He answered after one ring.

"Yes, Perce."

"Yes, Wrighty," I mimicked. "We are in."

"Nice," he said. "Go and ask for locker 426 at the reception desk. That's got all my stuff in it, buggy keys and whatnot. Then just- I don't know. Wait it out, I suppose. Til they shut."

"Won't anyone ask any questions?"

"No one ever notices the staff, mate. They're basically invisible."

"Right," I glanced over at Zig again. "Got it. I'll keep you updated."

"Have you spoken to Rob?" his voice jumped a little. I almost felt bad for Rob. Almost.

"Yeah. He's down in Devon, isn't he?"

"I think he's taking some time out, yeah."

Rob had, understandably, not been in a good way the night before. He'd informed us he was taking time off work to stay with his parents in Devon. Stress and anxiety, apparently. Poor guy.

More importantly, though, he'd given me the green light. To take care of the job.

So I'd spoken to Wrighty last night to ascertain a way into the club without alerting security. Ziggy had laid next to me, analytical, silent, casting me knowing looks and rolling his eyes whenever boys, banter, or beer were thrown into the conversation. We shared silent, shuddering laughs at his expense.

He'd shown shallow affect regarding the news about Rob. "Oh, not the R8?" he'd said. "Shame. Nice bit of kit, that. He'll be fuming."

He'd paid attention to the bottle though. Did you see where it came from? He'd asked.

No, I'd replied, not at all.

Me and Ziggy had talked a lot after that, too. About why we did what we did. About what we liked about it.

He got the big thoughts, too. He got the ache. He loved it.

"You ready?" I pulled a holdall out the boot- just a hedge trimmer in case anyone asked what we were doing.

Ziggy was giving me the sort of puppy-dog, wide eyes look of total adoration. I think he liked it when people took charge.

"Yeah, sweaty." He kept calling me that. Like a pet name, I suppose. "Let's go."

As we walked, I felt peace.

Hearing the scrunch, scrunch, scrunch of him walking beside me, the wood pigeons, the wind in the trees. The gentle *thud* of a golf club. Peace.

You never got peace in London. You got traffic and rain and people. It felt simpler out here.

I felt heavy suddenly. Too much relaxation, maybe.

But I had to stop walking. I had to just- stop.

Take it all in a sec. All that nothingness, all around me, still and perfect. I shut my eyes. Ah. You do really appreciate the calm before the storm sometimes.

"What's the matter, sweaty?"

I jerked awake. He was still looking at me with those dazed eyes.

"Oh, nothing. Just catching my breath, that's all."

"Okay," he said, leaning in for a kiss. I stepped back.

"Come on, now," I was firm. "Be professional."

His face darkened, pupils flickering. He fell silent. Just like me, he was sensitive to minor changes in tone.

"Listen," I said. "No PDA. We can't do PDA in the golf club. Surely that makes sense. Look at that guy-" I pointed at two rotund white men, caps, sleeveless sweaters, talking loudly near the eighteenth hole. "If *they* see two groundsmen pulling each other, they'll gossip. We don't need gossip. We *can't* have gossip, can we. Whole point is we aren't meant to draw any attention."

But he still looked sad. "Just seems like you're a bit embarrassed of me."

"No," I said. "No. It'd be the same if it were anyone. You're just gonna have to keep your hands off me for a few hours."

Picking up the buggy, we drove out to the edge of the course, parking up near an anonymous looking hedge. I surveyed the scene again, big rolling plains, far-off laughter, golden light as the sun cast shadows. Ziggy, by his own admission an inside cat, lurked in the shadows again.

"Come and stand in the sun," I said. "It's so nice."

"I can't," he mumbled. "I'll burn. I wanted some SPF 50, but someone wouldn't get it for me."

"Okay, okay. But just for a bit. Bob Ross said that to appreciate the light, you have to have dark, and dark to have light. You'll appreciate the shade if you stand in the sun for a bit."

I felt him draw closer. "Did he really say that?"

"Well, he said to have one to have the other, yeah."

He drew into the sun and winced as it hit his eyes. "You know," he said calmly, "it sort of does look like a Bob Ross painting. Especially with that lake."

There was a lake in front of us, perfectly still, the sun arcing down the centre, carving a line to half it in symmetry. A Canada Goose floated on top, so still. I could hear tweeting just above me. It was so peaceful, so beautiful.

I saw another buggy pull up to another brace of blokes on a nearby hole. Its driver handed over a hamper, to the evident joy of the men. The buggy sped off, and soon the men were clinking champagne glasses, a spread on a cloth out in front of them.

Ah, that could be me and Zig, drinking in the heat, nothing but fields and nature around us in the heart of the green and pleasant land. With anything we wanted at our beck and call.

Like an egg cracking on my head, I felt the chill cover my temples, my eyes, my jaw, and my shoulders. I felt everything relax.

"You alright, there?"

"We could live like this," I said. "Honestly. We could live like this. Just you and me."

He looked at me for a while, just letting the thought sink right in

But then he laughed.

"Why on earth would we want to do that?" he said. "All the way out in the middle of nowhere? It'd be a bit... *lonely,* don't you think?"

I stood in shock. My fingers began to tingle, and I forced myself to do something to get our of my own head-

-OH I GET IT, SO I'M NOT GOOD ENOUGH AM I, YOU'D WANT OTHER PEOPLE AROUND? WELL THEN DON'T COME, STAY IN LONDON, GET ARRESTED FOR ALL I CARE-

"Woah," he said. "What got into you there?"

"Eh?"

"You started twitching," he said. "As you were opening the bag. It looked like you wanted to beat the shit out of it."

Sinking, embarrassed, I swallowed as I unzipped the rest of the bag, feeling sick.

I am fully, properly, losing control..

"About time," we heard a loud, American accent behind us. It was the brace of gammon that had been sharing the hamper. "That damn hedge has needed cutting for so long."

Three

We worked in near silence, cutting the bush into right angles. The sun arced in an ellipse through the sky until it began to get low, casting long shadows, bringing a cool breeze with it. We both knew it was near time to toss the coin, but, obviously, neither of us wanted to say it.

I took another look over the sweeping scenery.

"You know, I almost don't want to torch it," I found myself saying aloud.

I felt a change in energy behind me.

"Don't then," came the reply. "I'll do it. But remember, you did have your reasons."

"I did?" God, it was SO beautiful. Just picture perfect. All those happy little trees. Even trees needed a friend, you know, Bob Ross would say. Everyone needs a friend.

"You- you literally talked for about an hour about how much you hated the idea of this place," he said. I heard another thud as he threw his hedge trimmer to the ground. "How it's unnecessary, how its elitist, how it only shows the difference between the have and have not's. You told me you hated the people here. You told me the- the company, this Lola Pink, and her franchise, they're human rights abusers. You told me you wanted it wiped off the face of the earth, this monument dedicated to corruption and manipulation and extorsion, you told me you wanted it sacrificed to the elements, back to mother earth. That's what you said."

Tweets from the birds in response.

"I said all that?"

"Yes, you did."

"Wow." Shit. I really don't listen to myself sometimes. "Probably cos I'd never been here."

"Do you want to do this-" I heard a squeak in his voice- "or not?"

Need to rein it in here. I turned and gave him a quick kiss, watching his expression soften again as I did so. Too easy.

"Course I do. But only one of us can go, remember. One of us needs to get the car."

"I'll do anything."

Oh aye, I know you will sunshine.

"You take the car," I said. "I want it to be me."

Alright, yes, I KNOW, I'm a convoluted character, OK? But hey, you're still here. I'm still here. Sort of.

After that, I had to get into the boot.

"You'll never fit in there," Ziggy was whining again. "You're too fat. I'll do it."

"No," I gasped, trying to swing my leg into the buggy trunk. "I'm fine."

I could- just about- fit two legs in. Crammed in like frankfurters in a jar.

"Get on your side," he was saying. "Get on your side. Like you're in the daddy position."

"The daddy position?" I spat. "What the fuck is the daddy position?"

"No, sorry. What's it called? The *baby* position."

"The *foetal* position, Zig," I said heatedly. "Where'd you get daddy from, anyway? Right," I'd just about nestled myself into the compartment. "I'll squeeze in, then just- slam the door, OK? That's the only way I'll fit."

My logic to this was simple. On a long journey, or a move, or anything requiring a lot of baggage in a car, you always overpacked. Right? So the baggage would be sort of- hanging out the back, like a big, fabric, haemorrhoid. Unfit for mere pushing.

So you slam the door. It goes back in the- er – back passage, compressed a little, and you go on your way, fine and dandy.

However, my logic was flawed. I was the haemorrhoid; I was the pile. A human pile. Humans don't compress very easily. And I was about to be squished into a compartment roughly a metre cubed.

"Jesus," I yelped as the door slammed. "It's a bit small."

"One sec," I heard him say. "It's on the catch. It hasn't shut. Hang on-"

I felt another push as the boot came down on my side. My back cracked. Cheaper than a chiropractor.

"Woooaaahhh," he laughed. "Was that your *back?*"

"Yes, Ziggy," I gasped. "Now hurry up. Go."

The plan was, again, simple. Security would do a sweep of the garage they kept the buggies in, I would stay in the boot til they were gone, then undo the catch. I'd noted that the garage had left machine oil and all sorts of lovely flammables all over the joint.

Then, business as usual. Hoo-hah.

The buggy buzzed off, minimal attack in it, every bump a punch. Soon the cracks in the corners went dark, and the buggy ground to a halt. I heard a whisper near the cracks.

"Okay," his Manc voice was calm. "I'm going to go now. I'll be in the car, outside the gate, on the verge. If anyone sees me, I've broken down, waiting for assistance."

"And how long will I be?"

"An hour. I'll get going. Love ya."

I felt a bit sick hearing that. Or maybe it was being trapped in a tiny boot, with little air and seething heat.

Four

And now I had to put up with it. For an hour.

Now, heat does strange things to a strange mind. So does compression. So does lack of air. You hear stories about animals acting out in their impossibly hot cages as they head to the slaughterhouse in a tin trailer, ready to be burgers and sausages.

I was beginning to sweat, unable to stretch, unable to adjust my clothes. I wanted a bit of cool. I wondered how long had passed.

I remembered locking myself in the airing cupboard, playing hide and seek with dad, only to be in there a full 45 minutes while he went out for drink. I cried and screamed in there, but no one came. I was so scared.

Mum left him because of his drinking. Shame really, there weren't a bad couple. Relaxed, faithful, all the rest. But she couldn't be seen with an alcoholic. Her parents hated him, always drunk, never willing to push beyond his industrial cleaning job, always the dumb goofy grin on his face. They hated his clothes, how he'd always buy the minimum to save money for drink, they hated his friends, they hated our house. But I think most of all they hated his happiness, as they would discuss in much detail- how could you be *happy* with that job? How could you be *happy* with that house? And yet, happy he was, and frequently tipsy.

I hadn't wanted Mum to leave. Like, I really hadn't. But they never paid any attention to me.

Dad had dismissed the fires as a quirk. He even got it in his head that I wanted to be a firefighter. I think Carlsberg special brew really had killed off his grey matter by then. He'd even said I used to do a little dance when we went to a bonfire, round and round in circles and thrown myself on the ground and scream, a man possessed, in sheer joy of the heat and the light.

Back then it was a little bit different though. I just liked fire. Big. Hot. Dance-y.

I heard footsteps outside the buggy and snapped back. What time? How long had I been in? I wanted to wriggle, just the tiniest bit, but any noise would give me away. Lactic acid was building up inside me, filling my muscles to burst, my calf went into cramp, ow, JESUS, so much pain-

I imagined God up in the clouds, Zeus like in stature, his huge hammer smashing on top of me, pain, pain , pain, all the pain he could inflict, I wanted to scream so badly-

Footsteps fell around me. Still, now, Perce. Control. Can't be much longer now, surely. Basting in my own sweat, cooking, my outside crisping up and my inside softening, fluffy, unstable.

After Grandad died there was no whiskey left in the house, so Dad just drank the bitters. He winced and spat, crying, getting it all over his shirt.

And did those feet in ancient time

Walk upon England's mountains green??

And was the holy lamb of God

On England's pleasant pastures green?

Mum and Dad were choking up. It was his favourite hymn, apparently. And I really did try to cry, then. I really did. I made a lump in my throat and I pursed my lips to a frown and I wrinkled up my forehead and I thought about all the sadness in the room, the grief and loss everyone was suffering, the sheer unfairness and cruelty of the old mans passing. I tried and tried and tried to eke out some scrap of humanity in me.

But try as I might, I just could not cry.

"Ian?" I heard in the garage. "Ian? I'm locking up, mate." I heard a chain rattle and the roller shutter door creak. A beep of an alarm system. I was a million degrees, clammy and hot with pain shooting everywhere it could-

We cremated Grandad after that. I walked up through Acklam crematorium, *We are the Champions* playing, at his request. The priest said his piece and the curtains shut, Dad wailed out, no, no, he cried. I walked out the pew, trying to follow Grandad, to see the big hot dance-y fire take him, but Dad held me back-

No time for losers

Cos we are the champions

Of the world

"Dad, I want to see it," I said. He slapped me. "Fuck sake, Tom," his face was red and veiny and tear streaked. I didn't understand.

Later, we scattered his ashes. Me and Dad and Uncle Alan and my cousins, James and John, walked up Roseberry Topping to throw him to the wind. It's a big hill near Middlesbrough, quiet and proud against the backdrop of industry.

"See that building over there, son?" he pointed way out east. "That's the steelworks. That's where Grandad used to work."

Dad handed me the urn and I scooped out a handful of ashes.

And that's all he was- ash. My Grandad, who had a big fat body and a bald head and a beard, who brewed his own wine and listened to the Beatles and classical music, who ate fish and pasta for every other meal, who had frogs in his back garden and a big snail in a fish tank in the living room.

He was just ash.

White specks against the colossal green and purple of the North Yorkshire countryside dotted with wildflower, basked in the evening sun. This kind, generous human, who was once flesh and bones and a brain and a soul with warm eyes and a loud laugh.

He was just little flecks of white papery dust.

I thought about him then, quite clearly, in the furnace, his body and all that came with it dissipating into dust. And then the wind took him, and the ash blew over the hill edge.

Watching him go, I realised fire could even change a human. That was important. That was a big moment.

"Grandad Bob," Dad said tearfully, "will always be our friend…"

Five

I zoned back in. All quiet. No light from the crack.

The pain was back. But this time it was unbearable, every gram of my flesh filled with fire ants, stinging and biting. My fingers grasped for the clasp to let myself out- where was it, WHERE WAS IT-

I found the clasp and the boot swung open, cool air flowing over my body. I stripped, so desperate to feel it.

The garage was cool and dark and I stood there, dripping with sweat, cooling off. Deep, cool breaths, in through the nose, out through the-

Ah, fuck that. I didn't need to do that anymore.

It was a liberating feeling, to stride around inside a golf club wearing nothing but sneakers and a mask. Would highly recommend. Only when there's no one there, of course.

The mask was to shield me from CCTV. I'd be seen, of course, but without a face what could they do?

And the sneakers, well, they were for sneaking. Obviously.

I strode around the golf club in all my new found exhibitionism. The place was huge but old fashioned, those purple and blue 70's carpets and isometric décor all over. The walls were painted gold, the stairs and bannisters were painted gold. The opulence was breath-taking, but tasteless, it was a hollow canistes, shiny and polished on the out and so one-dimensional and numb on the in.

Like Wrighty and Rob, I suppose. And maybe even me.

The kitchen echoed the one at the midpoint. All stainless steel, big gas burner, immaculately clean. But one thing was a little different here. They had a pinboard.

For the staff, obviously. There was some little notes and pictures pinned up.

A family picture, I guess in the lakes, a man, and his wife and two kids and dog all looking happy.

Two child's handprints in bright orange paint, with the name 'Kyle' underneath.

An old wedding picture, black and white, a girl with a big perm and her husband, so young looking, long hair and huge collars.

A team picture, all wearing Santa hats, Christmas tree in the background.

I looked at this for quite a while.

And then the thoughts hit me.

"Why me?" I said aloud. "Why do I have to do this?"

A five-a-side team holding a trophy. A woman with a racing number on her front, holding a sign- "I raised £216 for Cancer Research UK"-

Four men in a pub, glasses raised. A young mother and her newly born baby. An abstract, almost Picasso-like painting of a human with the words "I LOVE YOU DADDY" next to it.

I wished I was normal. I wished I did normal people things.

Movie nights, going to the pub, normal friends, normal relationships, small talk, laughter, trust. Family, kids, pets, all the rest of it. Why couldn't I have that?

You CAN, came a voice from somewhere. You CAN!

I walked over to the stove, fingers hovering over the dial. Why *did* I have to do this?

Glancing back at the pinboard, the picture of family and the dog looked happily back at me. There was a picture of me and Mum and Brandon like that somewhere. We were in London, right in front of Big Ben. All smiles. All teeth. But we hadn't been happy.

I turned the dial.

"Fuck you," I breathed, "that's why."

I *did* use to like normal things. I used to do normal things. I used to have a normal brain.

Grabbing a metal pan, I walked to the microwave at the other end of the kitchen, stuck it in, and twisted the timer dial right as far as it would go. It clicked and set off.

I used to ride bikes, play Pokémon, have friends. I used to look forward to the happy meals at McDonald's, play in a paddling pool, chase the ice cream van when it rattled down the road...

But now that was gone, and replaced with this- this desire to hurt-

I stormed down the corridor, stamping, frothing at the mouth, hating them and their normal lives-

And then a wail.

A deafening, two-tone wail.

The alarm screamed, unimaginably loud, cutting my eardrums-

Oh, no. Oh, shit. A burglar alarm.

I ran to the door, twisted the latch and it opened. I shoved with all my might, but it didn't open-

Ah, bollocks. Magnetic locking system. Probably triggered from the burglar alarm. To, you know, stop burglars escaping when the police arrive.

I shoved the door again, and again. But there was no hope. I was locked in. In a golf club. Naked. And the golf club was about to blow up.

I was going to die, tonight, naked, masked, burned.

I sat down on the floor, alarm still wailing. Squeezing my eyes tight shut and holding my head in my hands, but they didn't feel like my hands... I was tiny, now, a tiny little action figure, plastic arms and plastic limbs- I wasn't alive, and I never had been-

Dad had given me an Action man that could swim in the bath.

People look different when they're on fire.

The alarm wailed and wailed.

Me and Dad had a bonfire after the funeral.

The alarm wailed and wailed.

"Grandad Bob will always be... our friend..."

The alarm wailed and wailed.

Dad looked different when he was on fire.

THE ALARM WAILED AND WAILED-

He didn't scream straight like you think people would, he went awful quiet at first, flames licking him, and he was so gentle and poor and old and the flames covered him and he was grasping at his head and I didn't know what to do and he struggled with his top and his hat AND THEN HE STARTED SCREAMING.

THE ALARM WAILED AND WAILED AND WAILED-

I jumped awake. I felt some force, some presence within and around me.

Everything went white for a second.

"What are you *doing?*" Dad had yelled, "WHAT ARE YOU DOING?!" But I was too scared and awestruck to do anything-

"What are you doing?" Ziggy was yelling. "Come on!"

The glass walls were smashed. Gone. Dead.

Shaking, I stumbled over the floor of broken glass, towards the car, opened the passenger door, and fell in.

The whiteout was flashing, coming, and going-

"Why are you naked?" he said. "Bit weird."

"Just get us out of here," I wheezed. "Now."

I felt the car lurch off. He was a good one, Ziggy. Mad that I'd only met him for the first time four days ago.

Behind me, there was an almighty crack in the sky as the building took off. I caught the red in the windscreen mirrors.

This time, I didn't feel anything, really.

Six

"Listen to the wind blow

Watch the sun rise"

When Zig had stayed at mine that night- two nights ago now- we hadn't slept. No, not like that. Well, a bit like that. But mainly we'd just talked. Talked and talked and talked.

He used to be in the circus, did Ziggy. A gymnast. A tightrope walker. Explains how he did the thing with the telephone wire. See, it all comes together, doesn't it?

He's from Bury, originally. Was nearly right with the Manc accent. Spent a lot of time in the care system, you know, pupil referral units and that. Foster homes. Adopted parents. Jealous stepbrothers and sisters. Apparently, he just never felt like he belonged. He told me all this on the first night together.

And I listened, and I told him things back.

"Running in the shadows..."

But not everything I told him was the truth. I just wanted him to stay. I just really, really, badly wanted him to stay.

"...damn your love,

Damn your lies."

Two individuals, bonded by a fear of abandonment, could be a dangerous thing. Co-dependence, they call it. It's unhealthy.

But with him, still asleep, next to me, I felt like I belonged to him, and him to me. I liked his weird spindly little fingers and cracked lips. He was beautiful in all the ways society tells us we are not beautiful.

I watched him roll around and doze in and out of sleep. He put his arm out and I saw his face scrunch up, finding only pillows, and not me. It was nice to be needed. I liked that I'd convinced him to need me.

Last night wasn't ringing in my ears as much as it should. Clean suit, clean shoes, hair slicked back. Back to work today.

He rolled over and opened his eyes. "Morning," he said, rubbing his temples, "You're up early."

"Gotta go to work, don't I," I was preening myself in the mirror. I went for the Hugo Boss aftershave, citrusy but powerful. Made me feel like a real gent. "Gotta go and earn some bread."

"You *hate* work," he grumbled. "Come back to bed."

This was becoming a half-truth.

"Can't. They'd know something was up." I finished my hair, adjusted my tie and my jacket, and admired myself. I looked better than usual, a bit more put together. Yeah, not bad, not bad at all...

.

Seven

"I've said it again, and again, and again, London just isn't secure enough. We have this huge system of surveillance, but there's crime everywhere, Perce, literally everywhere. There's blind spots, you see, Perce, blind spots in the system. And that's where the crime happens. Imagine a set, mate, like a TV set. You look at your telly, you see it from one perspective. Boom. That's it. But there's loads of shit happening everywhere else, isn't there? Things that people don't pick up on. And it happens everywhere. And once you're in a blind spot- that's it. Anything that happens is unaccountable. You know what I mean?"

Wrighty's rambling had reached a frenzied level. We'd got in early today- a lot of businesses affiliated with Ms. Pink to fiscally ransack. The shop floor was quiet. A calm before the storm.

But Wrighty was tense. "Look at this," he was saying, opening a tab on his laptop. It was a map of West London, filled with dots and tiny cones.

"This is the CCTV coverage for West London," he said. "The black dots are the cameras, and the red space around them is the area it covers. But look how much it doesn't cover, Perce? There's- literally- swathes of land, that aren't safe. No man's land, I call it," a grim, stoic look in his eye. "So I've changed my route home, now. Before, it was down here- now, I walk this way-"

He traced what looked like a figure of eight shape around where he lived, following the black dots.

"-so it's miles safer, see? I can always be seen." He sat back, a relieved look on his face. I got the impression some time and effort had gone into this.

"Let me see," I said.

The map stretched from Central out to Brentford. So many little dots.

"There are a lot of blank spots."

"Like I say," he said again, an undertone of terror in his throat, "No man's land."

"Are you worried?"

He shut the tab. "No. Just interested."

"Okay." I loaded up my own screen. Ten to eight. Not long now. "You heard from Rob?"

"Yeah. Back in tomorrow."

"Tomorrow? What the hell? I thought he was off for at least a week…"

"Nah. Wants the money, he says. Like, he really, really, wants the money. He's trying to speak to Lola Pink directly, set up a meeting. I don't know what he plans to do, but…yeah. He's still in."

Two minutes left.

"So," he whispered. "Last night. How'd it go?"

The siren cut into me again. The picture of the family and dog.

"Yeah, fine. Long drive, and all. But it was fine. Like you say, no one paid us any attention."

He laughed a little. "Caused a scene inside though, didn't you?"

He flicked onto another tab. BBC News. Live reporting.

Appeal after 'deliberate fire' at Isle of Sheppey golf club

Officers are investigating the blaze at Applespeake Golf Club, which happened within the area of the kitchen at Cornborough Road around 9.30pm on Monday.

The fire is being treated as wilful.

The blaze caused extensive damage to the kitchens, atrium, and function rooms before being extinguished by firefighters.

No-one was injured and the roads remained open.

The suspect -an exhibitionist arsonist who appeared on security footage naked with a mask and trainers- is still at large.

Bizarre CCTV footage captured the man strolling nude across the floor of the golf club, in Kent, with a mask pulled over his head.

He is shown making his way towards the front entrance, before a security alarm is tripped, triggering a locking system on the front door.

However, despite this, the suspect did escape, and police say he is still at large.

Police are looking for this man- shown here- and are appealing for any information.

Lola Pink, the owner of the club, declined to comment.

I burst out laughing. Real, uncontrollable laughter. Wrighty looked confused.

"What?"

"Just the way it said," I gasped, "Lola Pink declined to comment. Like, she's just sat and watched a video of some naked man blowing up his golf club. Of course she declined to comment," my voice rose to a squeak- "what the hell do you say about that, Wrighty? What do you even say about that?"

I don't know what got into me. Tears rolling down my face and everything. Mad.

And Wrighty just sat there, a confused smile on his face. "Erm, yeah, so…was it- was it you?"

"Huh?"

"Was it you, who torched it? Or the guy you hired?"

Oh yeah. I'd told Rob I'd hired someone to help.

"Yeah," I said. "Yeah. That's me, there," I pointed to my whole naked self, masked up, there on the BBC website. "That's me."

For the first time- maybe ever- I saw his eyes light up in awe.

"Respect," he said dumbly.

Twenty seconds left.

"Where's the list?" Time was tight now. Wrighty pulled out a folder. Names and details of businesses. All of them owned by Mrs. Pink. All of them flammable.

"I'll take A-R," I said, pulling the top two thirds of the pile off. "You can have the rest."

"That's more than half," he spluttered. "That's, like, three hundred grands worth of sales, Perce."

I shrugged. "I started it, didn't I?"

The bell went.

I picked up the phone and keyed in the number to A.R. Atkinson.

The dialling tone droned on.

Life as we know it is just one big old struggle. A struggle for power.

A click. I was ready.

"Hello, A.R. Atkinson, Sarah speaking, how can I help?"

"Hi. Can you put me through to accounting please? It's Tom calling from Benson and Fletcher. Your premiums gone up."

Eight

"Now, that one's nice. But the location? I dunno, I've heard Acton's a bit...low-income, isn't it? Now that one's good, but it's a bit of a walk to the tube- this one, this one here, now that is my jam. Open plan, garden, roof terrace- I like the décor , too, what's your thoughts on the décor?"

"Yeah. It's nice. Simple."

"Loads of natural light, too... now, if I'm a good boy, and can rein it in on the old- you know-nose candy- I could get my deposit down by, say, end of the month. Fuck it, end of the week, maybe, at the rate we're going! I think I'd like Battersea, too, you know. Mate, I went there once, you know, me and the boys went down to some pub, few beers and all that...literally, mate, *swimming* with gorgeous girls. Swimming." He beamed, eyeing up the £1,300,000 Victorian terrace on the front of the estate agents. "You know," he went on thoughtfully, "I think I could be really happy there."

Struggling to hide my shock I scoped a quick look at him. His face was sincere. He'd never mentioned being happy before.

"Is it on a blind spot?"

"Oh, shit-" his face froze, and he grabbed his phone. Thirty seconds of tapping later and a look of relief was on his brow. "Yeah. It is. Hmm, but it's...not *that* near a camera...anyway. Yeah. That could be mine."

We were talking big, big money now. Even in our world, six figures…
that was some senior management stuff, that was some big boy money. Not
just suits and flinging white up your conk every night.

Big, serious money. Property. Ownership.

'Oh, yeah, this? No, I own it. Yeah, it's mine. I bought the place.' And in
London? I mean… that puts you in the elite, right? No doubt about it. No
one owns homes in London anymore.

But we had done very well today. Very, very well.

A girl with a sleeping bag around her neck approached him. "Any
change, sir?"

Wrighty ignored her. "Sorry, no money on me."

She shivered and walked off.

I waited for everything to go dark, or pixelated, or the big kaleidoscope to
whirl around my vision, like it used to when I felt stressed, or alienated or
whatever…but nah, it just didn't.

It just…didn't happen.

I bought Zig a little number on the way home. Just an impulse purchase,
you know? He loved something a little different, did Zig. I had this old *Drop
Dead* tee that I wore when I was lounging round. Ancient, it was, but he
loved it. He liked the alternative look.

So I bought a look for him.

A purple crushed velvet jacket, collarless shirt, black bow tie, black
braces, deep purple brogues. He'd look so good.

Oh go on then. Why not. Why not live a little when you can?

Gold cufflinks, a gold Gucci watch, a thin gold necklace. God, he'd look
such a peach! Now, I'll go and pay, get home, and he could get into it-

My phone started to buzz. Who…? Rob, probably. Probably anxious to
know my winnings.

I pulled my phone out my pocket. Now, I could do with a new phone, too. Fancy one of those new iPhones, you know? Might pick up one of them, too-

I gulped when I saw the name on the screen.

Dad.

"Hello?"

"Ow, son," a deep Teesside accent replied. "Ow are ya?"

"I'm good, thanks. How are you?"

"Yeah, I'm sound, kid," his voice was still scratchy. He still can't have quit the fags. "Listen, err, I've got these coupons, yeah? Got them from work. Fifty quid of Morrisons vouchers! Fifty quid, Tom, how mad is that? Cos I've been in the warehouse two year, now, haven't I? Anyway, I'm- I just thought I'd send you them down, so you can treat yourself."

"I-" Traffic jam in my throat. "I- I think I'm alright-"

"Ah, g'wan," he laughed. "If you don't shop there, just give it to one of your pals, or save it, it doesn't run out til next June-"

"I'm fine, honestly.Thanks, though. But I'm fine."

"Sure?"

"Yeah. Sure."

"Sure your mates don't want it, or owt?"

I imagined handing over a fifty quid Morrisons voucher to Wrighty. Or Rob.

"No. Thanks, though."

"Oh, alright," he sounded a bit sad. "No worries. Well, I'm finished me break, anyway. I'll have to get back to it."

"Bye, dad."

"See ya." He hung up.

I looked at my hand. There were white marks where I'd been gripping my phone so tight. I had pins and needles in my feet, and-

-I remembered walking home, through the little walkways in Ormeston. I thought they were so cool, little secret tunnels in a maze of houses to get lost in-

"Card or cash, sir?"

The assistant had a wide smile on her face. I took a shallow breath.

"Card."

When I got home, arms draped in bags, I made Zig get into them immediately. They fit perfectly, of course- he looked like a little toy in them. He was wide eyed as he pulled out the jacket.

"How much was all this?" He pulled on the watch. It glittered on his wrist.

"Doesn't matter."

A grand or so.

When he was done, I guided him to the mirror, stood him in front of it, and put my arms round his waist.

"You look amazing," I said. "Don't you like it?"

"I love it," he said. "Thanks so much."

He was smiling, but there was something else in his eyes. I couldn't quite catch what it was.

Nine

Rob was already there when I got back into work.

He looked more functional than his usual peacocked self, just a shirt and trousers and shoes. And...glasses?

"You wear glasses?" I said to him as I walked over. "I've never seen you wear-"

"PERCE," he barked, as I approached the aisle he sat on. "Stay there."

I stood six foot away from him, watching him type furiously. "What's up? Are you OK? Feeling better?"

"Never better," he said breathlessly. "Never better. Busy day. Busy, buuuusy day. And I don't wear contacts now," he said, still typing. "Takes too long to put them in."

He picked up the phone, tapped in a number, and drummed his fingers restlessly on the table. "Come on, pick up, fucking pick up…"

"What are you doing," I said, advancing on the stack of paper next to him. "Are these new leads?"

"NO," he shrieked, causing a few other early birds to turn round in shock. "These are *my* leads," he said, hunched over, still drumming on the table. "I found them. Now piss off."

He propped up a large folder on his workstation, shielding himself. I wandered back over to Wrighty.

"He's upset that he missed yesterday," Wrighty whispered. "Been buying stocks and shares in fire cladding companies, privatised bits of the fire service, extinguishers…anything. He's jacking up premiums on anyone that he can get his hands on." He drew closer. "He's gone *mad*," he said, a touch of urgency in his voice. "Honestly. Been in since 6. He was on the phone yesterday with Big Neil, negotiating a salary cut so his commission can't be capped. He's really, I dunno… *involved*." He looked over my shoulder and nudged me.

Rob approached.

"You two," he said, scurrying over, "I'm going to speak to Lola Pink. This afternoon."

"*The* Lola Pink?"

"The very same," he said. "going to discuss her assets, and how we can protect them."

His tone was clipped, but his aura was bursting, fit to explode with excitement and nervous energy. "Now. I need to make some calls. A lot of calls- and then I am going to her office. At five. I will update you later tonight." He turned on his heel and walked back.

"Wait," I said. "I'm going to come, too."

He stopped, arms twitching in rage. "You *can't*, okay? We cannot fuck this up-" he spat every word, as he whispered them furiously. "We can *not* fuck this up!"

But even in that, his power had gone.

"Well," I breathed, "You best find someone else to do your job then. Someone who can play with fire."

We both looked at Wrighty. He hung his head.

"Besides," I continued. "Lola Pink. One of the wealthiest women in England. And you're going to meet her, dressed like *that*?" I scanned him, head to foot. "You look like you work in IT, man. No offence, obviously."

A look of horror struck him. He looked down, at his practical shoes, his practical, loose-fitting trousers, his creased shirt. His mouth opened and closed like a fish. He took off his glasses, gazing at them, mortified.

"Oh my god," he said, aghast. "I need to go and get changed." He ran out the door.

"He is involved, isn't he?" I remarked. "I best take some of his workload."

Wandering over to his desk, I took a few leads. Then a few more. Then a few more.

By the time Rob had returned- adorned with an azure three-piece and trademark pocket-watch, we were running late. I'd advised Wrighty that he should stay behind- he'd wanted to pressure Rob into allowing him to come, of course, but I told him no.

"Four hundred thousand," Rob was saying breathlessly, "Four hundred thousand. They're risky investments, yes, but if they all play off- and, you know, I think they will- then I could make four hundred thousand."

We walked at some pace out of the building. It was cool now.

"Hey, Rob," I shouted. I ground myself to a halt, and he turned and eyed me.

"Come on, Percy. We're going to be late."

"You never even asked me how the job went," I said. "Like, I went out and did this job for you. A fucking dangerous one. And you never even asked me how it went? What's that all about?"

He looked embarrassed. "I was meaning to," he said. "I know it was a success, but-"

"And then, you started shouting at me, second I got back in. What was that about?"

It was the strangest thing. I was wailing at him, a rage, a vex I'd never been to emotionally.

"You know, I just think it's rude, mate. I did all that for you. And you never even said thanks."

Good GOD, I think I could feel hot tears welling. What- what the hell was this?! My god, this is what real people do! They get angry, they get emotional, they get upset! Was I a real human? Did this make me human?

For a second felt like laughing. But I guess that would have ruined the act. Normal humans don't juxtapose crying and anger with laughter.

But then he cracked too.

"Perce, I'm sorry." He stopped, his lip trembled, and then he burst into tears, grabbing his head, bent over. "I'm so, so, sorry." He advanced over, so small in his sadness, and embraced me, sobbing into my expensive jacket. "I just- all this shit that's happened, with that fire and everything, I just feel so *scared* now, like, I can't stop thinking about how near it was to me, and how- I could have died, and what- what am I doing, Tom? What happens when I die? What's it all even for?"

Oh god. Nah. I was out of my depth here. Must have got all the human out my system in that little outburst. I stood there, with this little well-dressed rich boy crying into my shoulder, feeling absolutely nothing. Nothing at all. I wasn't a real human. Just a good actor.

I took a sigh of relief. False alarm.

Ten

"Stop sniffling," I said urgently, as we walked through Canary Wharf. "People don't cry round here."

They really didn't, either. Well, maybe those who worked in hospitality, who everyone else thought they were entitled to treat like shit. But besides that. No tears in Canary Wharf.

I used to hate the place. I really did. But now I was bowled over by it, sort of like a New-York-lite, you craned your neck to see the top of the immaculate glass towers. So dull and grey, but so beautiful and timeless. The streets were pristine. There was a pleasing symmetry about the place. The air felt cleaner than Central. No wonder no one cried here.

Lola Pink owned Ultion Capital, a building on Upper bank street. Much like the rest, it glowed yellow on the storm clouds, imposing, powerful. You felt like an ant stepping inside, the scale ridiculous, unnecessary, overconfident. The buildings here were showboaters, posturing rivals to each other, all looking to be the tallest and the cleanest.

"Hi, we have a meeting with Lola Pink."

The girl at reception, much like everything else in the room, held herself in perfect symmetry. Her face did not change as she probed us.

"Lola Pink?" her palms rested on the keyboard.

"The very same."

"And what is your business, sir?"

I glanced at Rob. Jeez, were his eyes still red? For god's sake.

"A meeting with Robert Winter, please. He should know we're coming."

She picked up the phone and tapped in a four-digit extension. "Hi, yes. A Robert Winter here to see you? Thanks. No problem."

She hung up. "They will call when ready to send you through. Just take a seat. They should only be around five minutes."

"How are you?" I said suddenly.

Her brow raised. She prepared herself. "Erm. I'm fine, thanks! And yourself?"

"Yeah, good." I held her eye contact. "So. How has your day been?"

"Oh, yeah, well," she laughed nervously. "Busy as ever. Glad it's nearly over. Well- you know. Not that glad!" She threw an anxious, but perfectly practised, business-laugh around the empty lobby.

"You like working here?"

"Erm, yeah, I do. It's lovely. Everyone here is- well, it's a nice place to work." Her smile showed no signs of fading. Wow. *So* practised. "I've been here over six years now."

"And they treat you well?"

"Well, they-" her smile remained intact, but the little wrinkles round her eyes had disappeared. "They- they're very orderly," she said. "When I first started, if I made a mistake, they'd come down on me, and I'd be like, 'no, please, I need this!'… but I don't make mistakes anymore."

"Mhmmm."

"I mean, I always wanted to work on Canary Wharf. Like, always. So, after Uni, I got this job…"

"…six years ago."

"Yeah, six years ago. And…well. Here I am." Her smile was pulled up at the sides by strings of floss now.

"Cool. "

The phone rang and she answered it within a second.

"Hello? Yes. I'll send him up now."

"They're ready for us?"

"Yes. Floor twenty-eight."

"Well, have a good day."

Without a word we walked to the elevator, which slid open automatically. I tapped the twenty-eight button.

"I think the receptionist is depressed," I said to Rob. "She hides it so well though. Impressive."

The elevator began to rise. The elevator's back wall was made from glass, so as you go up, you can feel yourself getting higher...and higher...and higher...

The superficiality of Canary Wharf was starting to make sense. It didn't matter what was going on in your life. Not a jot. You glued your smile on, and acted like everything was OK, and in return, everyone else did the same to you. You didn't have to be a human here. In fact, I got the impression you were encouraged not to.

We rose up and up, steel beams crossing my vision diagonally. This must be some power trip, some elevation to the heavens type thing. King of everything you looked out on. Amongst the sea of grey, the sun peaked out and lit the river a deep yellow.

This is all you.

I heard that voice again, the demon. Only, there was no guilt, no sickening feeling of power. This was a friend now. Comforting me, congratulating me.

I'd worked hard for this. I deserved it.

As I looked out onto London. About to meet a business magnate. About to rise even higher. About to own the city. This is all you, the voice kept saying. This is all you.

Eleven

Lola Pink was no conventional businesswoman.

Somewhat a myth in the world of finance down in old London town, she sought the finer things in life. But still she clung to the common touch, adorning herself with jewellery, designer streetwear, limited edition trainers. A woman in her forties, she dated grime MC's in their twenties, drove a Ferrari, was no stranger to five figure bar bills, and had acquired a notoriety in the tabloids. The first and only female member of Oxford University's Bullingdon Club, she was well schooled in its ways- trash first, pay later, do whatever the hell you want, money will reimburse your damages. Money could repair any damage, soothe any woe, and she damn knew it.

She also swore like a trooper.

"Oh my fucking god." She shouted over, positioned on a tiger throw on top of a leopard print sofa. Her suite, predictably, was the penthouse. A domed glass ceiling, latticed with white metal, patterned above us. Low, ambient lighting accentuated the shadows. The place was impeccably adorned- oak tables, huge orange trees. The floor, jet black marble with illuminated flower beds embedded into the ground, shone up around our feet. But all we could concentrate on was the woman in front of us, in a black and gold tracksuit and black trainers, platinum blonde hair cropped at the shoulder, dark eye shadow and a diamondized whiskey glass in her hand. She broke the mould of the room, intimidating us with her pressure.

"You two," she said, still languished on the sofa, "Walk like a pair of virgins. Grow up for me, would you? You've come to talk, now, act like professionals, not a pair of schoolboys, Jesus Christ."

She took another sip and stood. Despite being little over five foot, we had to take a step back. Too much ego per square metre.

"Take a seat, you two."

We obeyed.

"So," she said, swilling her drink, "You have come to talk about how you can protect my property."

"Y-yes," Rob stammered. He was a millimetre from the edge of his seat, front row to his own casualty. "We're concerned for your estate, Miss Pink-"

I caught her roll her eyes.

"-and we wanted to help. There are preventative measures we can put in place, you see, to save some of the… irreparable damage that has come to you."

"You're not concerned for my estate, you clown," she said. "You're concerned for your own pocket."

The silence hung in the air. Rob, two lines into the script from his starring scene, was down and out.

I would have really loved to help but watching him flap was just such a joy.

"No, honestly, Miss Pink. We wouldn't normally reach out to a customer like this, not so personally, but we do really want to help-"

"Oh, you wouldn't *normally* reach out, would you?" she laughed, a furious look in her green eyes. "You wouldn't *normally* have anything to do with your customers, but as soon as one of them's on the ropes, you go sniffing after them like a pack of dogs? You're all the same, you brokers, you'll say anything, won't you? Any damn thing to get what you want. I-honestly, I don't know." She took another drink, laughing again in her anger. "Normally. NORMALLY. You're so false."

Rob wobbled, but did not stand. I think his nerves must have tensed up or something- he didn't look up to walking.

Time to intervene.

"In his defence, Miss Pink-"

I was shocked at the voice that came out. Boom, crackle, thunder. It roared around the penthouse, striking down the stale air that hung in the rafters.

"In his defence. Oh- sorry. Before I start, could I take a drink?"

Her pupils narrowed another notch. An eighth of an inch thick, they flashed over to the decanter and back, daring me. I reached over, smelled the bottle, and poured a dram. Keeping eye contact, I tasted it.

"Now, that's nice. Peaty, isn't it?"

She said nothing, furious dagger eyes blading me.

"Sorry, where was I. Oh, yeah. In his defence. He said we wouldn't normally come out to see a customer. And he's right. We wouldn't. Now, before, say, last Thursday. Things *were* normal, weren't they? I can remember last Thursday. It was a normal day at work. I was going to go and buy some popcorn afterwards. Do you like popcorn? They've just brought out a Peanut and Almond butter flavour. It's delicious."

Rob's expression was rapidly changing to one of horror.

"Anyway. I didn't go and buy popcorn. I went out with one of our team, for some cocktails. And on the way home, we were attacked by an arsonist. Since then, nothing has been normal, has it?"

I couldn't tell if her expression had softened.

"You've had- what. Three, four properties, all damaged by fire? In the space of a weekend? Do- do you think these aren't linked, Miss Pink?"

CRACK.

She looked down and raised her hand to her head. Bingo.

"Rob, here, had his car torched just the other day. You think these are all just some coincidence, Miss Pink?"

"Lola," she said quickly. "Just say Lola." ·

"Lola. Things are moving quickly. There's some…insidious threat in London, and we have literally all been affected by it. Which makes us in this together. We need to start behaving as such."

I took another sip.

"There's, like, almost a vanilla to this, isn't there? What do you think, Rob?"

His mouth was dry. I offered him a sip, and with a trembling hand he took it.

"Yeah," he whispered. "Burnt sugar."

"Burnt sugar, of course! It's very light, isn't it? You know, I'd heard psychopaths prefer bitter flavours? Something to do with like- a sensation seeking personality? Apparently, it stems from when we were in primordial times, bitter flavours were associated with poison, so only the braver ones in packs and tribes used to actually, you know… go ahead and eat them. Crazy, that, isn't it? Anyway, I'm glad you're on the sweet stuff, for that reason."

You know when you- like- catch yourself? You're so busy running with a narrative that you don't even pay attention to what you're thinking or saying or doing? And then- BAM. It hits you. This is real life. I had that just then. Felt a wobble and all. Luckily, Lola filled the silence.

"What do you want?" her mouth moved like a tiny snake, contorting and flexing in ten different directions at once. "Why are you here? Have you come to threaten me? Do you know who I am?"

The glasses began to tremble as she bellowed.

"I own- I OWN- Ultion Capital, my dear, we are the largest business outsourcing provider in the UK, we're on the FSTE 100, we OWN EVERYTHING," her eyes lit up, like a 1930's rubber band cartoon- "And you think you can just welch in here, with your demands? You're just here to make a quick buck out of my misery. It's disgraceful. You're a pair of nobodies, working for some no-mark company. I'd have never even heard of you if not for the last few days."

"Blimey, that's mad, isn't it."

The tension in the room was of the highest pressure, but me and the demon, well. We liked pressure. We used it to diamondize.

"Just a few days, isn't it? Since this all happened. It's so hard to believe its all just…. Exploded in just a few days. Like what's happening here, this is ridiculous…funny how it can all change, right? It can all change so quickly. Has it even been a hundred hours, Rob? Since that first fire?"

He took a painful-looking swallow. "Um. Well, the fire was Thursday night. And it's Tuesday afternoon. So… five days. That's a hundred and twenty hours."

"A hundred and twenty hours, huh." I swilled my drink again. "Not a long time in the grand scheme of things, is it? I think whiskey takes about three years to mature. That's what- how many hours, Rob?"

With a more than noticeable twitch of anger, he pulled out his phone and nervously tapped on the calculator app.

"Twenty-six thousand, two hundred and eighty," he said finally.

"Wow. Now, imagine what could happen in that time? We don't know if this is a one-time thing, or if it will get bigger. But it's odd, isn't it? How a few fires can change everything."

Something changed then, quite abruptly. Maybe she'd been on autopilot this whole time- auto-CEO mode, aggression and conviction and assertion all in one.

But she very suddenly stopped, cast her eyes to her drink.

"Yes, it is strange, isn't it? Very strange."

She rested her glass on a table in front of her. "Give me a moment," she pressed her fingers to her temples. "Just give me a moment, please."

The silence became oppressive very quickly.

And I had a question that was just burning a hole in my lungs that I needed to ask Rob.

Sat on the other end of the impressive grey sofa, I typed in a text and hit send.

Do you want out?

Zzzzzzzzzt. I heard his phone buzz and he checked it immediately. A stony-faced man in business normally, I was starting to see his tells. His pupils stretched to the size of pills when he saw the text.

A long beat. Heavy breathing, unmasked from Lola, stifled from Rob. He looked at that text for a whole minute, without even paying me a glance.

Eventually, I heard two pops as he entered two letters, and a little whoosh as he hit send.

I knew what the reply would be but had my phone at the ready. It came through.

No

As I thought. But as I was about to send him another communication, I received a text I did not expect to. An unknown, +44 number. What the...

"Heyy it's Ziggy what u want for tea tonight x"

Wait- what? How'd he got a phone? Thought I told him not to leave the house...

"Do you think there will be more fires, then?"

I startled. Lola, still catatonic, had regained the power to speak.

I couldn't respond.

"Well, go on," she said again, still unmoving. "Do you think there will be more fires?"

What the hell was Ziggy doing? Did I need to up sticks, now?

"We can't answer that," Rob spoke, finally, with a brewing air of authority. "Do *you* think there will be more fires?"

Wow, credit where credit is due, he's pulled it out of the bag there. A real homing missile of a question.

"I don't fucking know." she mumbled.

She gazed up at the latticed glass ceiling.

"What is going on, lads?" she didn't address us at all. "What's going on? Five days, five fucking fires, I've never seen anything like it in all my life. Do you know, I've literally never felt depressed before, not in my life. I always thought depression and anxiety and all that shit were just for people who are weak minded. But I think I am depressed."

I felt just a flicker of red lightning creep in from the corner of my vision.

"I own all this shit," she went on, "and a few days, that's all it takes, and it all goes up in smoke. Literally. And it's not just the money, it's people's lives too, their livelihoods. You get all that shit on your shoulders, too."

The red lightning intensified. I was losing hit points fast here.

"Like, why do people do this? What kind of... sicko, goes round targeting someone's business, and literally setting fire to it? So there's absolutely nothing left there? You know, back at that club, there was this old jukebox- it was useless, it had no good records- but the workers, they loved it, even though the music was weak. Why, why do they do it?"

This was a bullet hell video game, swarms of red lightning streaking everywhere around my vision, frantic jazz in the background as I struggled to avoid its shock, block it, BLOCK IT-

"They do it for control," I heard myself say. Through the chaos on my inner screen I saw her look at me.

"It's the ultimate form of control, isn't it? To use an element to irreversibly take something? To reduce time, money, capital, material, into nothing, and everything that comes with it. There is no rebuilding after a fire. That's why they do it. They enjoy it."

She was a little surprised at this monologue.

"Why would you enjoy that?"

"Well,"

Don't say it, the voice of reason said.

"It's a defence mechanism, Lola. I mean…you go through those early steps of life with no control over one damn aspect over anything, then you begin to relish control, fetishize it, treasure it. Control becomes your number one goal, your priority in life. It becomes a *need*, Lola."

She regarded me with equal parts concern and contempt.

"You certainly know a lot about this subject, don't you?"

"Did a free elective on psychology at uni." To be fair, I had. "You ever heard of Sigmund Freud?"

"No," she sat up, exasperated. "I haven't. So, you think they're going to do it again, basically, that's what you're saying?"

"I think so. Maybe not anytime soon. But they will."

"Hmm." She was apathetic now. Did we have it?

"Well. I suppose there's assets that could use it. And, if we do have some…maniacs on our hands, then it's worth it."

"We will discuss tomorrow," she rolled onto the sofa again, pouring another large measure. I'm tired. I want to go home and get into my jacuzzi."

She stood, wearily. The meeting was over.

"Set up a meeting, tomorrow morning. A few others and I will come and see you to discuss. Now, if you don't mind. I'd like you to leave."

"I think you should insure all of your assets," I said quickly. "We could finalise it tonight. Shake on it."

She paused for a moment, then erupted in laughter. "Shake on it? Good lord, you think you're straight out of a film set, don't you?"

We are in a film set. I could have sworn we were in a film set.

Twelve

Ziggy had cooked me a beef stroganoff. Only, the beef was super noodles, and the stroganoff was popcorn.

"I used the rest of the aged white cheddar popcorn, you know, to give it a bit of a tangy funk." He'd set the table elegantly, glasses of red, placemats, two sets of knives and forks for one course. "And I paired it with the chicken and mushroom noodles, to make it creamy and rich. And then I paired *that* with the Malbec, cos it's got that smoky, oaky aftertaste, which I thought would play well with all the flavours on the plate."

He spread his arms real wide, genial smile on his face. "Ta-daaa! Hope you like."

He came in and kissed me, that weird obsessed look about him.

"I've been meaning to ask you something. But I've forgotten. Let's eat."

"What is it, smelly?"

"I don't know. Something from work. I can't remember."

The meal was not good. The flavour of the chicken and mushroom noodles did not marry up well with the tangy funk of cheesy popcorn, resulting in a bland, salty dish that reminded me of eating the mud in my garden infused with weed killer when I was three.

Regardless, Ziggy wolfed it down. "Try it with the wine," he said. "The undertones of cherry and grape really go well with it."

I tried it with the wine. This time, it was like mud mixed with vinegar. I tried to imagine it was Asian fusion food, pickled fresh noodles with Himalayan goat's cheese. But it wasn't working. It was hard to swallow, and for a second, my throat didn't want to accept it. I threw up a bit in my mouth.

"You don't like it?" immediately, distress welled in him. So quick to change.

"I do," I choked. "Just feel a little sick."

"Don't eat if you don't want to."

A forced apologetic look on my face I slid the plate backwards. He promptly took it and ate the rest.

"Shame you can't eat," he said. "It's so good. And I made it just for you."

"I know. Thanks."

Then I remembered.

"Wait. You texted me earlier. How did you get a phone? How did you know my number?"

In the one hundred hours I'd known him, I knew he tended to respond to urgency with even more laconism.

"One sec," he said, almost forcing himself to slow down. "Let me finish this. Mmmmmmm."

He ploughed through the rest of his sordid meal with boundless joy, proceeding to lick the plate clean. I resisted the urge to throw up in my mouth again.

"So," he began, wiping his mouth with the kitchen towels he used as napkins. "Exciting news! I found a bag. Just this holdall, outside the apartment block. I saw it when I was looking out the window. So I went and got it. And it had a phone in."

"You *found* a bag?"

"I didn't steal it!" His smile was still genial. "It was just- well. It was kind of hidden. I saw it poking out from behind that massive bin on the other side of the courtyard. I think someone hid it. And," his smile broadened, "There was something else in the bag. A couple of other things, actually."

He exited and brought back in a large Sports. Inc holdall. His body was buckling against it- must be heavy.

"So this- this is the phone. You like it?"

It was a burner phone. I could tell by the fact it was marked 'BURNER PHONE'.

"I've never heard of burner-phone before," he mused, turning it over in his hands. "Sounds a lot cooler than Vodafone though. Have a look."

"Ziggy," I felt my heart pound. "Do you know what these are? They're designed to be thrown away. They're designed to be untraceable. Drug dealers use them. They're illegal."

His eyes lit up again. "Well. Wait til you see what else is inside."

He reached in, and, with some difficulty, removed a crossbow.

"What the-"

Now, I'd never seen a crossbow in real life. It wasn't like the old medieval types you saw in museums, or on *Lord of the Rings.* This was a pure mechanical beast, gleaming in chrome and brass, with a gunstock mounted on the end. This wasn't antiquity but rather army-issue, built to kill.

"Ziggy," I breathed. "Why is there a crossbow in my house?"

"How cool is it? And look, it came with arrows-"

He withdrew a drawer of them. Again, these weren't traditional- full carbon metal save for a few black fins of plastic at the end. Again, built to kill, not for cosmetics. The ends were wrapped in cheesecloth, tied to the end with wire.

"Smell it," Zig said. "The ends smell like sparklers."

They *did* smell like sparklers.

"Ziggy." Blood was beginning to run below freezing. "Is there- is there anything else in the bag?"

"Just this."

He removed a small tub, no label. I opened it and sniffed. My nose burned.

"Kerosene," I said. "It's kerosene. Zig, did anyone see you pick this up? Anyone at all?"

"No. No one. Maybe a dog. But no one. Like, no humans saw me, for sure. I was careful, smelly. Definitely."

I stood and looked at it for an age.

"Was it for you?"

"No," his voice rose. "No. Honestly. I just found it."

Another age passed. I was starting to get that feeling that my shadow was following me. That it was catching up.

"Okay. I believe you." I turned to him. "I think someone else round here was trying to start a fire with that. I think we've just spoiled someone's plan."

He genuinely looked surprised. "What makes you say that?"

I sighed. "I will explain," my voice felt heavy. "You know how you said those arrowheads smelt like sparklers? It's potassium perchlorate. The same material as the end of a match. It's got a high energy density, see, so it ignites easy. And this- this is kerosene. Lamp oil. So, when it's lit, it burns well. I guess when you- when you fire the arrow- the combination of the two stops the wind from blowing it out-"

"Oh, okaaaay," Zig rolled his eyes with a laugh. "Didn't need a science lecture on it, Mister Degree."

Stop now, stop now, said my brain. Slow down, stop now.

"Ziggy, this is MENTAL," the words burst out. "This is mental! Someone, round here, is trying to shoot working flaming arrows. Flaming arrows, Zig! Who the hell has a use for flaming fucking arrows in Maryland? Do you know, I think- do you think you were meant to find it? Was it obviously placed? Did you see who dropped it?"

He looked a little embarrassed. "Well, actually. It wasn't behind the bin. More in it. I'd seen this lass, she had a big bucket of fried chicken. And she just left it over there, on top of that bin. I thought, I'm having that, me...you know I like fried chicken. And when I tried to get it, the lid on the bin, it broke. And it was in there."

My legs paced the room as my brain whirred.

"Okay," I said. "okay. Okay, okay, okay. Maybe it was just... in the bin. Maybe someone just binned a crossbow and some modified arrows and a tub of kerosene."

We both knew I was lying. Only one of us seemed to care.

"Shall we try it out?" he beamed. "We can get up on the roof, can't we?"

Thirteen

"It's a bit like *Zelda*, isn't it? You play that game? You're this little elf looking thing, with a sword, and green clothes, and you have to save the princess from a big monster. Reminds me of that, you know? Cos there's...puzzles, where you have to light the tip of your arrow from a torch, and fire it at another torch, and when all the torches are lit the door opens. That would be cool, wouldn't it? Like a locking system based on torches being lit?"

"Course I played it," I said. "He had a longbow, not a crossbow. Get your facts straight."

There was, mercifully, only a little wind on the roof. The sun was just dipping below the horizon, the sky turning watercolour navy. I was bathing the end of one of the arrows in kerosene.

"I loved that game," he said. "I really, really loved it. I remember playing it getting ready for a trip with my friends in the orphanage. And it was so innocent, you know? It's just a kids game, right?"

He was looking out over the edge of the building, hair and baggy clothes swaying in the breeze. A bit like a *Zelda* character, I suppose.

"Just thinking about those...flaming arrows-" he laughed, at the ridiculousness- "it just reminds me when there were virtually no cares in the world for me besides homework. And you know what, it's a beautiful memory. I'm glad I can have memories, you know? Even with all the shit that's happened." He laughed again. "Anyway. Sorry. My names Ziggy and this has been a TED talk."

He said that with such peace, looking out over London with all its money and its nine til fives and commuters and complex unnecessary adult bullshit. He was cast away with a scene on the lid of a dreamer's eye, lost in the happiness of it.

But I did not understand.

I had no happy memories.

Fuck you, Zig.

I boiled over.

"Memories are nothing." I stood and walked over to him. "Memories are the fucking past, Zig. They serve nothing, nothing but a constant reminder of the- the cruel- unidirectional flow of time. Don't you- don't you *simp* on me, with your bullshit video game recalls. It's pathetic. Tragic, Zig, tragic, you know what I mean?"

Oh god. I think Wrighty just spoke through me.

"Alright, no need to get antsy and all," he said quietly. "It's just a story."

I stood, panting, all red and veiny and gammon-y. God I was angry.

"Match," I said quietly. "Got a match?"

He offered me the book of matches.

"Light it," I said. "Light the arrow, then."

I pulled the butt to my shoulder, loaded an arrow in, and clipped it to the wire. I pulled it back. The mechanism clicked into place.

"Light it," I said. "Light the arrow."

He looked for a shred of compassion in my face but found none. Hands all trembly, he lit a match and hovered under the cheesecloth wrapped round the end of the arrow. With a fizz, it lit.

"Move out the way," I said. "What shall I shoot?"

We were looking out onto the courtyard. I wanted to take something away from all the shiny happy people here. I HAD to.

"Nothing down there," he hissed. "Someone'll see us."

"Fuck you," I said, very quietly, and pulled the trigger.

Now I never even though there'd be a recoil on a crossbow, but by hell there was. A big old TWANG and the arrow loosed.

I'd been aiming for a big square bush in the middle of the courtyard. But, alas, my aim was poor.

The arrow flew straight, missing the bush by a good couple of feet, and thudded into a bench. The flame stayed lit.

"Oh, well done," I heard him jeer. "Memories are nothing, are they? Is that why you couldn't remember how to not shoot like a total divvy?"

"Shut up." Tar started to drip from up top of my vision. "There's someone there."

There was.

Now, we couldn't see them properly- it was too dark, their face shrouded in shadow. They were tall, though. Broad. And whoever it was made its way over to the flaming arrow.

"Oh, shit."

The figure stood like a zombie, staring at the arrow. Then they walked to the bin, looked inside, and slammed the top.

Then the figure looked up at us.

"Get DOWN!"

I yanked him down as hard as I could. Heart thumping in my mouth, I peered over the top, trying to get a look at them...but they were hooded, cloaked. Could have been anyone.

But they were still looking up at me.

And then they began to walk toward the building.

"Oh no," I whimpered. "Oh, god no. Ziggy. Ziggy, get inside. Now."

Ziggy was already on his feet. I grabbed the crossbow.

"No, man," he said, "leave it, could be anyone, could be anyone..."

My finger on the trigger, tar dripping all over my brain, not working properly, I was in my old room with a lion and an elephant and a-

"Look," he said softly. "He's going."

And he was. His hand on his ear, on the phone, striding back to the alley from where he'd came. I could hear the echoes of a voice. It was a man.

Fourteen

Some purple sky this morning. Birds sound like guitar strings on max distortion. The clouds are all red, like big evil teeth on a cartoon monster. And nah, I hadn't slept. Again.

Silver Springs sounded calm this morning, though, all harmonics and voilined guitar chords and gentle vocals. My brain producing some echo that wasn't there. The house over the street contorted into a sphere, and when I started breathing, it came out as rainbow smoke.

You could be my silver spring
Blue green colours flashing
I would be your only dream
Shining autumn ocean crashing

My tie kept attacking my fingers. I think it was a milk snake, but through the brain fog you couldn't be sure of anything, really. Ziggy was an angel though, all feathers and a halo, the crossbow he cuddled turned into cupids bow.

When times like this happen (I've heard they're called 'episodes', but I hate that word, makes me sound crazy, hahahahahahahahahahahahaha) you just gotta roll with it. You just gotta roll with it, take your time, accept it as the new normal. The second you take stock, start thinking 'oh, I feel really weird' or 'oh, I don't feel like I'm really here' or anything like that, your head goes. A toxic catalyst goes off, turns your brain inside out, you get the chills in your neck, and you start thinking the real nightmare fuel.

Did you say that she's pretty

And did you say she loves you

The crescendo hurt. The word love hurt. Roll with it, roll with it, kaleidoscope it. Did I look OK?

I checked in the mirror. Ah, I hated looking at myself when I was like this. Especially my eyes. They always moved towards me, looking all around me.

I can't go to work like this.

Call in sick.

Take a sleeping pill.

Don't go in.

My chest hurt from hyperventilating all night, but it seemed to have gone all warm and full of pins and needles. It made me want to laugh. But hell, if I started laughing on my own. Then I really would know I'd lost my mind.

I took a stroll to the balcony. Fresh air will sort me out.

And it did, for a second. So cool and crisp. The morning light all shimmery. Things looked normal again. I drew closer to the balcony edge.

TOP YOURSELF

CHUCK YOURSELF OFF

WoOoAahh there, partner, that was quite an intrusion just then! I best just…step away…

Ahhh. The floor feels weird. Spongy. Like I'm on a big bouncy castle. Maybe I *am* on a bouncy castle. Have you heard that conspiracy theory, that the government put things in the water? Just to keep us acting normal? Maybe all this real-life malarkey is actually the thing I'm feeling now, and the water just creates a big boring hallucination…

I didn't want to walk in the road. It looked so deep, a big vat of black death miles below me. Pavement was safe. Stay on the pavement.

For a moment, things did seem normal then. My feet clacking off the concrete.

There's a crossbow with flaming arrows at my house that we stole, and someone came looking for it last night and THEY KNOW DAMN WELL ITS US-

It's weird being in the limelight, huh? Especially on the metro. I mean tube. I mean autobahn. Where am I...? Either way, there the spotlight was, shining down on me, in my fez and tap-dancing shoes, mother had always told me I couldn't dance but what did she know? I was born to dance!

My brain wasn't dripping the tar anymore but everything was very rainbow rhythms right now. The tunnels kept collapsing in on themselves but I could walk through, I was Harry fucking potter, striding through walls to get my own train to my own platform...oh, damn, what a day this was going to be...

The jostling was unnerving. They could well be all demons. Or lizards, or zombies. I mean I didn't really know any of these people. They had the human skin, yeah, but what besides that? Those damn lizards, with their sharp teeth and claws, scratching me up at bank station. Who are they? Did they start fires?

One person in London right now is looking for his crossbow.

One person in London right now is looking for his crossbow.

ONE PERSON

Beep, why couldn't they make some nicer noise for the ticket barrier? Why so functional, so cold? Had I taken my- oh, shit. I hadn't taken my meds. Is there time to go back to get them? Best consult the watch;

Perce: Good morning, timekeeper. May I request the time?

wATCH: Pls insert 14p

Perce: Give me one for free.

wATCH: DELETESYSTEM34

Hmmm. It didn't want to tell me, today, ne'er-do-well that it was.

I was just going to have to grin and bear it.

One person in London right now is looking for his crossbow.

He's going to go to the flat.

HE'S GOING TO STAB UP ZIG

HE'S GOING TO STAB UP MY BOYFRIEND

And I sang that cheerful four-line ditty to the tune of the chorus of "You can go your own way", by the Mac, as I walked down Penny lane towards work.

I t w a s

It was becoming

It was becomomomomoming

It was BECOMING increasingly clear to me I was on a knife edge. Or an arrow edge. Or a cliff edge. If I went too far one way, I would fail.

I needed to calm down. Just a bit. Just for a bit.

…popcorn…?

Fruit twist?

I had to find somewhere quiet to eat it. This place ended up being an alley. Behind a bin.

The trick was, to focus entirely on the popcorn whilst you ate it. I had bought your standard butterkist toffee stuff. Now, it was standard but had a good crunchy texture, good golden glow, nice squeaky voice, long lasting sweet honey flavour. You have to screw up your eyes tight, block out all the noise. Isolate taste and touch as your only senses. And then, begin.

No judgements, only acknowledgements.

If your thoughts wander, bring them back to the popcorn.

If your thoughts wander, bring them back to the popcorn.

If your thoughts wander…

ONE PERSON IN LONDON IS LOOKING FOR

If your thoughts wander, bring them back to the popcorn.

If your thoughts wander…

It was getting easier. And easier. I didn't feel like such a psycho anymore.

But then I hit the end of the bag.

"Now son, if you go and help us pick some courgettes, I'll buy ya a bag o' popcorn."

"Got an A in maths, did ya, son? I'll take you for a bit of popcorn, shall I?"

"Happy 18th birthday, Tom lad! I bought you some popcorn."

It's OK. You're allowed to do that, I think, at the end of spirituality. Let your mind wander. And, you know, me and popcorn go way back.

I dared to open my eyes.

It felt cold. A little windy. It was spitting. I felt uncomfortable, squatting in some ugly alley eating popcorn.

Must be back to normal, for now.

Time to go to work.

Fifteen

Work smelt of bleach. Must be a weekday. I think after my vision-colours had worn off I was feeling a little tired, so I elected to go for a triple scoop of coffee.

"Perce," that old familiar voice of superiority. "Just use the espresso machine. So much better. Know what I mean?"

Wrighty filled his own cup, a statue of overflowing energy. His hand looked like it was shaking. He looked like his cup would have cracked.

"So how'd it go? What did she say, did she say yes? Did you get- it? Did she-"

"She's coming in today to discuss it," I poured the boiling water over the dry coffee granules. The familiar muddy scent hit me in the nostrils. "She'll be here soon. An hour, maybe."

"Oh… mate, that's brilliant, I'm really pleased for you."

No. He was not. Because he'd have never said that. This was the first time I'd have ever gotten above Wrighty, the gold-leafed oozeball. A man who could slide through anything from parking charges to sexual misconduct with his wealth and his Teflon shoulders. He did not want to lose out on this. But he was going to.

"We spoke about insuring all of her assets, too. But, you know. I doubt that'll happen."

His eyes glazed over.

"That's, like…like…"

"She owns a lot," I went on. "One of the great estates, Wrighty. You know how much rent is worth there? Something like seventeen thousand a square metre, John. And those houses are big, too, unfairly big, some would say."

"You should have let me come," he said, and there was more than a hint of anger in his voice. "You should have let me come, Perce. I would have done it, I can handle it now, I could have spoken to her-"

He got small in front of my eyes. No, really, he did. It was like he'd stepped down a level. Hunched, crouched, tiny.

"This is like, a four-million-pound deal, what you're talking about," he squeaked. "Coverage of all of her assets. That's ridiculous."

"Yeah. I suppose it is ridiculous. But hey. It still might not happen."

"You invited me into this," his voice crackled. "You were the one who bloody started all this. So now you've changed your mind? I'm not productive enough for you, am I?"

"I never said that, Wrighty." It was weird, you know. Having this poor little man standing up to me. I just- I couldn't take him seriously.

"Anyway. Have a good day, yeah?"

Damn, that instant coffee tasted sweet.

By the time I'd got to the meeting room Lola was already there, as was Rob.

And by God, Rob was terse. The bags under his eyes looked like big purple grapes. Lines etched into his forehead. I felt like I could see his skull.

"Morning," my voice was coming out behind an invisible wall of tinfoil. It buzzed like a train tannoy. "How are we all?"

Rob's hand was quivering. He'd been a bag of nerves, recently, hadn't he? So strange that, but a week or so ago, him and Mr Wright were giants of the office, tall necked carnivores ready to slay anyone and anything to gain their capital. Now, they were withering wrecks, dinghies burst in the sharp rocks under the current. Very strange. Still, though. Great character arcs, eh?

They crawled with dark red energy, menacing, corrupted. There was some knowledge of wrongdoing here, some evil at work. Perhaps that was me. Or perhaps it was us.

I seated myself directly opposite them both, growing comfortable in my cold blood.

"So. Shall we begin?"

Sixteen

So, what do you think of me? Be honest. You've been listening to my thoughts a while now.

I've always felt genuinely sick at the thought that I exist outside my own perception and that other people can form opinions of me. Like, I really, really hate it.

So come on. What do you think of me? Do you find me funny? Awkward? Endearing? Cold? Terrifying? Do I... turn you on? Hahaha, no, don't answer that.

No, but seriously. Since I got that deal, I've had this odd feeling.

Like, I dunno. It sounds kind of crazy, but it seems like someone else is in my head. And they're writing down everything that I think.

And once the thought has been, well, thought, it is irretrievable, it is irreversible, it is there for fucking everybody to see it.

Now, imagine my distress when I began to feel like this? My distress and excitement. Of the horror people would see when all the thoughts of I, little old Thomas Percey, spilled out onto paper, all guts and warts and ink and all.

So, so, so, come on then.

Tell me what you think of me.

Tell me what you think of me.

Answers on a postcard below.

Oh, yeah. So I secured the deal.

Lola Pink had agreed to insure with ourselves as a sole provider, all of hers and Capitol Ultion's assets and buildings. Now, for the uninitiated, this wasn't just a few thousand. Or even a hundred thousand. Once this came through, I was going to be a millionaire.

A millionaire. Millionare's club. Millionaire's shortbread.

I was going to own a million pounds.

The money doesn't matter. What would I even spend it on? I had a flat, and a car, sure. But I owned a million pounds. There's something that comes with that word. It even *sounds* amazing. Say it slowly. Mill-ee-on-air. It rolls off the tongue.

You know him? He's, like, a millionaire, you know.

But there was something not right.

Someone had tried to start a fire last night.

There'd been a report of another attempted arson on one of her estates over on Mayfair.

It wasn't me. It wasn't Ziggy. Nothing to do with us.

Must be a coincidence. Got to be.

What was I doing in the bathroom? Oh. I've been sick. All that money in my stomach, that paper and pulp triggering my gag reflex. Where's all my stuff?

Every time I moved- are you writing this? And can you hear all the- the background noises? Them too? There's fourteen conversations happening in my head right now, and every time I blink, they're all there, Picasso-esque monochrome nightmare slendermen reaching out from the void of the inside of my eye, pulling me to the dreamer's land-

One of them was crying. He was remembering when I got called bogey boy in school- I always had a runny nose-

Millionaire.

Millionaire.

Millionaire.

I was powerful, now. People at work had been talking about me. People who I'd never met looked me in my eyes and made those jeery, one-upmanship comments I used to hear from Wrighty all the time.

"Done it now, haven't ya, well done mate, drinks on you tonight, waheyyy,"

Where was Wrighty?

I'm looking in the mirror now, forcing my eyes to be wide, wide, wide open, cat's eyes, unblinking…if I shut them things will start to speak again, especially that chap at the back of the head with sunken eyes and no nose and a C shaped mouth-

"That pride and that love and that confidence is built on a foundation of sand!" shrieked the chap at the back, *"that pride and that love and that confidence is built on a foundation of sand!"*

He knows the score, god, what I'd give-

Rob was shaking my hand again, enthusiasm turning to emotion, glassy-eyed, humble.

"No, Perce. I underestimated you. I completely underestimated you. I'm sorry for the way I was before. You and me, we're a team, we're still a team, right? Aren't we?"

The chap at the back spoke again.

"But you'd give it up in a heartbeat just to feel like a normal person again!

Act like a normal person again!

Talk like a normal person again!

You'd give it all up in a heartbeat, my lad! "

I was being sick again. Should I go to sleep? On the toilet seat? There's a bit of popcorn.

Millionaires don't go to sleep on loo seats.

Who's got a match?

Who's got a match?

Who's got a match?

This wasn't one of the fourteen little voices. This was my voice.

Who's got a match?

Who's got a match?

Who's got a match?

I pushed my jaw shut.

Who's got a match?

Have you ever lit a match?

I used to play a game as a kid. Well, not a game, per se. I was told that the purpose of games is to have fun. But this game was different. It wasn't fun- it seemed more like a necessity-

WHO'S GOT A MATCH?!

"WHO'S GOT A FUCKING MATCH?!"

Rain. It was raining on my cheeks. I- I was outside. I think.

"Waheyy!"

More banter around me. Thumps on the shoulders. Strangers. Pretending to be my mates.

Someone offered me a match and stuck a cigarette in my mouth. I lit it and smoked.

A lot can change in a week.

Money flying over the sky.

I came to, still stood, through the static and the fog everyone was bouncing around outside me. Seven figure deals never happened, literally never. They'd want to know what I'd do with all that paper.

I pulled out a twenty and looked at it, calm amongst the chaos around me. It was just paper, really, wasn't it?

Lots and lots of paper…that can make people, you know. Do things.

Wrighty was staring at me, big green monster eyes boring into my soul, fear and loathing in there. I had the paper now, Wrighty, I thought, I have more than you, the paper that makes the people do the things….

Where is all my stuff?

Now here you go again, you say, you want your freedom

Wait.

Wait.

I'm coming now.

There was some business to attend to inside.

Lola Pink had offered me a job.

She was a lizard, you know? Cold blooded. When I shook her hand I could feel her reptile skin. Cold and clammy. And her pupils, they were…vertical, you know? Like cat's eyes. She's a lizard.

Maybe William the Conqueror was a lizard, too. Maybe that's how he won, after all. Maybe they're all bloody lizards.

Perhaps I am one, too.

"I don't know what you do," she said, her huge devil yellow eyes luminate in her skull, "I don't know how you do it. Give me a call."

Maybe the fire that was nothing to do with me tipped it over the edge.

Because someone had tried to start a fire last night.

There'd been a report of another attempted arson on one of her estates over on Mayfair.

It wasn't me. It wasn't Ziggy. Nothing to do with us.

Must be a coincidence. Got to be. Unlikely to be.

I had to go and be sick again after that.

"I remember the day he got here; I remember the day he got here. Hey. I remember the day he got here, you know,"

Rob wanted the attention. They were clamouring over me. I think because I had the paper.

He wanted to be the centre…" yeah, I remember the day he got here, couldn't sell a damn thing-"

But big bars and a lock and key and a chain wrapped round his head, he wasn't the number-one, that was me-

Purple haze, all through my brain

People were breathing fire as they spoke, cool blue gas flames, but it didn't singe my skin, oh no, I was immune now, pins and needles and tacks and razors on the inside of my skin, all that metal bursting to get out, consummate with machine energy, twisting, turning, hacking, slashing-

It was still raining outside. Now, the drops hurt, a bit. Some boy had told me once I was a Sagittarius. A fire sign, apparently. A fire-type. I guess that made sense. Water was super-effective against me. It stung, it was, urgh. Making me feel dizzy…

Someone had tried to start a fire last night.

There'd been a report of another attempted arson on one of her estates over on Mayfair.

It wasn't me. It wasn't Ziggy. Nothing to do with us.

Must be a coincidence. Got to be.

It wasn't a coincidence. Of course it wasn't a fucking coincidence.

"Perce. Percey. Ey, Tom, mate. Hang on."

Rob was running from the building toward me. The rain began to fall harder.

"Perce. You left your phone on your desk."

He handed me it. It felt hot, heavy.

He allowed me a moment of silence. I remember what he said to me a week ago. If you can't improve, we can't continue. And oh, how I had improved.

"So," a squeak whistled through his teeth. "Are you…going to take that job?"

Everything was a phantasmagoria. Everything. Was it right to act, at this moment?

I opened my mouth. Slowly. Felt like it was moving through sand.

My voice box engaged.

"I-"

Seventeen

When I woke up things seemed normal again.

Take your meds, Perce.

Hurriedly, I squeezed out a tablet each of Chloroprozamine and Fluoxetine. One green and white capsule, one tiny and circular and red. I didn't even know if they worked anymore.

Every fibre ached. My head hurt. My eyes felt like golf balls squeezed into shot glasses, mouth dry, face numb. I hadn't drunk or anything. Rolling over, I pulled a pillow over my head, blocking out the light. God I was tired.

I love to sleep when I can get it. I can tell when I'm starting to drop off cos I can see weird little cartoon images flash up in my mind's eye just as sleep takes me. It was a powerful enemy, sleep, and a good friend. It washed over and through me, numbing all the pain.

There's nothing left to do today, I thought again, nothing at all.

I was probably expected in work but what was the point? Baby I'm a rich man, a fat cat now, an obsessive, an execution-heavy technician of the trade. Yeah, I can be the narcissist for once.

I don't need to go in. I got paper.

I dipped in and out of sleep, fleeting dreams I didn't recall, flashes of traffic. Intermittent warmth as Zig got in and out of bed.

I had a dream I was selling a book, out at a convention. People told me it was so good, how interesting and unique it was to read. But when I opened it, it was all in Cyrillic.

Ah, well, I thought.

I was a dinosaur, now. I looked at my big hoof hands, wiggling them. How'd I become a dinosaur? There seemed to be a HUD in the corner of my vision, first-person-shooter style, with the caption *10000 B.C.* I must have gone back in time, I suppose.

Ah, well.

I was tired. God, so bloody tired. No energy to speak, nothing.

They say winners are constantly moving forward.

They're not obsessed as such with winning but with the execution of it…
I'd read all this after one of Brandon's sneery friends had given me a wealth
of self-help books, designed to help people like me- common scruffy no-
marks from council estates in Middlesbrough- become preened
entrepreneurs.

But nah, I say different. Success is built on destruction. Of rivals, of
reputations, of livelihood. For all your success, there is a failure elsewhere, a
crushing defeat.

And all that was done now.

The demon was letting me sleep. For once

I got a call later. Much later, in fact. Four p.m. was when I heard my
phone go off.

"Hello?"

"Hi. Thomas? Is that Thomas?"

"Yes."

"Hi, it's Detective Constable Olyvia Rocca."

"Hi," I said. "I like how you always introduce yourself as the full title."

A laugh. I could say whatever now and get away with it. "Oh, is it a bit
much, do you think? DC Olyvia, maybe? Or just Olyvia?"

"Nah, I like the full name. Powerful. A statement. You gotta say the full
thing, people will respect you for it."

"Oh, thanks! I do wonder sometimes. Anyway, how are you? Free for a
quick chat?"

"Sure. I'm not busy."

"Okay, great." It didn't sound like she cared either. "So. I'm calling about
Mr. Winter. And his car."

"His poor car, eh?"

"Yes. And you were a witness to this, I understand?"

"I saw it happen, yeah."

"Okay," a rustle of papers. "Am I OK to record this?"

"I don't get the feeling I have a choice." This was tiring already.

"Oh, no- I mean- do you, er, consent... to being recorded?"

"Yes, Olyvia."

"Okay." Another rustle of papers, then a click. "Okay. I'm going to bring the recording to a start. My name is DI Olyvia Rocca, the time is twenty past four, the date is May the eighteenth, two thousand and nineteen." She sounded bored, automatic. "I'm here with Mr. Thomas Percy, first line witness, case IKIWY705. Thomas, can you state your name and the date please?"

"Thomas Percey. May eighteenth."

"Thank you." She was running through the motions, the same damn journey she took from voice to laptop to meeting to filing cabinet a thousand and one times a day. "So. The incident concerned occurred on the fourteenth of May, at 20:24 BST. Can you confirm this?"

"Yes, I can."

"And why don't you talk us through your version of the events, Tom?"

"Yeah, no worries." I didn't have to pretend. Wasn't me who torched the damn thing. "It's not much of a story, really. Rob parked- illegally- in the courtyard outside my flat. I walked him down, we spoke for a bit, then I saw this thing smash into his car. Then it set on fire. It was great."

"Pardon me?"

Oh. Did I think that or just say it?

"Yeah, great meaning big. It was a big fire."

"Ah. I'm sorry. Do go on."

"Well, that's it, really. He called the police after that."

"And what did you do?"

Ah. Now *that* I couldn't tell her.

"Well. I went and had a lay down, to be truthful. It was just so overwhelming. I got into bed, pulled the covers over my head, and lay there all night."

"Sorry to hear that." Oh, so insincere. But hey, she probably gets it all the time. "Now, did you see where the projectile came from?"

"Just…above, really. I saw it fall from above us."

"And was it at an arc? Or dead straight?"

I thought back. I remembered Rob talking about Trellick tower.

"Dead straight."

"Thank you." More scribbling. "And did the car go straight up? Or take a while to take hold?"

"Took a while."

"Good. Now. I've just got a few more things. I don't want you to be alarmed when I ask you these, okay, Tom? They're just questions."

"OK."

"Have you been attacked or threatened at all in the last week?"

Yes.

"No."

"OK. Have you noticed anybody try to follow or contact you, whom you did not previously know?"

"No."

"Have you felt threatened in your home over the last week?"

"Yes."

A pause.

"I mean…no."

"OK. And have you received any phone calls from any private numbers?"

"No. None."

"OK. Thanks. I'll bring the recording to a close."

Frantic typing. I felt like I was starting to come to.

"Now, just a quick one. If it came to it," she said, "Is there anywhere else you could stay? Apart from your current residence?"

Okay. Now I *definitely* was coming to.

"Why?" a vein of defensiveness. "Why do you want me to move?"

"Listen, Tom," she went on through a stifled yawn. "It's just procedure. You've been witness now to two arson attacks, both very similar in nature, both against people who you affiliate with. And even though there's loads of fires at the moment, I think- I think you ought to be out of London, Tom."

I sat upright.

"Wait- leave *London*?" I could have laughed. "Wait- officer, I don't need- I don't need to run. I'm not in any danger. Seriously, I don't. I'm not."

"Be that as it may," she droned, "imagine, Tom, what it'd look like on me. Now, you're right, you probably aren't. But let's say you are. And I sit here and do nothing. Imagine what that'd look like on me? A direct witness to two of his friends being attacked with fire and he's not offered protection? Come on now, Tom. We're not savages."

A long beat as she waited for me to protest. Hearing none, she continued.

"I'm going to have to ask you to think about alternative accommodation, Tom. Or the department will think about it for you."

"Okay."

"Well, I'll let you get back to it. Stay safe."

"You too."

She hung up. I let my head crash back onto the pillow, the weight of my water balloon blimp skull pulling me down.

"Who was that?" I heard Ziggy say.

I couldn't answer. Too tired. Didn't even bear thinking about.

I wasn't in danger.

Was I?

Wait-

I sat up again, deadlifting my head from the pillow.

"Did she just say there'd been loads more fires?" I said aloud.

Eighteen

Fuck being a millionaire. I could be a billionaire if I wanted to. Now that's where it's at.

Of course, to do that, you have to be either very clever, very hardworking, very exploitative, or a member of one of the British imperial, royal, noble, gentry, or chivalric ranks. None of these applied to me. Well, maybe one.

All of these, however, applied to Lola Pink, who sat opposite me in a suite in the St Pancras Renaissance hotel, quiet, staring into the depths of some stock app on her phone. Never one to shrink into the wallpaper she was dressed in a gold power suit and cravat, a gleaming knight in shining armour- or just another billionaire in tinfoil, depending how you look at it.

With her were some of her friends- the Duke of Speyside, and the honourable Earl of Guisborough.

The honourable sixth Earl of Guisborough- a man one year younger than me- insisted on being addressed with the prefix "Your Honour", although he had been introduced to me as Felix.

He was a strange looking man-baby sort of guy, sunken beady little eyes, a tiny mouth, almost no eyebrows and a stern expression. His skin and hair were very fair, and he had almost no stubble. Despite his youthful looks his mannerisms held no indication of any serotonin in his brain- he sat with his hands clasped, industrious, serious.

"You're from the North, then?" he snapped.

"Yes, your honour," my voice dripped with fake meekness. "It's close to Guisborough. Middles-"

"I've only been to the hall," he went on. "It's my land, after all. I suppose I should visit the place, sometimes."

Plain and proud, he stared off into space, again.

The man to Lola's right- The Duke of Speyside- was older, and smelt overwhelmingly of butterscotch to the point I could smell him from ten feet away. He hadn't spoken at all, but sat very calm, very confident of what was about to unfold. I didn't know what his name was. But I really hoped it was Glen.

We were at an Eindhoven meet.

And the Eindhoven were legendary.

A group of some of the world's greatest influencers. Academics, political leaders, CEO's of some of the biggest banks. They met here, once a year, to discuss... things.

I'd heard that there were conspiracy theories that they are a global ruling class that can start wars and decide who becomes the next US President.

These people controlled the world that I lived in. And I was about to be inducted.

Lola wasn't thick. She knew I knew something. But she possessed the diplomatic sense not to accuse me just yet. Either way. It must have been evident, to someone with a socio-economic sense as potent as hers. That I knew the fires were going to happen.

And despite the megalomaniac devil whisper-whispering in my ear all the time. I felt uneasy. I didn't feel right.

Because my mind was lies. It had been for some time.

A million sharp-toothed, narcissistic tales whizzing round my ears, each one ready to manipulate, tear, freeze, and shock.

But you must know this, by now, right? That I'm a liar? A fantasist? An unreliable narrator?

Look at the carpet, Perce. Green and gold. Your feet push down on it, it pushes back.

I never desired to feel wealthy or high status. I just desired to feel like I existed. And for nothing to skew that feeling.

Green and gold, Perce. Green and gold.

But as I greeted Florin d'Hereault- the social secretary of the 2019 Eindhoven Conference, a man who I'd been told could often be found relaxing in his castle in rural Anjou- I realised things had changed.

I had become covetous recently. Covetous of their existence.

"Ah, and you are?"- he extended his hand and I shook it.

"Tom Perce. I'm an associate of Miss Pink."

"Tom has been helping me forecast," Lola chimed in. "I'm putting together a new business strategy of sorts. Big data, disruptive tech, you know how it is. London is different now, than how it used to be." She cast me an icy look. "But I would like to understand it more."

I was starting to understand why I'd been brought here. As rich as she was Lola's stakes were high here; she could become the forgotten cell, left to die in the flesh of capital. I was supposed to mole, dig, sabotage. I was supposed to plant lies, swing things in her direction. I was the imposter. And only she knew.

A bell sounded and the huge oak doors, three times my height, swing open to reveal a dinner hall lined with long tables.

They burst with food. Roast turkeys, blood-red, size of a boulder. Plates piled high with every kind of food you can imagine. My party began to surge forward, eyes wide and greedy at all the delicious death.

And I thought for a second of how stressful this would have been for my Dad, who carried home his weekly shop in two *Iceland* bags…so much waste, he'd say, turning green, so much is going to go to waste-

"Come on," Lola nudged me. "Time to move."

She walked ahead of me. I noticed the tremor in her voice, and in her step.

Nineteen

Florin took a particular interest to me that day. First, he'd sat next to me at dinner.

"You are not liking your duck?"

I was picking at a duck confit, but it's hard to use you're motor skills when planning.

"I'm not hungry, to be truthful. How's your calamari?"

"It is awful," he said, equally truthfully. "It is all greasy and crunchy. You need to be able to taste the seawater that calamari grew in."

"You enjoy the taste of seawater?"

A laugh. I was making progress. "No, but it brings character to a dish, you know? There is no character here."

"I mean, with all due respect, it's a dead invertebrate, sir. I don't expect that it would have much character."

He laughed again, but this one was faker, and his gaze lingered on me.

"Where are you from? Not London, yes? You are from the North, uh, Manchester, Liverpool?"

"I'm from a town in the North East. Middlesbrough, it's called. It's an old industrial town. Used to be quite a metropolis, apparently, before the steelworks there closed and whatnot. It's quiet now."

I allowed myself to think of my little street back home. The gossip that'd go round, I wondered, if they knew Alan Percey's lad was in with the big leagues at an Eindhoven meeting, with caviar and cognac and champagne and money...

"Do you know," a red mist had drifted over my vision. "there are people here who could buy my entire *street*, back home, with the money they make in an hour? Just think about that. I've got a neighbour, he works sixty-hour weeks at a factory that makes washing machines. He's called Colin. Colin probably won't even pay off his mortgage until he's past retirement age. Crazy, that, isn't it?"

Ah, shit. Word vomit. Just fell out.

Luckily Florin took this aggressive socialist dogma as a genial joke.

"Wow, yes, crazy world that we live in!"

We talked quite a bit. He'd studied economics- just like me- and he liked football, too, like me. He didn't like popcorn though- he'd never tried it, apparently- and also his dad owned some kind of firm, and he'd worked there before going on high-risk, high-reward business ventures with the vast fortune he'd amassed. So, despite my greatest fears early on, we were not entirely similar.

He asked me more and more about my roots, and I told him as best I could. I told him about my Mum and Dad splitting up. I told him about her moving all the way down to Watford, with her nightmare new partner. I told him about school, how I was the quiet kid with the long hair. I told him about my Dad's allotment that I'd travel up and visit at half-term. I told him about my disillusionment with college, but how I stuck it out to escape the place. I told him how my self-imposed misery wherever I moved meant I never made any roots, no friends, no connections. And then how I'd gone off to Uni and felt the same damn thing there.

But I didn't show a scent of what I'd felt back then. I turned it off. On the contrary, I felt pretty happy. I was letting him get to know me. I was letting him get his guard down.

A plan had formed, now, see.

And just like we were in a film, or a book, or something, about my life, being written down, a young man on the far side of the room stood, tapped his glass with a spoon, and the clamour of the room fell to silence.

I looked at Lola. Mouth smile, eyes glazed, empty. Many in the room echoed her expression.

Adoration.

"At our party conference last year," he began, "I said that the task in which we were engaged - to change the global attitude of mind - was the most challenging to face ANY administration since the war."

He spoke with diction, clarity, thick received pronunciation.

"Challenge is exhilarating. This week we have been taking stock, discussing the achievements, the setbacks and the work that lies ahead. Our debates have been stimulating and our debates have been constructive. This week has demonstrated that we are a party united in purpose, strategy and resolve."

His words rung out. Felix, the honourable sixth Earl of Guisborough, seated a few down from me, bristled with pride.

"But now is not the time for complacency. Now is not the time for ease. Now is not, sadly, the time for contentment. Now, my friends, is the time for MORE."

The O shape his mouth mate became an abyss, sucking the room in.

Poker face, now, Perce.

"Contentment," he went on, a thimbleful of bile bubbling in his voice, "Is the shackles that the working man binds himself to. Contentment is weakness. Contentment is loss. And this…politics, of contentment, means that the working man's ambitions have steadily shrunk. When their ambitions shrink, our ambitions shrink. This- this poison of contentedness is seeping into our very skin. Are we happy with that?"

"No!" mouthed Florin.

All at once I felt myself become thick and lump along with the plan in my head. Sickness welled in my stomach.

"The Earth, and our time on it, is but an opportunity." He was smiling now. "And who are we to disrespect the Earth, and the life given to us by God, by not using up every ounce of this opportunity? We owe it to the Earth. We owe it to our staff, to push their limits, if they are not willing to do it themselves. And, we owe it to ourselves, of course. Thank you."

A tremendous applause. A standing ovation, no less.

I caught Lola looking at me again. Fear, respect, suspicion. Oh, I bet she knew.

Twenty

It seemed like a while since I'd spent proper time with Zig.

I'd been busy, though. Busy. Like, I'd got back there and just slept the last few nights. When was the last time I ate there? When was the last time we spoke? My head was normally spinning so much when I got back-

Where is my mind?

Where is my mind?

-spinning so much since I'd got back, yeah, that I couldn't think. I wasn't sure if I *was* thinking, anyway? Like, is it me, thinking these thoughts? Or is it you?

God it was really spinning now, so much I wanted to be sick, spinning around, get out of my way, I KNOW YA FEEL IT COS YA LIKE IT LIKE THIS

I alighted. It was quiet. Warm. Getting dark.

I can feel the wind between my fingertips, the ground beneath my feet. I can see a sign. I can smell cut grass.

Better. OK.

So anyway. I was going to treat Ziggy. To the finer things.

I'd booked something special. Roof terrace at Muy Bilbao- an exclusive, Michelin Star tapas experience. Well, it was a restaurant. But they called it an experience on the website, which people like me buy into these days.

It had cost a lot of money to book out that roof terrace. But oh, how magical it was going to be. Sat on a wee circular table, moonlit, waiters topping up our drinks. He'd look all sweet in his little napkin, tucked into that suit I'd got him. How his eyes would light up when that food was brought out; food with wilder and more exotic flavours than a street urchin like him could have ever imagined. How he'd smile when he tasted it, tears welling in his eyes.

It would be perfect. Everything was set to be just perfect.

He'd been pacing the kitchen when I got home. He always did that. I loved it though- his little mutters in front of the mirror, the way he wrung his hands when I got near. It was cute. He'd been doing it more and more this week.

"Hello," I walked up and planted a kiss on him. "How are you?"

"I'm alright," he said quietly, looking down and smiling with his big Disney overbite. "Nice to see you for once."

"I've been busy." I'd prepared that. "Very busy. Very very busy."

"Veryveryveryvery busy?"

"Yes, very much so. Meetings, conferences, you know how it is. But tonight's going to be different. I'm taking you out tonight."

"Oh." His mouth smiled but his half-moon eyes downturned.

"What's wrong?"

"Nothing! I'm looking forward to it, sweaty."

I gave him my nod of approval. "Good. Well. Go and change into your suit. And we'll walk over there in about a half hour."

"Your voice sounds different," he said quietly. "Your accent has gone."

"I-"

Wait. What?

My- accent?

"I- must have…"

C'mon, use your tonsils, Perce. Teessiders talk through their tonsils, deep and gravelly. Southeners talk through the roof of their mouth, posh and light.

"It must have been talking with all of those posh buggers," the back of my throat vibrated. I sounded vaguely like where I was from. "Aye, all those posh buggers from the conference today! What am I like?"

"You're trying too hard now. You just sound different." There was a note of distress in his voice.

Connection withered. Isolation prevailed. My head spun-

"Is something the matter?" said my dummy mouth.

He didn't answer.

After we'd got all dressed up, we walked slowly down the cracked streets with illuminated power-buildings reaching up to the sky, left and right, left and right.

They couldn't seem to fix potholes round here, but by heavens, could they build a high-rise.

The buildings shone pale in the moonlight, eerie and green. The colour seemed to have drained out of real life tonight, but Ziggy walked along beside me in vibrant orange, the silk hugging his body, his hair all blow-dried and tousled and lovely.

I gripped his hand and gave it a squeeze. He did the same, but the squeeze was shorter. His eyes, those big blue eyes, were translucent in the light.

As we drew towards Muy Bilbao, I pulled him aside into a doorway, his back to the door, and kissed him. He pecked me, but laughed like he was afraid, looking down.

"Stop embarrassing me," he said, but his tone seemed warm and inviting. I went in again, but he resisted.

"Can a man not kiss his partner? This is the 21st century. Let me at those lips."

"No." the reply was shorter this time. "You are very...friendly tonight."

He weaselled his way out and walked toward the front door. He giggled again, higher in pitch- but I saw his face in the window as we approached. It was squarer, the skin tight and wrinkled round his eyes, his mouth a toothed oblong of discomfort.

Galacian Octopus. Foie Gras sliders. Iberico pork. Aged Manchengo. Monte Enebra. Saffron Croquettes. Oysters. Quail Eggs. Almas caviar, Kobe flat-iron. Goats cheese and white truffle souffle. The table was laden, so much it heaved under the weight of all. The plates were huge urns, deep and wide with the tiniest amount of immaculately presented food on each one.

The idea of tapas is that you pick and choose bits of each dish, discarding and moving on to the next once you're bored- making it perfect for anyone in London under 30.

The roof terrace was exactly as I imagined. So quiet, save for the downstairs music of acoustic guitars, cellos, pianos. The night was just swimming- it was ambient, a mild night at the end of a hot day. We could see the river from where we sat, the north bank in all of its lit glory, stretching out to the wetlands. I basked in the current, content, the switch turned off.

"Try the Quail eggs," I said. "You'll like them."

He hadn't touched much. A few cubes of cheese on top of the complimentary focaccia has gone down his neck but he'd been staring into the table, past the food, lost. He'd have never seen such grandeur in his life.

"Go on, try one. They're beautiful. I'm *egging* you on, eh?"

He picked one and ate it. "It's good," he said. "really really good."

I beamed. Nothing to worry about after all.

Now, I'm not a big eater, by any means. Few bags of popcorn normally does for lunch. But tonight, I was ravenous. The flavours, as I told him repeatedly, were so deep, so rich, the thick umami flavour racing through my blood and making my skin tremble.

It was…winnings, to me. I'd won. All of this rich food. I was eating my winnings.

"Cheers to us," I pulled myself out of the salt-induced daydream, raised my Dom Perignon to him. "Cheers."

He smiled and clicked my glass, but his smile was still oblong, like he had snooker balls in there. He was- very gingerly- eating a rye cracker with a small amount of caviar on it.

"Eat a spoon of it," I said, grinning from ear to ear. "Try it, go on!"

He took the spoon and I watched his lips as he opened, his tongue flashing to the side as he bit down. His face contorted more and I laughed.

"Strong flavour, right?" my glass was still in the air, waving, dancing for joy.

He winced. "It tastes like Marmite."

I threw my head back and laughed. Lola would have laughed at that. Wrighty, Rob, they'd have loved that one. Oh, god, they'd have tortured him. He could be so funny and silly sometimes.

"Once you get a taste of that stuff, you'll never be able to get enough. But it's alright, Zig, cos we can have as much as we want. I can- I can give you anything you want, Zig. Anything. You and I can do and have anything we want. And it's all because I met you that night, remember?"

He hadn't looked up.

"Remember that night, Zig? How we set Wrighty on fire? How we fucking, oh, ohhh-"

The fever and chills got me, god, god, it'd felt so good-

"We lit him up, we lit him up," I sang, "We lit him up, didn't we? We were in charge, that night, just you and me! Now, come *on,* eat, eat-"

"I- I'm sorry-"

His hand, holding that silver spoon, weakened. His grip loosened and down, down it fell.

I remembered looking at him, when Wrighty had pulled him out of that corridor, in a headlock. He'd looked so scared,

The clang when it hit the bottom concussed me, tinnitus in my ears ringing and ringing.

He hung his head so low, a dog after eating the chocolate, in disrepair.

"This- this isn't really- me," he confessed.

Everything lit up a garish yellow, the moon an extra-terrestrial sun. Zig had hands full of eyes, his head stretched out like a rugby ball-

"This isn't really me," his voice choked. "This isn't me. This isn't me at all. I don't know-"

He jerked his head up, Punch and Judy style, his eyes royal blue laser jets searing anything in his path. His mouth was still oblong, wide, you could fit a fucking plank in there-

"I don't know what I'm doing here. I don't know what I'm doing here at all."

He stood, the force of the backs of his knees pushing away sent the chair to the floor. "What am I *doing*?" his voice turned to laughter, "what the hell am I doing here?"

I watched him, my eyes in another dimension. No. This wasn't happening. It's a psychosis-

"Ziggy," I said, a terrified sternness coming through. "Sit down. Please."

But Ziggy did not sit down. A wild look about him, he stormed to the edge of the building.

"No, no-"

I had his wrist.

"Please, Ziggy. Come and sit back down. Eat with me."

His royal blue eyes burned straight through my skull. He said nothing.

"Please, please. Fucking, PLEASE-"

I yanked as hard as my could, even the muscles in my head pulling with all my might, a full body twist, every ounce of my being pulling for him to conform-

But suddenly there was no resistance, and I was on the floor. I held his jacket, and he was further away. There was emptiness in his eyes, and that stupid half smile on his face.

But when he spoke his words reached a hollow anger.

"I really thought you were the guy," he said. "The way you treat me that first night. The way you spoke to me. All that shit you told me about your Mum, and Dad, and your stepdad, and what he did to you, and how much you fucking hated it here and how everyone is…fake, plastic, how much it upset you that money is the fucking be all end all of every single person's life here, and how you've chained yourself to it-"

He gulped. His next breath was a stammer.

"And how you wanted it to come crashing down. And you said that to me, and you made me do it with you. You said only I understood, that's why it had to be me-"

He was seeing. The truth cut me more than him, though-

"Zig, no, no- don't cry, it'll be OK-"

"You used me," he said simply. "You're not who you said you were. I really, really thought you were the guy, Tom. But look at all this shit-"

He gestured wildly to the table.

"Fucking caviar? Who do you think you are? You're just one of them, that's all. Just one of them."

"Shut up," my brain ran vibrations quicker than frames in a video game- "shut up, Zig-"

"I'm going," I heard him say. "Goodbye."

My head really hurt now, Gods mighty hammer striking me in the temples again and again and again.

"Don't abandon me," I heard myself say. "Don't abandon me. Don't abandon me. Don't abandon me. Please. Please."

But when I opened my eyes, the night was back to normal. The music still played. The moon still shone brilliantly. The river ran calmly through the city.

But he had gone.

Twenty-One

The dialling tone droned on and on.

The dialling tone droned on and off.

Dialling tone drone out and in and off again-

Why won't he answer?

I'm- like, I'm really worrying and really fretting now, cos, cos-

My phone buzzed in my hand and I jumped. But it was Rob.

Hey man, how've you been? Heard you were at the Eindhoven, check you out, moving up in the world-

Fuck that noise. I didn't even finish the text.

The dialling tone droned on and in.

The dialling tone droned in and on.

He wasn't replying. I needed him to reply.

I had become so powerful over the last few weeks. But now , once again, power eluded me.

The phone cut off. *This is the voicemail message for 0797...*

I got a text through from him.

I don't want to talk tonight.

Clasping my head in my hands, I battered out three urgently tapped texts, deleted each one after drafting it, sat with my head in my hands some more, then sent him a sentence.

This isn't about us. This is urgent.

Oh, I did want to tell him. How I did think he was special. How I'd never felt love as powerful as his. How I wanted companionship, so, so badly, and that our broken pieces fitted together.

How I didn't know how to act around him, well, because I had imitated others my whole life, making me a weird tapestry of mannerisms.

And how I really, really just wanted to show him the real me. I didn't mean to change, Zig, I wanted to say. I don't want anything but you. I don't.

But something had changed.

Through the sickness, I'd gotten home, blurry with tears, sick with guilt, light-headed from disseverment. But when I'd gone to the big cabinet to get a whiskey, I'd realised something. Something was very, very wrong.

He finally called. I answered after one ring.

"Ziggy," I breathed.

"Tom," his tone was fine and curt. He wanted a fight, an explanation. I wanted one, too. But things were moving a little too quickly for that. "is this really an urgency?"

"Yes," I gasped, "where's the...where's the..."

I couldn't breathe. Blood pounded in my ears, my eyes went numb and full of static, like they were going to fall out my head, my chest, argh, Jesus, my *chest-*

"Oh, fuck's sake- where's what?"

I just needed a little air. A tiny bit of air. But it was no use. The more I realised I couldn't breathe, the more the anvil pushed down on my chest.

Pushing and squeezing and biting and mauling, squeezing and contracting my heart, beating ten to the dozen, *I couldn't breathe-*

"You know what," I heard him say. "I'm just going to hang up, if you're going to play games like that."

Just a little air…

Just a little…

Crossbow…

"Ziggy-" I heaved in air. "Where's- where's the crossbow, Ziggy? Where the fuck is the crossbow?"

Silence on the other end of the line. I could hear a car go by. He must be next to a road.

"I- I put it outside," his tone was confusion. "I put it outside, a few days ago, like you asked."

"What?!" Air trickled into my lungs round the knife embedded in there. I rasped and rasped- "I didn't tell you to put it outside, you stupid fuck, you mean to tell me you've lost it?! You fucking idiot, do you- do you realise-"

A click and the phone went dead. The tone flatlined, and I lay on my back, pulling air into my diaphragm, waiting for it to pass.

I can't have told him to put it outside. Can I? I pulled my phone with heavy hands toward me, opened my message chain with him, and scrolled back. And back, and back. Through kisses, lol's, haha's, dinner plans, gossip-

And then there it lay. Four days ago.

Hey, can you do me a favour? I need you to stick the crossbow back where you found it. In that bin. I don't want it in the house.

The reply had come three minutes later.

No worries, sweaty! Whatever you say.

I didn't tell him to do that. I didn't tell him to put the crossbow outside.

…did I?

ACT THREE- FRAGMENTATION

One

I did not want to go to Mum's graduation. Not one bit.

Reasons had been flitting through my mind again and again why I couldn't go. I was tired. I was blue. I kept- seeing things.

But the main reason was Brandon. Obviously.

Now, I'm aware there's been a lot of foreshadowing about this, hasn't there? Well, here it is.

He's my stepdad. I'd learned to forget him, through time and absence. But every time a flash of him did come back, it fly-tipped a vat of toxic into my heart. I'd shake with anger. Lash out at whatever was around me. I couldn't control it. There had been a lot left unsaid to Brandon. It had been eight years since I'd seen him.

I would normally meet Mum in Central. We'd go and do tourist things. I'd give her a card, and a little gift, which she always loved, and we'd just talk and chat like nothing was wrong. I would ignore the fact she stayed with him, and she would ignore the fact that I was quite clearly rather unwell.

But this time, it was a ceremony. She had insisted that I attend.

It had been a week since I'd lost the crossbow, a week since Zig had left. I hadn't really eaten much since then- food made me want to be sick, the textures were gloopy and tasteless- so I'd more or less just stayed in bed, in suspended fucking animation, unable to sleep, wash, or masturbate.

I had informed work that I was sick. They had feigned concern and left me to it. Thank God.

Zig had turned off his phone. I'd look at the news most days, all the connected stories surrounding that fire at the Midpoint. But he had not been seen. He was still at large. And for a boy that slippery, he would just disappear into smoke, I knew it. I wasn't going to see him again.

The ice of severance sent nitrous oxide into my belly, a horrible cold burn every time him in that suit popped into my head. But I couldn't have been as toxic as he made me out to be, oh no. The second you accept falsehoods like that, you crumble. My foundation was sand. The walls could not break. Ever.

I'd hoped, while travelling up to Watford, that something would happen. A train strike, a power failure. Awful weather halting transport. You know, one of those things that actually DO happen when you really do want to be somewhere.

But no. Everything ran very smoothly. They didn't even check my ticket. Why can't these things happen when you *want* them to happen?

They lived in a big house, did Mum and Brandon, in a wide street lined with nice cars. Detached new houses out in the suburbs, all glitz and white stone and metal and glass, not a chipped brick in sight, not a hair out of place. My dad would tut when he saw these, complaining they weren't built to last, not proper houses like his 1960's 2 bed pre-fab.

A man was laid face down in the grass, but this was no murder victim. He often did this, along with a pair of scissors, to ensure every blade of grass was trimmed to the same length. This echoed the values of the entire street; tight, strict, orderly, perfect. Flawlessly executed to an obsessive extent. The second you started letting that grass grow, the entire street would be tutting and gossiping, about how they never put their bins out and their kids were badly behaved at school and the house was a mess. You better be sublime in the suburbs.

The house at the end of the street was theirs. It was the biggest, with a square and empty extension tacked on to the side, amounting to a total of five bedrooms. Obviously, I was given the smallest one, to make room for Brandon's home theatre (the 55 inch TV was no good for his tiny eyes), his 'war room' (he had amassed an almost disturbing collection of flags, maps, crosses, and uniforms) and office (he owned a computer, therefore it needed a room on its own).

There was a spare bedroom, sure, but they used it for guests. I had the box room. Not that I'm bitter.

The steps were so smooth. I remember slipping on them when I used to come round here. One time I'd slipped and banged into their car, he'd got angry. Two Mercedes were parked on the drive, personalised number plates.

BRAND07

BRAND08

Must have cost a lot of money, them. He must be doing well for himself. That pig, who was wrong in almost every way-

I resisted the urge to throw up and key both cars in one fell movement. I stood, shaking, looking at the big fake perfect house with its inhabitants living big fake perfect lives.

I heard a key rattle in the door and felt even sicker. They'd seen me.

The door opened and Mum stood there, all happy and excited, already dressed into her graduation gown.

"What are you doing, Tom? Stood there like a…. a big weirdo! Come on, come here, get inside!"

She was really short, was Mum- about five foot, mousey brown hair, brown eyes, heavy wrinkles around them from all the smiling. She hunched when she walked but came to me with her arms outstretched.

"Hi. Lovely to see you."

"Aw, Tom, it's lovely to see you too. Come inside. We won't be long! And Brandon's dying to catch up with you."

I went stiff and she saw it. A reassuring laugh followed.

"Don't worry. We had a chat last night, me and him, and we agreed that it's my day, and that he's going to be kind and polite and charming, to all parties."

"Well. If he's civil, I will be too."

She beamed. A sad day it was, when that was the very best she could hope for, from partner and son.

I followed her in to that perfect porch, with a cream carpet, pine furniture, Italian white leather sofas positioned around a perfectly square and clean room. The air smelt of bleach and a clean cotton scented candle, and I remembered that sense that I always felt when I came here- that there was something *deeply, deeply, deeply wrong with every single thing about me-*

Come on, Perce. Not now.

He was stood over the dining table, messing around with something. He didn't look up.

Breathe in through the nose, out through the mouth.

He was a short man, thin hair that curled on top. He hunched when he walked, he was skinny as a rake. The kind of guy you'd think very harmless should you pass him in the street.

But he was powerful, was Brandon. Very powerful.

I took one more breath and advanced. I was going to be the bigger man, the stronger man. Invincible, impenetrable to his vices. I was going to be so iron hard, so bulletproof, that it would upset him, and he'd be racked with doubt over whether he had any power left at all.

"Hi, Brandon."

I advanced, like the bulletproof robot I was, electrical circuits heightened to an elevated response rate. My armor was thick, but the machinery in me had been ill-maintained-

He glanced up. Not a flash of emotion passed his eyes.

"Tom." His voice came out like thunder, from his weird small wrinkled mouth. "Shoes."

An system error forced me to my knees. Brandon's command mode was a master override.

"Sorry," my voice box whirred on automatic, coded to respond like I was. "Sorry, Brandon."

"Well, not there. Take them off in the porch."

His voice was gruff and quick and loud and deep, commanding.

And I complied. I bowed down to it. Instinctively.

Crouched down in the porch, fumbling with my laces, I thought about all the things I could have responded with.

Two

I did not speak during the graduation ceremony. She had attained a Batchelors degree in Pharmacy from the University of Hertfordshire, and this was a moment of great pride of her- you could tell in her high pitched voice and ditzy hand movements, excitedly painting a picture in signs as she struggled to find her words.

She had to go and sit on the other side of the Guildhall, and me and Brandon were left to go and sit at the side. I beckoned him in first, but he did not move- his eyes were cold and hunting, impassable.

If you've never seen a graduation ceremony, I'll talk you through it. The person who you've come to see will, inevitably, graduate last, and you sit and watch hundreds and hundreds of identikit students mill over a stage, taking a scroll, and leaving.

The scroll is a prop, by the way. They send you the proper degree in the post.

You are also asked to clap after every single student. Every single one.

The clapping starts loud and enthusiastic, and dwindles as people's hands get sore, and they get restless. Occasionally, something funny happens- someone's hat might fall off, or they trip on their robe. About half way through, you get an honorary graduate- normally a celebrity from the area who's donated to charity or something- who gives a speech, which would be fine if the speech wasn't so petulantly boring and everyone wasn't already sore and tired and pissed off.

During the ceremony, around me, there'd been plenty of partners gossiping quietly with each other. But me and Brandon, well, we had little to say.

I thought of how desperately I'd wanted to win his approval in the beginning. How I'd pick up things he'd thrown on the floor, and made his mates laugh. His little weird questions to me at parties, that I didn't understand, but by god, *they* all did-

No. This is her day. Today, of all days. Let it be her day.

One day, I'd lied to him. I'd taken some chocolate out of the cupboard and said I hadn't. But he found out. He made me-

I twitched and he felt it. I thought I saw that crawling, incredulous, smile of mockery pass his lips. Pride swelled in him, but not for his wife, who was about to walk up the steps onto the stage.

I thought of the KEEP CALM AND CARRY ON mugs, that everyone seemed to buy. That's what I needed to do, KEEP CALM. And the KEEP CALM would always be attached to some pointlessly niche imperative, like KEEP CALM AND DO THE DISHES, KEEP CALM AND PLAY VIDEO GAMES, KEEP CALM AND IGNORE YOUR VICIOUS GUARDIAN-

Another twitch in my elbow. I locked my head at ninety degrees, set forward, rolling my eyes to the left until they hurt, trying to get a look at his face without it being obvious. He looked calm, satisfied.

Brandon was, I suppose, like most people in my life. He was smart, superficial, charming. People, in passing, enjoyed his presence. He had that knack of appearing interesting and interested at the same time, but only if he wanted something- be that a promotion, sex, a favour…whatever. They were all the same.

But he had a streak of nastiness about him, unpredictable like a cat. He revelled in his ability to destroy people. Even Wrighty, the plastic man-child brat that he was, did not match him in that department. Rob could intimidate like him, but he could be knocked, too. Brandon was completely and utterly unshakeable. And how I envied his self-esteem, his lack of doubt- and how he could sow doubt in the minds of those around him-

"Susannah Tymond," the University Dean read out, and I saw Mum's face light up, and she advanced up the stairs, six hard years of graft under her belt for this moment. She was smiling, walking proud, ten feet tall, across the stage, arm outstretched, a symbol of all the distance she'd overcome to get to where she was-

And then, very, very quickly, Brandon's ring hand flew toward my face.

I'd learned to respect that hand, and quickly.

Age can grow your body into a thick, strong, lump, but some parts of your mind never grow. His hand was small, and when I was younger, it was covered in jet black hair, all up his wrist plated with gold watches up to his fingernails, which were long but scarily immaculate. A ring hung from one finger, a symbol of his ownership of my mother, and by default, me. It was smooth, but cold. It could nick the skin, with enough force.

The hand that fed was not to be bitten. It was to be obeyed. It would flash unpredictably, when you were least expecting it, and for no reason. That was the power of it. When you didn't know when to expect it, it taught you to be alert all the time. It taught you to do as you were told.

They began clapping then, the hundreds in there. But the loudest and most painful came from my left.

BANG BANG BANG.

"*KEEP GOING*," he was saying, back in the bedroom, all those years ago, "*KEEP GOING*."

Every single clap was a gunshot. I raised my hands, but I couldn't clap, I was too hot, everything spun, I covered my ears-

I was in the paddling pool again, eighteen fucking years of age and still unable to stand my own ground, dancing, naked, him and his friends drunk in the sun crying laughing, my awkward pale wrong body trying to twist and jive-

The clapping ended. She walked down the aisle to join the rest of her group, doing a little fist-pump of joy as she passed- Brandon gave her the thumbs up. Then he went back to staring forward. Looking contented.

He'd done that on purpose. I was sure.

"You didn't clap," he said, that stern self-assuredness in his voice. "You should have clapped. That's your Mum. She's worked hard for that qualification."

He still looked contented.

And sat next to him, all these years later, I couldn't figure out why. I couldn't figure out why it was me.

I felt the flames of all the fires I'd started lick up inside of my skeleton, burning me alive.

Three

You'd never believe it, but I used to be a real blast at parties.

Now, I'm talking when I was like seven. All went downhill after that. But yeah, I was the go-to guy at parties. None of this awkwardness and apathy, none of this overthinking an entrance, none of these lone protracted periods in the loo on my phone unable to engage in even a second more conversation. No, I was the guy, telling jokes, doing handstands and shit. Those were the halcyon days of partying, back in 1998.

But now, a decade later, they had become unbearable. So physically unbearable that now I was sat on the loo, on my own. Again.

Some course-mates back to the house after the ceremony, for tea and drinks and snacks. I wanted to go home. Or just leave. But I couldn't- Mum had chained me in on account of being her son. I didn't think that would be an excuse but apparently it was.

A heavy rap at the door signalled the end of my time. I stood up, and opened the door, to see that familiar bony scary face staring back at me.

"Hi, Brandon," I shrunk down to the size of an iced gem.

"You didn't wash your hands. You didn't even flush."

"I, er, didn't go."

I remembered when I'd broken one of his mannequins, playing about with it one day when they were out. When I'd confessed, I'd wet myself. I was seventeen.

He didn't say anything, but his gaze fixed me down like a tack. Then he started laughing, his horrible high-pitched croaky laugh. You had to watch out for that laugh as much as the back of his hand. It meant you were doing something weird, something that wasn't right, something you deserved to be humiliated for.

Even after almost nine years of not seeing him, I'd heard his laugh in my head just the other night.

I shuffled off, quickly.

"Eeeh, dear me." The door closed and my flight sense switched off. I bit down on my hand as hard as I could.

The party was passing me by.

"I never take the M1 anymore, when I go north, you know. Too full of potholes, too much traffic, not enough scenery. Do you know where you want to go? Up the M11 to Cambridge, come off on to the A1M there. Now *that* is a road. And the service stations are just fantastic, you've got Greggs, Subway, Burger King…"

So, I couldn't be the life and soul of the party, like it was the 90's again.

But I *could* be a conversation robot. Willing to go to the absolute mundanities of discussion.

Here I was talking to Carol, 59 and from St Albans, about roads.

"I've been," the metal mouth sounded off. "it's great."

I had to listen as intently as I could. By doing that, maybe I could evade the limelight.

I just had to hope there wasn't eyes crawling on my back. Words about my character spoken.

"I'd like to raise a toast, everyone-"

An unidentified, shrill voice cut through the afternoon balm. It was Adelle, another course mate to join this afternoon. "I'd like to raise a toast. To Sue. Now, I don't think I can really put into words how- how honoured we are to have had you with us, Sue. You're one of the kindest, most supportive people we've ever met. Even if you did copy off us all on that E2735 assignment-"

A shared snigger between the guests. Some inside joke I didn't understand.

"But seriously, hats off to you, for being the loveliest pharmacy student- oh, god, why am I playing this down so much! Three cheers for Sue, the loveliest bloody woman we know!"

A rapture of applause, Mum all glassy-eyed and proud, glass of champagne in her hand.

But the high pressure was bringing a storm. Clouds yellow, I could feel it looming.

"Ah you're clapping now," he said.

When a voice has brought you so much pain you tune to its frequency. Your ears become hyper-sensitive to it. It cuts to your cortex. It owns you.

"Yeah, he's clapping now." Even his voice, so quiet and severe, could cut down a wail of congratulations. "You didn't clap when she was on stage, did you? Ha. He just sat there like a lemon, staring into space."

His thunder echoed into the party, the humidity of it stifling all conversation. Mum looked at me, upset, concerned, the joy of her moment ruined. Because of me.

Her eyes were tears, a fresh distress melting her down into liquid, and even as she fixed herself a smile and walked to her friends to forget the moment, I could see her pain.

I looked over at Brandon, so calm, so serene in his evil. He turned into a stone statue, cracks down his torso, every ounce of his flesh ground to a halt in granite and erosion.

I could only see him. The outside world was a blur, an apocalyptic black. The ringing was back, my body was huge and full of acid, scorching me from the inside.

I almost sighed when I realised, he was going to have to die today.

Four

The war room was hilarious.

Now, the concept of war had evolved somewhat for Brandon. A somewhat maniacal lover of WW2, despite having been born some fifteen years after it had ended. He had adorned it with poppies, crosses, and strange pictures with silhouettes of soldiers on the frontlines over some faded background of the Union Jack.

These days, however, there was no such war, and so he had invented one-the war for freedom of speech. Along with another plethora of middle-aged men he had taken to uploading videos of himself, stood in front of a map, shouting about feminists and the Islamification of Britain.

I'd seen the videos. Knowing that the man did feel hate, such seething, red-faced hate for those different to him, filled me with comfort. At least he could feel.

Brandon had a dodgy ticker. He took ramipril to lower his blood pressure. But a drop too sudden could be fatal.

You do wonder, sometimes. Am I going too far? Is this really justified? Who am I to decide who should live and die?

But then I remembered the night after the last day of school.

Opening four of the capsules, I tipped them into the glass of champagne. I followed this with two propranolol, which Mum took for her stress headaches, a sachet of Diaralex, and then four crushed tablets of Viagra. Toxicology would reveal a combination of meds that offered no explanation-other than he used more than perhaps he should, and wanted to fuck his wife.

If all else failed, I'd somehow get him to sniff the poppers I'd accidentally left in my jacket pocket.

As I walked back to the party, and over to him, sheer cold trickled up my neck. My vision hadn't altered; the outside world was black and subterranean, only a firefly lit him. When he was gone, would everything be as black as what he saw?

"Brandon," I said. "Hi."

He was stood to the side of the party, now, on his phone, pretending to look important.

"Alright." I stretched out my arm, with the drink. "Brought you one over. Cheers."

He took it but did not sip. Quite contentedly, he scrolled through his phone.

I needed his attention. I needed his goddamn reaction. I needed to make him feel something.

"Why did you call me out?"

An innocent question. A just question. But still no reaction.

"Because you didn't clap."

"That's because you made me flinch."

He glanced up. Only for a second, though.

"No, I don't think I did. I was just clapping."

His cool infuriated me.

"You pretended to hit me," it took all my effort to lower my voice, as more darkness closed in. "You pretended to backhand me."

A flash of his pupils to the left told me I was right. He laughed gently.

"I can't take you seriously, Tom," he drawled. "Anyway. It's not my problem."

"I want you to explain to me," everything was rising now. "I want you to explain to me. Why me?"

A long, irritated sigh told me I was getting somewhere.

"I don't know what you're trying to pull, Tom. But listen, hey, it's your Mum's day. We don't want you around to spoil it."

"Why me, though?"

I was going Paxman on him. I would get there. Eventually.

"Like I said. I don't know what you're talking about."

And then he took the glass, took a long swig, and smiled at me.

Now, the demon and the devil and all the fifteen different sides of me rejoiced in that moment. Everything exploded into full colour. Birds sang, an angelic chorus sounded, a deep golden power washed across the land, bathing me in its warmth.

"Why me, though?" I started to smile, a deep, true smile. The reason for the fires was about to be extinguished. It felt spiritual. "Why'd you used to shove me about, knock me about? Why?"

My newfound glee was making him uneasy. "I don't know what you're talking about, Tom."

"Yes, you do." Streams of cyan and tangerine flooded the land, and I drank in the fluorescence, letting it poison me in all its brightness. "You know exactly what I'm fucking talking about."

"I don't, mate."

"I'm going to tell her, you know." My larynx was emitting purple poison clouds, some strong alkaline, making my skin all soapy and rubber. "I'm going to tell her, tonight. About when you came home drunk and found me in your room. I didn't understand then, Brandon. But I do now. So, I'm going to ask you again-"

God, I needed to learn how to extend some control over my voice. It just leapt about, some ungainly pogo stick of a voice.

I was always hard to hear when I wanted to shout. But when the colours came into vision, I entered a juggernaut gear-

"Why me, Brandon?" outlines of non-player characters glitched in my peripherals, aware of the confrontation. "Why did you do all that shit to me?"

A few more people had reared their heads, but, in the Britishness of the home counties, trying so very desperately to adhere to their own conversation.

He stood, sore, riled, but still with that skeleton smile, eight-bit, square and sharp. Cartoon character that he was, he stood, unblinking.

But even in the juggernaut state. A body of chrome and hydraulics and power. Something gave it away. I think- I think one of my independently mobile, stereoscopic eyes zoomed in on his glass.

And though he gave little away. He took in so much.

He sniffed his glass. I wished I had poured the poppers in now. That'd have got him.

And then suddenly. All my visions were gone.

The party was continuing. Happy shiny people making happy shiny laughing noises.

Brandon had stepped in towards me. I could smell his sausage roll breath. I was no longer a juggernaut.

"I don't know what's got into you."

But I forced myself to keep that dumb smile on my face.

"Why did you-"

It took every single ounce of strength to say it.

Every match, that I'd lit in lieu of it.

Every relationship I'd fucked up, every friendship I'd lost because I'd held onto this shit for too long.

Every fire I'd started.

"Why did you... make me toss you off?"

It sounded so childlike saying it.

But fuck. I was a child. I'd scarcely grown a day past that last day of school.

"Why did you make me do it, when I was just a kid. Why me? Why the fuck did you make me do that to you?"

It all came up, it all came out.

I was back in their room, looking for my Nintendo DS that they'd confiscated from me earlier that week. I wanted to play *Ocarina of Time*.

"Why me, Brandon?"

He'd come in and locked the door. I was so scared. I didn't realise.

He'd been wearing brown corduroy trousers. His legs were so skinny, pale, unhealthy. He'd made me kneel on the floor. Mum wasn't in.

"Tell me," I ground my teeth to a paste. "Fucking tell me, why you did it."

I was sick when it was done.

I washed a thousand times.

I wanted to break something.

Burn something.

And it never went away.

"Brandon,"

It never, ever, ever, ever fucking stopped.

"TELL ME, BRANDON, WHY?"

Still. In the light of day, eleven years later. His retribution was scarce.

He suddenly stepped very close. Whisking his body round so he could stand with his back toward the party, obscuring the rest of our bodies.

His hand was on my neck. Not tight. Just there.

"Listen to me," he growled, his face pressing over my ear. "You're not going to say that. You know why? Cos I-"

An impact on his side, a sudden scratch to my temple. His words stopped.

I'd never find out what he was about to tell me.

Because he had an arrow in his head.

I looked at his expression, as he hung onto me, blood tricking from his eyes. Finally, finally there was something there. Surprise.

His body pressed hard into me, and I began to lay him on the floor. The screams around me were beginning, but they were tin foiled, reverbed into an echoey mess.

The last ounce of understanding emptied from his eyes.

And then I looked at the arrow. Red feathers round the edge.

The kind that Ziggy had found with the crossbow.

Five

The dialling tone droned on and on.

Trains are boring. I miss driving. Thrust, acceleration, pollution, burn. Trains are dismal. The landscape is dismal. England's pastures green are fucking grey. In a steady, linear way, the countryside becomes more and more devoid of colour as you head north.

The home counties, just outside London, they have it all. Gold and green, fields of wheat, hamlets, scarecrows. The air is clean. Then, you get to the midlands, the outside becomes more incongruous with this green and pleasant land we sang about in school.

North, north, north. The towns even sound more northern. Peterborough. Doncaster. Leeds. Northallerton. That last one even has 'North' in it.

Must be nearly home.

The dialling tone droned on and on.

Rain streaked sideways down the window. I intermittently called and scrolled, scrolled and called.

It was ambient, but I was cold. The coffee was hot, but too bitter.

The dialling tone droned on and on. Then-

Welcome to Virgin Mobile. The person you've called is unavailable. Please leave a-

Why won't he answer?

I scrolled and scrolled and scrolled, cobwebs forming on my still expression as I did so. I was Schrodinger's cat, neither here nor there, alive nor dead.

Visibility was low. The rain got harder.

British summertime is the biggest damn hoax there ever was. They reel you in with postcards from the 60's. Permed mothers sunbathing in Skegness. Discounted barbeques. 14-day weather forecasts with high pressure and cloudless skies.

Then it rains. A lot.

I didn't want to go back to Middlesbrough. I didn't want to go back to where I came from. It meant a step back. And when you start taking steps back, and it's raining, and you're already on a slippery fucking slope, well...

A buzz in my pocket. Phone snapped to ear.

"Rob," The rain pounded in shockwaves over the screen. "I need to-"

"Rob?"

The voice on the end was not that of him.

"Who's Rob? When does your train get in, son?"

Ah. Dad.

"I'm going through Eaglescliffe now. So about 10 minutes. I'll just get a taxi through."

"What do you want for your tea, son?"

Been so long since anyone had asked me that.

"I don't mind. We could just get a parmo."

"Alright then. Yeah. We'll do that. Alright, son. See ya."

It was cold at Middlesbrough train station, concrete floors with ominous spills of paint on the floor. The only thing of note is a timetable, which no one uses, because smartphones. A tannoy belts out service announcements that no one pays heed to, because smartphones. The vending machine is still broken. It was last time I was here.

The taxi driver talks to me. Now, that never happens down in London. Normally your location will have been sent to them on an app or via text. They have all the information they need. That's it. A few taps of your phone and you're whisked off without a word. Utopia.

"Travelled far?"

"London."

"Blimey. And where you going, son?"

"Ormeston, please."

"Oh," a note of surprise. "You don't know Big Lew, do you? Big bloke, blonde hair, big beard. Brown eyes. Got a Boro tattoo on his hand. Can't miss him. Do you know him?"

"I don't, no. I've not been up here in a few years."

"A few *yee-aars*?" amazement pulled the jaw down and the brows up. "Oh blimey. You won't have seen the new retail park round there, then, will you? Got all sorts there, you know. Maplin, Carphone warehouse, TGI Fridays... my son, he's just got a job down at that Nando's. And they've said to him, he's doing well, impressing his boss. So they've told him they're going to put him through his production chef qualification, only problem is, he has to redo his GCSE Maths, didn't like it at school, see, had a bad experience with his teacher. But he's learning about how to manage a kitchen, it's interesting, you know, how they do it in Nando's, lean six sigma, it's called, so nothing goes to waste. He has to study operation management, too..."

He went on and on and on, about production mapping and the Kanban system and pay rises and how his son could never remember the formula of a circle.

And he sounded so happy.

His childlike glee at his son's new job as a chicken flipper in a huge conglomerate chain of fast-food restaurants, the knowledge it brought, the security and progression it gave his son. He was animated, talkative.

The red brick terraces fell into 1930's bay-fronted semi's, and then again into retail parks and warehouses, and then into a long, nameless, dual carriageway road. And then finally, into the streets I hailed from.

Ormeston looked different. The big, towering, pre-fab three-storey houses next to the Spitfire roundabout were still there, but instead of the pebbledash exterior they had all been daubed in white paint to hide their dilapidation. The houses stood tall and in rows like soldiers, but with only paths between them, no roads.

"Just here's fine." I handed the taxi driver a twenty and exited.

"Woah," he shouted back. "Hang about."

He handed me a tenner, a fiver, a twenty pence piece, and a ten pence piece.

"Mind how you go, eh, son?" he said, and left me.

Six

Dad's house- the house I grew up in- was in the middle of a row of terraces, opposite the youth club. Part of it hung over a link, a 'tunnel' as I used to call it- and when I was younger, I'd press my ear to the floor if I could hear people underneath. I always found it cool that I was in this floating bedroom with nothing below me at all.

There were some middle-aged bald men in tracksuits smoking weed underneath it now. As I approached, they stopped and stared, and I looked away.

I knocked. No answer.

"You after Percey?"

Always forgot my Dad's nickname was also Percey. I swung my head round the corner.

"He's gone out," one of the men was saying, struggling with a lighter. "He's gone over the allotment, mate. Wanted to bring his tomatoes and that back, didn't he, cos they don't do well in the rain. Something to do with the roots."

"Thanks." How on earth did people know so much about each other? The only thing my two so-called friends knew about me was that I started fires. People talked up here, and it was weird.

The allotment was about five minutes' walk away. I was wearing a shirt and trousers, and even though the sun came out and basked me in humidity, I was wet and uncomfortable. It was an acre or so of land situated just next to the estate, the big pink tower blocks and the crumbling red terraces starting to glow in the afternoon light. It looked...nice. It smelt good too, wet grass and fresh air and earth. Pushing open the gate- which had been daubed with *fuck off noncey farmers* since the mid-2000's, I walked down, looking for Dad.

He was in his usual spot, hunched on the ground, tending to something. He showed no sign of rushing tomatoes inside. Goddamn liar.

"Hi, Dad," I said. He looked smaller than last time I'd seen him. Must have grown. His blue tattoos looked even worse, and the circle on his crown had widened. He looked up, winced in the sun, and cast a smile.

"Alright, son."

He sounded much like I used to sound. Before the Russell group lot shamed me for my voice.

"You alright?"

"Yeah. Good. Yourself?"

We stood six feet asunder, worlds apart, the life I'd left. The sun beat down upon his face and cast a shadow over mine.

"Rotten," he said. "Look at this. Earwigs."

He held up a strawberry he'd been examining. There was, indeed, an earwig.

"Rotten, these. Honestly, I spend half me life getting shot of them. The lass on the reception desk said to put out eggshells, and little caps of oil and honey, as like, a trap. So, I only went and spend a bloody tenner on eggs and bloody oil and honey. And it hasn't even worked."

"There were some lads outside your front door. They said you'd come to get tomatoes."

He slapped his forehead and laughed.

"Ah, yeah, course. *That's* what I came over here for. Tomatoes. I come over here just for something to do, to be honest. Want a blackberry?"

I did not. But took one anyway.

"Shame it's rained, and all," he said quietly. "Could have had a little bonfire. You used to like them, didn't you, as a kid? You used to do a little dance whenever we had one, honestly, me and your Mam, we'd cry laughing-"

A sudden dark look crossed his face. "Your mam. Is she alright? After... Brandon? Are you alright?"

I remembered his eyes, apologetic for the last time. Bleeding.

My sins crawling on my back.

"I am, yes. Just- yeah. I'm fine. She's still in shock. Won't leave the house."

"I'm not surprised. Who's messing about with bloody bows and arrows, anyway, round that neck of the woods? Disgraceful. Long as you're alright, anyway."

"Yeah."

"Come on, then. Grab a tomato plant. I'll give you a croggy back."

A croggy, for the uninitiated, involves sitting on another's bike seat whilst they stand and pedal. Dad would always say it was like the passenger seat of a car. It wasn't. Especially when the rider hits every damn pothole along the way, and you are holding a tomato plant in each hand. I tensed my stomach, squeezed my hips around the seat, and prayed I wouldn't fall off, hit my head and die.

London is Venus, Middlesbrough is Mars.

"So the police sent you here, then, yeah?" he said breathlessly as we got home.

I was sore. My gooch hurt, and my hands were numb from pinching two plant pots.

"Yeah. They don't think I'm safe in London."

"You not been getting involved with gangs and that, have you, son," he said, matter-of-factly. "it'll only end bad for you, getting involved in selling all that cannabis and what not. I've told you this before."

"Dad. Do I look like I'm involved with fucking gangs?"

He looked me toe to top, examining my damp shirt and trousers, muddy shoes, shit hair.

"Er. Suppose not."

I'd spent the night in the Police station. Not in a cell, in the waiting room, whilst they sorted out witness protection. They wouldn't let me leave.

"I want to stay in London," I'd explained to Olyvia frantically. "I work here. I work for Ultima Capital. I stand- I could lose everything, Olyvia, if you send me away. I want to stay in a safehouse. I want to go to work."

The bags round her eyes seemed to swell and pop like popcorn as she explained to me how crucified the Met would get in court if a witness in danger was allowed to follow his normal routine.

"You're an intelligent man, Tom," her skin bubbled and melted under the light. "You've witnessed two arson attacks and one potential murder in about three weeks. The evidence that you need protection- whether you feel you do or not- is undeniable. We believe the man responsible for the Midpoint arson is responsible, also, for the murder of your stepfather-"

It's not him, I plead in my mind. *It's not him.*

"So. I'm afraid I must ask you again. Is there anywhere you can go, where you will be safe? Or must we do that for you?"

So, I had returned.

Against my will.

"Tom," Dad was stood in the door. "Oway, son."

Seven

We ordered some food later. His belly was paunch these days, almost comically so- it stuck out of his t-shirt like the cusp of a wave.

This was in no part due to his love of chicken parmos- a breaded chicken cutlet, deep fried, smothered in bechamel sauce and melted cheese. We'd ordered from *Parmo House: Home of the square pizza*, our local grease-house. Dad had enthusiastically informed me that it had been upgraded from a one to a three-star health and hygiene rating. Equivalent, I guessed, to eating off a relatively clean anus.

"I've started getting these," he said, unboxing his and lying it on his lap. "Parmo sandwiches, they're called. Can you see what they've done there? Parmo on the bottom, loads of donner meat on top of that, then a parmo on top of *that*. Few tubs of garlic sauce and you're good to go. Three and a half thousand calories, son! How about that!" he beamed as though it was something to be proud of, holding both knife and fork with one hand, and picking away at the chicken and cheese and bechamel and fat and spiced donkey meat with the other.

"'S'good," he mumbled gleefully, mouth food of the junk food that was sending him to an early fucking grave. "Mmm."

I opened mine and looked at the four shades of brown and yellow on the inside. I smelt the dirt and fat and could literally feel the grease seep through the flimsy cardboard box into my trousers and on to my skin.

And I felt content. I was home.

We watched a quiz show called *Never have they ever,* where contestants guessed what their families had or hadn't done. Then *Extreme hoarders: My OCD Nightmare,* featuring a man called Billy Bob who drove a mobility scooter and had populated his one bed council flat with all manner of weird Russian dolls. A perfect blend of tragedy and comedy. *Dirty Rotten Kitchens* followed, featuring Gordon Ramsey screaming at underpaid staff in unhygienic restaurants, and then *Railways of England,* which showcased the- yes- railways of England, presented by a laborious and uncharismatic ex- *Coronation Street* star.

The cheese and chips and chicken and bechamel sauce had left me so full I was almost in pain and now I slouched, wordless, on the sofa, the absolute drivel of primetime TV lulling me into a sleep. I was comfortable on the well-worn sofa, Dad was dozing off, as he normally did, and I felt for a moment like a normal person, living in a normal place, who did normal things.

My eyes closed as the credits from *Railways* played over some cut-and-pasted orchestral music. I was safe. I was safe. I repeated that in my mind, again, and again, and again.

"And now," a received pronunciation voice chimed. "It's time for the ten o'clock news, where you are."

I opened one eye as the fanfare blared. It was hardly necessary to watch the news in London- I mean, you were right there, it happened all around you. Life didn't exist to broadcasters outside of the capital. And local news was a beast of its own- somewhat sidelining huge national events in favour of a local primary school planting a tree, or a grizzled, racist war veteran celebrating his 105th birthday. Each sentence in the opening itinerary speech was followed by the sound of two hits of a drum.

In my tired mind, they sounded more like gunshots.

BANG BANG

"Tonight, on Look North. Ten dead as dinghies found on North East beaches, as the government increases navy patrols to deter immigration."

BANG BANG

"Teachers strike across Teesside, after a 'postcode lottery' exam marking scheme gives better grades to students in more privileged areas."

BANG BANG

"Middlesbrough F.C. suffer a historic defeat of 9-0 to Bolton Wanderers, at home. Chairman Godfrey Stevens says 'it could have been worse'."

"The lads just need to play it simple," Dad dribbled, halfway into a blissful, cholesterol heavy sleep. "I've always said. They just need to play it simple."

"But first," the reporter shuffled her presumably blank pieced of paper. "It's a very special day for Stockton man Lee Roaig, a former soldier in the second world war who turns 105 today! Our reporter Ben Wharton caught up with him-"

"The real problem in the UK today is… the *immigrants*," a grizzled old war veteran was saying to a placid, uncomfortable looking reporter. "Send 'em all back, I say, been saying it for years…"

Ah. Yeah. Nothing on the TV. I'd read somewhere that they had a quota of good news stories they had to put out every day, to try and pull the wool over the public's eyes, fool them into thinking everything was OK.

Still. There was nothing for me to be concerned about. No fires. No more dead bodies. No arrows.

Someone in London has a crossbow.

Someone in London is looking for me.

I turned those two sentences, beginning to buzz around my ears, into a snappy couplet with a jazz melody. A fun and creative defence mechanism, I always found. Someone in London, they have a crossbow, someone in London, they lookin' for me, dadadadadada…

No one knew where Dad lived. Mum had, by her own admission, forgotten his address. No one knew I was here. It was going to be OK.

Brandon's eyes, bleeding.

Someone in London, they have a crossbow, someone in London, they lookin' for me, dadadadadada…

My heart jumped. Probably just all the cholesterol from the parmo clogging my heart. No biggie.

Hey, you know what? If you hadn't started all of this, Brandon wouldn't have had to die.

Hey, you know what? None of that stuff even had to happen to you. You let it happen.

Hey, you know what? Someone in London has a crossbow.

Ziggy?

"And now," The reporter finished her piece about some pandemic in China. "He's made headlines recently for donating over fifty pounds to a local baby hospice. But what is a day in the life of Felix, our very own billionaire Earl of Guisborough, as he leaves the area to pursue a new life?"

And then it cut to him. That little jumped up arsehole from the Eindhoven. I recognised him straight away.

He was striding over moorland, flat cap, bottle-green gilet, beige trousers, high leather boots. He looked happy.

"An idyllic day in the North Yorkshire Moors," the voiceover continued. "But life here hasn't always been so simple for Felix. Embroiled in a feud with the department for environment and health, the young Earl is selling his assets, and relocating somewhere a little warmer- the Cayman Islands."

Oh no, no no no. My tunnel vision was coming in again. And once that started, one thing seemed to lead to another, and-

"So, for generations," Felix was saying, "My family have used the great moors of North Yorkshire for grouse hunting. As I say, it's a British tradition, extending back hundreds of years. And, to keep my land in the best condition, I burn it, once a year. It's quite common, for sport such as this. But the government have ruled it illegal."

He reeled off the lines with a jelly lip, voice smote with heartache, jaw all quivering.

"I don't think it's right that the government should tell ordinary folk what to do. If someone was to have a little fire in their back garden, it wouldn't be illegal. So why me?"

But his eyes were set in stone. There was no sadness there.

"Last year, Felix was hit with a twelve million pound fine for breaching environmental regulations surrounding the burning of moorland and peat soil. However, EU regulations ruled that widespread slash-and-burn degrades a protected habitat..."

"Bollocks to the EU," Dad dribbled in his sleep. "Breakfast means breakfast."

"Felix claims these regulations have forced him out of a county- and home- that is his. And as such, he plans to sell up."

"Yeah, I'm leaving it all behind," he went on, crybullying. "It's up for sale, my family home. Whatever I make will go towards a new life, you know, but there's that saying, isn't there? Money can't buy happiness. And I was happy here. Yes, I'll make money off the old hall. And the land. But money is just money, isn't it?"

And then he did it. His tell. His raised eyebrow. His smirk. Carefully hidden under onion tears, of course, but not so much that I couldn't see straight through his clingfilm disguise. The room went dark again, the clouds outside fell to the floor.

Uhhh, ohhhh, was it... happening again...

The room exploded in lightning, some almighty, earth-splitting crack, but when I checked outside the rain had gone, the clouds pink and peach and fluffy in the evening light now the rain had gone. I looked at Dad and back to the telly, and the smoking carpet that might not be smoking, and Ziggy outside and-

Ziggy?

I ran out the front door, peering round the terrifying white council courtyard. But there was no one. Broken bollards and blowing litter. But no Zig.

What did the therapist say, what did the therapist say, I mused, wobbling up the stairs to my room, trying to pull another Chloroprozamine out my bag. I was running out. I think the guidelines said one a day. But I needed one to get through the day, another before bed just to sleep.

The therapist used to say to write down thoughts. Link them up with feelings. Behaviours. Actions. Triggers. Visualise your own struggles. Figure out what sets them off. Figure out what makes them go away.

I scrawled out the words *Bad Stuff* on the middle of some paper, put a ring around it, started labelling everything I knew about it. What brought it on. What I saw. What made it better. Then, you link things up.

But the only link was fire, of course.

The thoughts went away for a bit, after that heady thrill. I was King Tinder, the world mine, no fear. But only for a bit.

So I was going to have to sit here and take fucking Chloroprozamine and sleep myself to death, or go back to the habit that'd got me here.

A crossroads, if you will. I knew the destination of both paths. Neither of them good.

A hum of my phone and I picked up. Rob

"Rob," I'd never been relieved to speak to him before. "How you doing, mate."

"A lot better than you." A howl of wind was in the speaker. "How is Middlesbrough?"

I could smell nothing but donner kebab, garlic, and regret.

"It's not bad. And you?"

"Um. Bit tense."

I felt that.

"I don't think anyone is after me, Rob," I lied. "Nor you. Especially you."

"You don't sound too self-assured."

"Has there been any more?" the demon caught me off guard. "I haven't heard of any more. Has there been any more?"

A long pause. Just the wind.

"Yes."

"Where? What were they like?"

"They were fires, Perce. One at the Paarsi Gallery in Chelsea. Another at…erm, Shell Island Risk Services. Outside monument. No link, I guess. Both Grade I listed. Both, I dunno. Associated with oligarchy. Different sides of the city."

"When?"

"Well. Erm. That's the thing. They happened at the same time. Five in the morning. Fresh for commuters to see."

"And no police information?"

"How should I fucking know, Perce," a flash of anger. "You tell me. You're the one that went- that took off, on your own, with your own agenda. You're the one who pulled us in and then fucked us off."

Hmm, fog in my room. Bright green. An image? Almost certainly. Get out, it meant.

"I suppose," I hastily covered my mouth with the decomposing pillowcase to shield my lungs from my own imagination- "I suppose you want me to think of one good reason why you shouldn't turn me in."

"Oh, I'm not going to do that. I thought- I thought it was you. I thought it was something you'd, I dunno. Organised."

"Ah. No. It wasn't."

More silence. The wind on his end seemed to have died down.

"So. I'm thinking of visiting somewhere whilst I'm up here. Guisborough House."

"Guisborough House. Right."

"I'm going to transfer you some money, Rob. Can you help me invest it, please? Into the right places?"

"Yeah. I can."

"Right." I looked up. Green smoke still there. But I could breathe it in now. It smelt gorgeous. Moss, basil, peat. "Thanks, Rob."

"No problem. Well, you take care."

He hung up, and I laid back down.

Guess I knew what path I was taking.

Eight

Woke up in a cold sweat. I'd been having weird dreams since I got back here. Maybe the change in location, maybe the potentially lethal mould that grew behind the wallpaper sppeing spores into the room. But, most likely, the fact that Dad ordered a parmo every single night. I think it's the cheese. They say cheese gives you nightmares.

Things were getting more and more cartoonish by the day. But I'd had to wait. I'd had to wait for a dry bastard day. And it rained every day. So I was alone, all day, every day, stuck in a 2 bed council house with nothing but a TV. When you have nothing to do, you devise a routine.

I would wake up and fling open the curtains, the first check to be the weather. It had rained for a while now. So it couldn't be today.

Then, I would make breakfast. Same every day, toast with peanut butter and jam. And a coffee. The coffee was "Rich Roast" from the local corner shop. Tasted like mud.

After that, I would clean the kitchen. Pulled on my marigolds, grabbed a bottle of bleach, and got everything really clean. Smelt like a swimming pool by the time I was done. But it was clean. No germs.

Lunch was a salad. I'd made Dad buy me some vegetables. The result was a one kilo bag of mixed vegetables from the shop. I mixed it with oil and white wine vinegar and crunched it down, in the hope it'd shift some of the cholesterol from all the fried food we ate in the evenings.

Then came the afternoon.

This was bookended by the News at 12- which I watched as I ate my salad without tasting- and the News at 6, when Dad came home. I filled the afternoon with *The Jeremy Kyle Show*. Because why not. Watching a wealthy, confident man rip the piss out of unwashed no-marks from massive dilapidated council estates, in towns like Middlesbrough. It served nothing but to pass the time. And served to make me feel better about myself in the weakest way possible.

Dad would come home and say the same thing.

"Alright son. Got us parmos tonight. Thought I'd treat us."

But he said that every night.

He'd fling his box open with the same wide-eyed enthusiasm, pull kilos of chicken and chips and cheese and fat out of it and into his mouth. We'd watch some programme on TV about the countryside, or meals in Morocco, or a DIY project on a house. He'd make condescending comments about the people on said programmes. Sometimes, his comments made me laugh. I don't think I'd laughed in about a month prior. I looked forward to the laughs.

And then he'd fall asleep. I'd stay up for news at 10, watch intently for any activity. Then I'd run a bath, wash away all the grease and the shit, and stay there, staring at the ceiling, listening to the sirens, til the water was cold.

Then I'd go to bed, and dream about morphing into a dog and being hunted by thousands of Wrighty clones.

Life was quiet. And as the days went on, I grew to like it. There was nothing to do. My head could switch off for a bit. I could just be.

"So how was work today?" I asked this, daily, when he came back. His response was always the same- "Living the dream," said with the most dour voice on earth. But this time was a bit different.

"Good, yeah. They've asked if I want to be head of freezers."

"Oh. Great." He seemed excited. "What does that mean?"

"Basically, everything you see in them big freezers in Tesco, yeah. I'm in charge. I have to order it all in, make sure it's stocked properly, make sure it's clean, properly maintained, that everything reduced is accounted for. Stock take and all that. Get a pay rise, too. It'll go up by nearly a pound an hour. Extra forty-odd quid a week, that's not bad, eh? Bit of parmo money, eh?"

"That's…great," double the responsibility for a fucking pound an hour more. But how could I say that? "That's awesome. Honestly. Well done you."

"And, you know, I keep that up for say… four, five years. I could be an assistant store manager. Imagine that, eh? Your old man, an assistant store manager!"

"Amazing, Dad. Yeah. That's so cool."

"So, I was thinking," his mouth was already half-full of donner. "Have you seen the weather tomorrow? Scorcher. Thirty degrees, nice and dry. So. Why don't we have a bonfire, eh? Down the allotment. You used to love doing that, as a kid, didn't you? We'll bring a few cans and that. Just you and me. What do you say?"

Oh.

Oh man. If the sun was out.

Then I had plans tomorrow.

But how could I disappoint that happy face.

"Sure. Sounds great."

He smiled and went back to his meat.

Later, when I'd finished, and he was deeply concentrating on the World Master Snooker championships, I sent Rob a text.

Tomorrow night.

Nine

There is no place in England like the North Yorkshire moors. God, they were beautiful. In summer, the heather bloomed a deep indigo, casting a purple spell over the tops of otherwise barren hills. Huge white jagged rocks cut imposing holes in the landscape. The sky was blue, ripples from heat rose from the sky. A mix of floral bouquets and soil and iodine waved in and out. A half-hour bike, or an hour's walk, from the south of Middlesbrough. The chemical plants faded into the sun, and you were left with a land of the purest splendour.

But by god, it was hot. I suppose that's good. That would make everything nice and dry.

I felt like a bit of a dick, if I'm honest. I pulled the oldest flake trick in the book, and told him I was poorly.

"What's up, like, son?"

I laid in my stinky bed, covers wrapped over me. Effeminate little noises, strained speech. The tone you'd use over the phone when calling in sick on Monday because you'd taken too many substances over the weekend. "Uhhh. Stomach... really hurts. Think it must be something... I ate."

"Really? Well, we both had a chicken tikka kebab parmo surprise with extra bechamel last night, and I feel fine. Hmmm. Well, maybe you had a rotten box. I'll have a word with Marco. You want anything? Glass of water? Cheesy chips, they're doing cheesy chips for a quid today-"

"I'm fine. Honestly. Go out and celebrate. I'll still be here tomorrow."

"...do you mind?"

Sure enough, there was a hint of relief in his voice.

"Just, some of the lads at work. They've invited us out in town. I said I was doing something with you, but…"

"No, go out," I said. "Honestly. You've earned it. We'll go and have a bonfire another day. Soon as it's sunny again."

He obviously wanted to go. But, in typical good-boy father duties, he pretended he didn't.

"Well….if you're sure. But, erm, if you feel any worse. Give me a buzz, and I'll be straight back."

We both knew that was bollocks. Dad liked to drink. He would be staying out.

I'd taken the bike out the shed and set off, weaving through the back streets of Ormeston, over the Parkway road, and then into the country lanes of North Yorkshire. It was quiet. No cars. Roads carve scars through the purple. One car wide, stretching up and up and up into the hills, into heaven.

I was panting by the time I could see the silhouette of Guisborough House on the horizon. The sun was beginning to set. Crickets chirped in the bushes. A cooler breeze fanned me. Almost there.

And when I collapsed into the bushes at the side of the road, it was very nearly dark. But I needed full cover for this.

So, I waited.

There were no lights on in Guisborough House. No car outside. The right Honourable Mr. Felix was probably at a country club, or some socialite party, or in London doing business…or whatever. But he wasn't here. He couldn't be here. There was no joy, to me, in bringing about his destruction. More, the look on his face as he drove up this very road to see smoke billowing out of his feudalism-built property.

That was what I aimed for. Balance.

Like any neurotic, I'd rationalised my decision to burn.

When the mind went sour, it was because the world felt sour. I sought to balance things, you know? Bring the evil down a notch. Bringing in the stinkers, the smiling hyenas who wore success and won everything they tried by foul play. I could relax when those things were balanced.

Remember when you thought, who's got a match?

Who's got a match?

Who's got a match?

You're the hyena, Tom Perce, you ruin what you touch. You're the hyena, Tom Perce, are you writing this down? You burn and pillage and fuck who you want.

Who's got a match?

And those people will do the same. They will absorb your hate like light and solar-beam it into anyone and anything they choose.

You can stop.

Put down the-

Put down the match.

"Shut up," I muttered, coming to. It was dark. Only… a bit of light in my hand.

I'd lit a match.

Fuck. Put that out.

I stubbed it with my foot. Not long now, Tom, and the crazy thoughts will be gone. If it would just get darker… argh, the ache. I couldn't wait for it to stop.

I touched the heather with one hand, desperately seeking stimuli.

Wonder what it'd be like to retire up here.

I could be someone who sat in on a Friday night, watching fucking re-runs of *Have I Got News For You,* laughing at jokes that I didn't understand from events happening years ago. I could go for walk and look at grass that was different to the turf in my back garden, and have a dog, and laugh at it running around. I could join a pottery group, in some desperate attempt to sow structure and meaning into a life or boredom, loneliness, anger. Realising all youth and vigour had drained from me, that all my mates were coupled up or just boring and reclusive, and that I'd never get it back. That the glory years were well and truly behind me, of going out and partying and fucking and all the rest of it, and even then I'd have to embellish the mundanities of my existence to appear interesting to people I didn't like.

And I'd still be fucking happy. Happy in that. Maybe... I wouldn't even think of it like that. Maybe those things would be normal to me. That's the normal way, right?

Darkness was falling.

Time for action.

I needed the darkness for the route back. Total cover. So I could duck into bushes, hide, avoid unwanted attention. Not that I'd need it. I'd be away before authorities could be called. I hoped.

Now, it was a big place, obviously. Multimillion-pound Grade I listed buildings tend to be that way. A huge, imposing hall, with the tiniest dirt track leading from my waves of purple grain to the entrance. Swathed in long alpine grass it looked rural, rustic, charming, perfect. Probably an amazing place to wake up to. An amazing place to retire.

But sadly, it had to burn.

There was no way a building of this stature wasn't going to be protected. I walked around the outer perimeter, peering in, looking for that tell-tale sign of a burglar alarm or the flash of lunar light on metal that would sign a security camera. It took me ten minutes or so to get around the outside- keeping low in the bracken and the bushes the entire time- but there was nothing. I pressed on.

It made more sense to approach from the side, off the path. I had eyes everywhere, looking for the slightest sign of movement or surveillance that would betray my position.

But still- none.

On the side of the building, the grass arced round to the rear. It was overgrown- perhaps the Honourable Felix had forgotten to hire a gardener? I stuck to the wall, looking every direction, heart pounding, the bloody thrill of it making me dance. I was James Bond, splinter cell, covert ops, a war hero, secret service… an icon…

My gloved fingers tapped the glass and it clunked, one sliding pane against the other. My heart bloody stopped- I froze, listening, listening, listening…. But all I could hear were the odd crickets, a bit of wind in the trees, and the cars on the A174. Nothing. No footsteps. No alarm. Nothing.

Windows clunked like that when something was loose.

I placed my hands on the pane, pushed in and up- and felt another big buzz when it slid wide open. My lucky day.

And guess what? It was the kitchen. Divine.

A scan of the place revealed no alarms, no motion detectors. I was losing my fear- so what if anything tripped? I'd be lost in the hills before anyone could make their way up that little path. I was the captain now. King of the castle.

The kitchen was big. What a lovely place to bake cakes in retirement this would be? Across the enormous tiled floor was another front facing window, allowing in even more light. Ah, this was just gorgeous. In a perfect world, I'd be pottering about, making a Sunday Roast for Ziggy and our adopted kids, before going rambling in the fields for sloes and blackberries, and finally collapsing into a big armchair for a dram and a re-run of *Have I Got News For You.*

Ah, if only he didn't live here. If only the demon hadn't singled him out for torture. This could have been a lovely place to buy, with my hoarded illegal wealth from all my fires.

Maybe I could just do that?

Maybe all this is…folly? Unnecessary? Destructive? Pointless? Cruel?

My feet weren't working. Solve the problem in your head first, Perce. Then motor neurone skills will resume.

I took the thought, crunched it up like a sprig of mint. Chopped it, put it away, in the back of my mind.

Now. Gas.

Yes, the gas.

A big range cooker. High supply. Oooh. I'll go for the oven this time. Mix it up, keep the body guessing.

Biiig breath in. Oooh. Yeah. Tingle tingle. God it just… grrrrarr, it feels soooo…

Push the dial down. Twist to the left.

….hm.

I couldn't hear anything.

I opened the oven door. Big heave. Can't smell anything either.

All the hobs go on. Can't hear anything. Can't smell anything.

He must have the gas supply off. Perhaps one of those nervous travellers, that goes and turns literally everything off in the case of a fuse shorting or accidentally leaving something on. Never mind. I'll go turn it on.

I checked under the kitchen sink and there it was, the meter, the safety shut off valve. God, this was really, really easy. I twisted the valve to an open position, and raised a hand to my ear.

….hm.

I still couldn't hear anything.

Couldn't smell anything, either.

Fuck! Was there no gas supply to this house? Jesus. I gotta go find something else flammable.

But the door to the kitchen was locked.

What the-

-who the hell locks a *kitchen* door? This is…ridiculous. How fitting, that the wanker in the hunting gear takes his petty little precautions and they actually end up *working in his favour.* Bollocks.

I walked over to the front window. What now? What now?

The chopped mint thought got slid over by some knife on a board toward me.

Go back, man, it said. Go back. You still have a choice.

Run through the events once more, in fast forward, said the therapist. And ask yourself. Was my reaction *proportionate* to the situation?

….hm.

I guess not.

Everything seemed a little greyer. A white bright floater appeared in my vision.

The fuck am I even doing here? This is ridiculous.

Biiiig breath in.

Can I just go home? Pretend like this never happened?

Can I?

Maybe I could…

Maybe I should.

Biiig breath in through the nose, out through the mouth. Things stopped wobbling. Everything was still.

Still. Serene. Calm.

Ziggy sleeping next to me after his bath.

Ahhhhh.

…

Peace.

I stood for a few moments, feeling the wind on the back of my neck, smelling that lovely muddy iodine piney scent of the Yorkshire wilderness. I was still. Perfectly still.

And then the floater moved.

Ten

The floater wasn't a floater. A shooting star? So close to the ground? A psychosis?

It hit the ground, fifty metres away in the bushland. Nothing for a second. Then fire.

Another floater hit ten metres to the left of it. Then another flew, then another. Low level flames, wobbly and red in the evening mist, played there, small and cute.

It's…. gotta be an image, right?

More came. They flew to the left of the building. The fire was shifting outwards- a teenager now, unruly, its growth spurting.

I watched the fire arc round the back of the garden, where I'd just climbed in.

Yeah. Surely. A hallucination.

But I smelt smoke.

And then clear as day my alarm system went off.

IT'S THE GUY WITH THE CROSSBOW, PERCE, THEY'RE FLAMING FUCKING ARROWS.

Just on the edge of the hill, I could see a tiny silhouette where the shooting stars were coming from. He was shooting fire. In a circle. Around somewhere I was hidden.

Someone in Guisborough has a crossbow.

That someone has found me.

Oh, fuck…

I scrambled out of the window, flames too close for comfort, now-

-ran round the outside, bones leaping up out the ground and pushing into my eyes, soon they'd be mine- I was going to die, here, on the moor-

The fire was hot. It grew big like a tidal wave, six feet, eight feet, twenty thousand feet high, a great snake leaping towards the stars, impassable, no way out-

I ran round the building again, but they were still there. Huge. No quarry, no route out for me.

No.

This can't be how I die-

I ran round, and round, and round, like a tiger in a cage getting smaller and smaller, panicking, my brain not advanced enough to find a way out- because there was no way out-

Smoke was blowing into me. The land didn't smell like scotch anymore, it smelt like death, as thousands of mice and hundreds of thousands of insects would be dying, right now, their deaths making no shockwave through the planet, no scream to the community, voiceless…. As mine was to be…

No no no no NO NO NO PLEASE, GOD, NO-

I was a dog, an old dog, sentenced to death, frantically picking my fur to pieces, too soon for acceptance, too late for grief- oh my god, I was going to die, tonight, and be sent wherever Brandon was, and he was going to fuck me, in the afterlife-

NO.

I couldn't let that happen. I couldn't. I couldn't follow where he'd gone.

Fuck, that fire could just be in my head-

All up inside, inside my head-

If I charge it, it could crumble. It could part like the red sea.

I burned up and the smoke got thicker…I crouched to the ground, gagging and coughing, but every breath of air brought more burn and pain.

I had to charge it.

Pushing my mouth to the ground, where the air was cleanest. I took one final deep breath. And stood, eyes stinging from the smoke. And ran.

Steps fell with more gravity than the centre of the earth, I was tripping and sweating and eventually it went ice cold and I smelt burning meat, and I screamed and jumped back-

No. There was no fire in my head. It was here.

I backed up, towards the safety of the house. But even then, I saw the fire leap in an arc towards the timber and the thatched roof- and that'd be enough-

No. There was no saviour for me here. The job that I'd employed myself to do was going to kill me.

There was a silence as that thought really took hold.

I would die, my body burned to a crisp, my charred remains found by my grief-stricken father.

Would there be an afterlife?

Would God forgive me, for my sins? Lust, avarice, buggery? Who knew.

Was there a God? Did anything happen after death?

Torn between fire and fire I laid on the grass. The fire would burn me. I had to make the most of the air, and the ground, and the feel of grass to my fingers in the last few waking moments I could.

So I stilled myself. Gathered my thoughts.

Took stock of everything around me and waited to die.

I remembered jumping from the high board, dolphin centre swimming pool.

Putting up a toy tent in the garden, three years old

Running round the estate, before it seemed scary, shouting at people, shooting them with a toy gun-

Having that book stolen from my bag, stones thrown at my head, first day, of the rest of my life- innocence dying-

The fall out, the argument over parenting styles-

The posh school, the poor boy comments-

The halls of uni, bleak and grey and beige, full of alienation-

Money-

Matches-

Ziggy-

Money-

Matches-

Ziggy-

Money-

Matches-

Ziggy-

Water-

Water?

Drops dotted my forehead. Sweat? The liquids of my body spitting out and popping in the frying pan? Was I crisping up? Water. I felt it again. More dots.

I opened my eyes. It was jagged with streaks.

Rain.

Was *this* a psychosis…?

Or was I going to live?

I slipped down bank after bank, hiding, as the flames were extinguished. And quickly, too- a sudden, vigorous quencher had poured from the heavens.

It was hammering down. I walked the rest of the way home. Another hour, along Flatts lane, past the old hospital, back into Ormeston. I was

soaking wet when I reached our little court, my head bowed, rain pounded me. Freezing.

There were blue lights outside.

Stop. Are they waiting? Did they know?

Oh, fuck, they must know…maybe it was a trap after all…

I pushed close to the wall, stealth style, and tried to peer round the edge. A van. Emergency services. What was on the front, though?

I peered further.

AM-

Oh, no.

AMBULANCE.

I dashed over. Oh, shit, it was outside mine, too-

"What's going on," I gasped, running towards the door. "Someone, hey, someone! What's going on?"

I ran over. The front door was open.

"Dad," I cried, "Dad, Dad…"

The kitchen light was on. There were people in there. I burst in. They had him on a stretcher. Grey as a cloud, face stretched into an upside-down D, gripping his chest with iron force-

"Oh, son," he said. "Oh, son-"

"Dad," hot tears rolling. "What the fuck-"

"Son," he gasped again. "I got home- went to check- you weren't there- oh, I got so scared, I ran round the block- god, my chest hurts, my shoulder hurts, fuck, it really hurts-"

"Come on," a paramedic said. "One, two, three. LIFT."

With some difficulty, they hoisted King parmo off the ground.

"We have to go," one said, almost apologetically.

And they took him.

I watched, dumbly, sopping wet, as they carried him in. The ambulance reversed around the court, sped off, and turned on its two-tones. They only did that when it was life threatening.

Eleven

I am the evil part of your brain. You can't beat me. Because you are the one who forced me into being.

...I forgot to look at my hands, for a second. They were so small. Why was everything close up again. I don't like it. I work too hard and want to go to bed.

I want some popcorn.

Why didn't I just go for popcorn that night, a few weeks ago?

...I think there might be some bombs in this house. But they're just like me. Happy bombs. Carefree bombs. The lightning was going again but it was jolly and happy.

Ha, ha. I had... such power.

But, power can be-

I'd had this song in my head all night. Like a distorted lullaby.

I think I had a good childhood until I corrupted it. And every time I thought of the bad things, a bad note played, a diminished chord, a minor interval. It was beautiful, harrowing. It played loud and clear as I laid on my bed.

All my memories lived and breathed life in this house.

There was dice everywhere, all over my floor. They were loaded dice. Dice were luck, dice were chance. Dice were loss. Mine all had to be weighted.

The outside was swimming, black and red, jagged outlines of spacemen and foetuses, a black hole sun-

- I am the evil part of your brain. You can't beat me. Because you are the one who forced me into being.

Was love make believe?

I'd kidnapped Ziggy. I'd forced him to stay. I'd rolled every fucking weighted dice at him until he loved me.

I French kissed Ziggy sometimes. Those French kisses of death.

The mattress was too many molecules.

They moved like sprites, and I twisted and rolled, afraid to engage them, for they were alive, with powers of fire and ice and electricity, paralysing me, poisoning me-

Molecules live and molecules die, and then they're sent back to the universe. And eventually, I, a set of atoms and bits of fire and pain would go with them, leaving nothing but my energy behind. And that energy was corrupted. Fatally so.

I am the evil part of your brain. You can't beat me. Because you are the one who forced me into being.

-who- who was saying that?

The floor was water. Green to blue to purple, all neon, all bright. The lullaby had turned into a humming. The dice rolled a little more freely.

My energy was corrupted. I couldn't pass that on.

I stepped off the bed into the water. My feet were wet.

I went to the window. The outside was still an electric battlefield, colours and screams and voids. We had risen high above Middlesbrough; I saw mountains and valleys cut their way through the industrial landscape, a road stretching out from the window- to a light-

But I could not go out there.

I must press forward.

I waded out to the door. Silver roots grew from the floor, trying to cut through my soles. Curled and gnarled, they were, dungeons in them, more lost souls trapped behind gleaming bars.

I am the evil part of your brain. You can't beat me. Because you are the one who forced me into being.

"But where are you," I said. "I need to come and find you."

Keep going.

I walked down and down and down and down until I reached a lake.

"Where are you?"

My voice echoed. The lake illuminated green.

Keep going.

I stepped forward. Brandon blocked the way. His eyes still bleeding, his mouth still smiling.

No.

"You're dead," I said. "Your influence is dead. Your energy is dead. I won't let your entropy continue. I'm free from it."

God, I could be so profound sometimes, eh. He still smiled. He still bled.

But when I stepped towards him, he disappeared.

The buzz of the lake was a low frequency, still a melody, a calm hum. Some whispers of high-pitched notes flitted from one side to the other.

I waded on to the living room. There was someone there.

"I am the evil part of your brain. You can't beat me. Because you are the one who forced me into being."

The voice was coming from that something. That something was me.

As I got closer I saw a light appear in his hands, and drop to the floor. Then again, another light- dropping to the floor.

I went and sat next to myself. The walls were glowing with a purple thick gloopy paint. The sea was still green. I looked focused on the match.

"Why do you do that," I said. "Why with the matches?"

"Because I can," came the reply. "I want to."

"But why?"

A pause.

"Everything pales in comparison to fire. An all-consuming flame. It takes and takes. I like the way it takes everything."

"There can't be more people like us," I said. "It stops here. Our work ends now."

Slowly, skin began to peel back from the other me. It revealed a demon.

"I bring you the things that you want. To lie and to cheat and to fuck and burn. Misery will lather itself all over you if you get rid of me."

It had a point.

"Maybe you're right. But I'll never know unless I try."

A pupil in the demon's eye tightened.

"I am the evil part of your brain. You can't beat me. Because you are the one who forced me into being."

"I know. You'll always be there. But I don't have to listen to you anymore."

He opened his mouth to say something.

And then, it was all gone. The water, the demon, the roots, gas, dice, fire, everything. The carpet was dry. My hands looked normal.

The phone rang.

Twelve

I always felt so weak when they wore off. Unable to pull my arm to my ear, I laid on the sofa, tapped the green button and laid with my head next to the phone. A private number.

"Hello?"

"Tom. It's DCI Olyvia Tamworth. Hi."

The acoustic distance was there. She was on speakerphone. And that white noise? Was she driving?

"I'm driving up to Newcastle for a conference tomorrow. So, I thought I'd drop by, en route."

"Right."

"Stay put. I have some evidence I'd like to show you."

"Ah."

"Don't leave the house. Remember it's your safe house."

"Yeah. OK."

"I'll be there by four."

"OK. Sounds good."

A pause. A quiet beep of another driver.

"Anything you want to ask me?" Her voice a little expectant.

"No. Am I in trouble?"

A laugh. "I wouldn't have called prior to arriving if you were in trouble, now, Tom. No, just some footage I want to run through with you."

"Ok. Well, see you soon then, I guess."

The second a pop denoted the end of her call, I let my head collapse onto the sofa, and fell into a deep sleep.

And for the first time in a long time. I dreamt of absolutely nothing.

No lakes, no dinosaurs, no Ziggy, no fire. Nothing.

The awakening came sharp. Jeez, you can tell she's used to knocking down doors.

Bleary, I stood up and answered. She looked bright, eager, hungry. Something had happened.

"Hi, Tom. Are you OK?"

"Yeah. Sorry. Just tired."

"You sure?"

"Erm. Well. My Dad had a heart attack last night."

"Oh my god. Is he OK?"

"I don't know."

"I'm so sorry," I didn't know what sincerity really sounded like. But her voice sounded throaty and hoarse, kind of like tears were coming on, so I guessed she was.

"Yeah. I've had a lot on my mind recently."

"I'll bet."

"I don't want my Dad to die."

"Yeah. After your step-dad, too."

"Oh, god, I couldn't give a shit about him. He sexually assaulted me when I was a kid, you know."

It came so matter of factly that it didn't even hurt this time.

"Oh. I- I'm sorry."

She shuffled uncomfortably, then hastened getting her things out her bag.

She pulled out a laptop and fired it up. "I've, erm. I've got something to show you."

Shuffling over to sit next to her I caught something in her eye. Her mouth and her voice were sad and empathetic. But her eyes were all smiley.

"We've checked a lot of CCTV recently surrounding the attacks," she went on. "but all of these places seem to have blind spots. Someone has exploited them. It's been…well, a bit of a shitshow, hasn't it. No continuity."

I agreed with her on that. Three weeks ago seemed like six months.

"So, take a look at these. Only evidence gathered from the attack at the Golf Club was from the car. Left burned in a ditch outside West London. Description of the buyer- well, it was a cash buyer, and it matched the description of the one you gave, the fellow from the Midland."

"Okay."

"So a repeat offender. Fair enough. He was seen in Fulham a few days before the attack on Mr. Winter's car. Again, no footage, nothing. But then, we did see him."

My heart caught in my mouth.

"Right here. A40, westbound."

The clip showed him ambling, quite carefree, along a dual carriageway.

"Now," her voice trilled. "Can you confirm that's him?"

"Yes." I had not a moment's hesitation. "I'm afraid it is."

"Ah," she said. "Yes. I thought so. Which means he can't have been the one to target your stepdad, Tom. Because that had happened at the same time."

I went numb.

"What?"

"Two days ago, there were two fires in London. At a similar time. One at the Paarsi Gallery in Chelsea. The other, Shell Island Risk Services, Monument. They seemed to run almost concurrent with each other. There have been other, smaller ones since, but more badly executed, more amateurish. And then, as I'm sure you've seen. There was a fire on the north York moors, last night, at Guisborough house."

I coughed. "Yes."

"Oh yes. And police found- wait- these. The same arrows used in the attack on your stepfather's property."

I glanced. Carbon fibre arrows. Black tips.

"Now," she went on. "What is the link, here? It's the same attacker. So what could be the link, between you and the Earl of Guisborough, proprietor of the house targeted last night?"

"I- it's me," I said. "I'm the link."

Her dark eyebrows raised, and she looked over, almost humour in her smile.

"No, Tom. That's not what I was thinking."

She shut her laptop and turned to face me.

"There's been…an atmosphere in London recently. A belligerence. A sort of…hate, I guess, to the haves, from the have-nots. Now, I'm sure you're aware of Brandon's internet activity? He had some quite strong views. On a lot of things. Not a YouTube star, per se, but he was prolific. You've seen his videos, I take it?"

"I-"

Wait. What the…?

"He was very vocal about some views," she went on. "he compared paedophilia to being queer or transsexual. He was critical of the welfare class, migrants, Islam… you get the picture. He had very particular views. And he made money off these claims."

"Right. So…"

"So," she flicked through a notebook to some datasheet. "If we look at Felix. A man of similar views. A man who heavily subsidised battery farming, who campaigned for cuts to welfare, who sent donations to vast amounts of MP's before a vote on same-sex marriage to sway them."

I had no fucking clue where this was going.

"So," she excitedly pulled her papers together. "I don't believe this is one person. I believe it is an organisation, Tom. A far-left, anarchist organisation, targeting those with extreme-right viewpoints. It'd make sense as to why Mr Winters was targeted, too- a socialite, young, rich. They hate all of that, you see. So, I think whilst our friend who assaulted Mr. Wright may be part of the group, I feel like it is something a little bigger than just him."

"No," I laughed. "Sorry, but I think you've got it all wrong. What group? That person- that crossbow- it was after me-"

She smiled, that horrid happiness in her eyes. "I think you need to get some rest, Tom. Why would anyone want to hurt you?"

A whole other storyline appeared, a normal ending, a pacifist route. I left the world I'd created. I chose redemption. Turn to page 222 to see this ending, like in *Goosebumps*, or something. It all flashed in front of my eyes, my dissolution.

But she made up my mind for me.

"I think you're unwell, Tom. Listen, rest up, and then you can return to London when you're ready. OK?"

"Wait," I said weakly. "It was me. I started…the fires. It's all me."

But I was delirious, slurring. Not to be taken seriously.

She turned, seemingly losing her patience. "Tom. Honestly. Get some rest. I'll call you in a few days to check in. We can assign you a social worker, a counsellor, if you need it. But until then, rest up. You've had a tough few days."

And she was gone. As quickly as she'd arrived. I rolled off my side and onto my back, on the tattered black leather sofa, cut to bits from where my Dad had picked it in his restlessness. The ceiling was exactly where it should be. The room was silent.

There was nothing here anymore.

Thirteen

Mercifully, Dad did not die.

He was in intensive care, alive, stable. He was not conscious. They did not know the full extent of the damage that had been done. But he was alive. I'd sat at his side, in James Cook hospital, watching him breathe, his heart rate quick and irregular. Nurses would come in and talk to him in an everything-is-going-to-be-okay sort of tone, even though his eyes were closed, and he was being fed off of a drip.

But he had dealt with the devil effectively enough, it seemed, and his soul was still firmly inside him. I'd waited and waited, buying more and more kitkats and expensive coffees from the little hospital shop, staying up and with him all night, scanning for signs of response. Still none came. But still his little tracker kept beeping and beeping.

When I wasn't watching him, I was watching the news.

Tinder was starting a fire.

"Our latest from Hackney," a breathless reporter squeaked, "Another arson, this time at 256 Eastway, the Headquarters of the well-known commercial law branch Sterling and Yellow. We're live from the scene…"

They'd been popping up everywhere. Places with money, power. Places with ties to corporations. If I didn't know better, I'd say Olyvia was right.

But I knew who it was.

"This follows a string of random attacks across the capital on investment and asset management firms. Some of the wealthiest firms in England have lost millions in stock to the fires, including TransAtlantic Tobacco Inc., valued as the highest market cap in the United Kingdom…"

Ha, ha, ha ha. Smoking is bad for you.

"Last night, an arson attack caused damage of over fifty million pounds to the popular department and home store Dartries in Belgravia, known for its high-end whiskies, foods, and furnishings. This is typical for the types of attacks we are seeing- no casualties, but many losses of luxury stock; or personal attacks on big business and enterprise."

It…did seem like a lot for Ziggy, admittedly. But it was out of my hands now. I did not need to start fires anymore. It was done.

I did think about it, of course.

I remembered that weird vision, the part of me, angry, bored, stubborn. He wanted to cause some trouble. The rest of me did not. The evil part of me was dormant, my anger lukewarm. It was the cause of my father's heart attack. It was the cause of my expulsion from London. And now, I had to learn to tame it.

The ideals would repel each other, stretching my skin out to its limit.

"Oh, fuck," I'd groan, too weak to stop them pulling.

But I stayed put. Somehow.

On the fifth day and something like the eighteenth fire, I got a phone call. Private number.

"Hello?"

"Hi. Can we talk?"

Shit the bed.

Fourteen

I remembered when I first came to London.

London is BIG. London is WOW. You can't get enough of it, walking round the hodgepodge chaotic streets with big glass skyscrapers dotted amongst the roman architecture. The hustle and bustle intoxicate you. You are a cell in the organ of the city, one of the tiny little clockwork pieces that make it all work. Everything is LOUD, everything is GO, you're rushed off your feet into its life-stream before you can catch your breath.

You just gotta make the move.

Fuck Middlesbrough. Fuck Hull. Fuck Newcastle. Fuck Manchester. Fuck Cardiff. Fuck Birmingham. Fuck Edinburgh. Fuck the UK. There is only one place for you.

Because London is the BIGGEST. London is the BEST.

It screams at you from every direction, cool and ruthless, until you bend to its will. You can't get better than London.

Yeah, I work in London now, I'd say. Yeah, I live in London now. I do my shopping in London now. I buy my clothes in London now. I get my hair cut in London now.

Those two syllables elevate every mundane fucking activity you can think of into the elite tiers of *everything*.

So fuck if you work in Glasgow, with its great nightlife and its gorgeous art scene.

I work in London. I live in London.

So you say these things in front of the mirror to yourself, praying to god that it will be the missing piece in your defective personality, that it will make you interesting and intelligent and cool and brave and loved.

You start making the dream into reality.

You accept the job offer. You stay on a friend's sofa. You look at apartments, house shares, flats. The prices seem too lofty to believe, but you do it anyway. You're moving to London. You pack your bags, the thrill of it making you sick, and book a train. You're ready.

You imagine what kind of person you'll become, as you move down there, to start your new life. You'll change. You'll change to fit in with the city. That's the whole point, right? You leave your post-industrial northern town to escape everything that comes with it. You turn yourself into someone new.

And oh, boy. Did I know what kind of person I wanted to be.

I wanted to walk down Bond street and have the security open doors for me. I wanted to sit in the bars in Covent garden, telling a rapture of colleagues and friends a story, drinking Pinot noir and people-watching. I wanted to stride into Canary Wharf, front of the tube, ready to go, excited and energetic, the day just ready to be seized. I wanted to go to clubs and restaurants and museums with my newfound clique, talking to anyone and everyone. I'd have my new partner round for meals, sitting on my balcony, the hum of the city rubbing against our hands.

And then. You get to London.

Its five pounds for a coffee. Six for a pint. Twenty-five for a haircut. The flat you looked at online is barely bigger than a studio, and you pay one thousand pounds a month plus bills just to sit in its squalor and say, I live in London now.

You commute for an hour on a brimful tube to get to work, silent in your approach, a maze of headphones and newspapers. You elbow your way off in silence, go up the escalators in silence, tap your oyster and leave.

The boss is hostile. The workers are unfriendly. You ask everyone *how are you, how are you, how are you*, until your throat is hoarse. They give you the same answer. *Good, thanks*. They couldn't give a shit.

You work hard, not smart. Staying late, being polite, complicit. You are crucified for mistakes, humiliated for anything that might discredit your work ethic. But you must prove yourself, you keep saying in the mirror, it's a frat, that's all. You just need to work harder.

So, you keep commuting. Your boss keeps screaming at you. You work harder, and harder, and harder. You are poor because everything is expensive, and you daren't ask for a raise. You lose your confidence, making commission harder to come by.

Rent drips from your account.

You go out, once, on a Friday, with some work colleagues. They didn't invite you, you just heard about it. And you sit in the bar and drink and drink and drink, trying desperately to talk to the people who regard you as little more than thin air.

You wake up to find you've spent all your money for the month, on one miserable night. You live off fucking tins of chickpeas and salt and rice to save money until the next payday.

And yet you keep going in, friendless, nameless, penniless. And it is endless.

When your dear old Dad calls you tell him how well everything is going, how you've settled in, had a few drinks with new friends. Been sightseeing. That kind of thing.

Because why wouldn't you, you ungrateful bastard. He works in a shop in a retail park 50 hours a week and he hates it. He lives hand to mouth. He will never leave the estate.

But you, you live in London.

And London is the BIGGEST. London is the BEST.

The woman asked me if I want coffee, for the fiftieth time. Everything is blue outside, the fields of wheat golden. The harvest would be bountiful, loads of grain to make the nation's low-priced sliced bread from I suppose.

Lots of chaff to feed the cows for our burgers. Lots of hay to mix with the shit for next year.

The journey was not going fast. I checked the window and my watch and the time and my map again and again like a madman, the table clattering as we hit little inconsistencies in the track. I was ambitious today, an apostle of rage, just want to get going, get running, get the job done... but we're still only at fucking Peterbrough...

I needed to see Ziggy, he was going to do something stupid.

I need to see him now; this is going to blow up...

Checked the time. ETA one hour. Enough? Hope so.

"I need to see you," he'd said, his throat slashed, tearing up. "Tomorrow night. I need to see you."

"Why? What's going on?"

"I'm doing a job," a stony remorse in his voice, high and low and black and white all at once. "I'm doing a job and I want to…see you before I do it."

A crumble of drywall in the cavities of neuroplastic.

"What the fuck? What do you mean," real me was scrambling now, eager to reach the precipice, halt the damage.

"Tom, can I see you? I need to see you. Tomorrow night."

"Ziggy," my vision went. I slumped down against the corridor of the ward, tiredness toxifying me. "Ziggy. What is going on?" I hushed my voice to a woeful whisper- "I'm not in that game anymore. I'm just not. I can't help you. I can't. I can't do it."

"Ohh." His cadence rose a full octave to a whimper. "Yeah, I get that, just- I'm a bit, er, worried about the job, and- and I might not make it, see-"

"You might not *make* it?"

"We all won't. We're doing the job together." A tuneful optimism cut through his tears. "Its- it's Ultima Capital. The only way, the only way we can do it is with us inside, and there's- it'd be hard to get out of the building, when it's, you know, all torched, all lit up, full of smoke-"

I laid down in the corridor, phone clasped to my ear, overworked nurses spilling past me with stretchers.

"That's the only way we can do it without getting arrested, and I can't go to jail, none of us can- but I have to do the job-"

"Okay." I sicked, wincing through the migraine, "okay. I'll come down. Just- don't- let me speak to you first, okay?"

That was this morning. I'd got the first train I could. I still wore my shitty *Rubber Soul* t shirt, shorts, trainers, hair a mess, ragged little beard from not shaving.

I was going to London now. Had to get there soon, before he did…whatever he was going to do.

I felt myself throw up in my mouth again. Hold it back. You can do this.

We were still fifty fucking minutes away. The sun was setting.

Fifteen

Canary wharf tube station is weird, I've always thought that. It's dark, spherical lights in duos dotting the cold metal of the infrastructure. It's alien, theatrical, isolated, grand. Much like canary wharf itself.

I was arriving as the stragglers of the main working day were on their way home. They rarely spoke on actual phone calls; this new breed was all about voice notes.

"Yeah, this activist chick who's coming round later, she's cool and kind and committed and all that, but she just won't fucking shut up, you know?"

Phone still had no signal. I clattered up the escalator on the right, vans slipping on the briny surface, desperate to get outside.

I stopped on hitting the air. God it was cold. Cold and dry for the summer. It bit my skin; it stung my eyes. It was quiet. I was disorientated. I was rushing. I wasn't thinking logically.

The sandstone rose up and bit my toe, sending me colliding to the ground, and when I looked up, I saw it.

The big screen. The huge plasma right in front of the station, normally littered with the markets and all their nuances, was dead. It was blank.

Canary Wharf seemed to have simply turned off.

Back in the day when I started, in the winter months, I would leave late sometimes, having done a large work of the team's admin after they gaslighted me into thinking that I didn't do any. I'd leave at nine, my ears ringing, and still notice lights on, silhouettes of traders gabbling into phones.

There was none of that.

The buildings were quiet. The hustle was short. The pavements gleamed in the nuclear light, the silent army of cleaners not out yet to scrub and shine.

I laid looking up, not one of the exeunt helping me, at the blank, dead, full HD screen.

Ultima was off.

Ultima was silence.

Ultima was petrified.

And I just stood outside, aware of the three hundred cameras on me, hoping to God this would work out, and that I wouldn't be arrested, or worse.

I do this thing, sometimes, in these situations. I give myself an ultimatum.

If he doesn't contact you in the next half an hour, go home.

If he doesn't stop harassing you at work, speak to HR.

If he touches you again. Tell mum.

The thing about my ultimatums was how often and how easily they changed. They were more malleable than hot gold, and a thousand times less valuable.

Half an hour passed. I swapped weight from foot to foot. Hold the ultimatum.

I'll ring him. If he doesn't respond. Go home.

I redialled his number. The dialling tone droned on and on.

Ziggy did not answer.

Wait another ten minutes. If he doesn't respond, go home.

I stood, pacing in circles. Hold the ultimatum.

If he doesn't call back in the next hour, go home-

"Excuse me, sir," a figure from behind barked. I swivelled to see a security guard; the private, gun-for-hire, Thugs-4-U menaces that patrolled the money state, ensuring not one rough sleeper dared pass into its reaches. His face was shadowed by the dark. "Everything alright?"

I bristled. This was a code. Stop loitering, you low-income nobody, get out of the Nucleus. He had a mind to move me on.

"Yes, officer. Just waiting for a friend."

In hindsight this man could have been my saviour. If he'd been harder, tougher, less fair, his cruelty would have paid off. It would have been kind to move me on, to deprive me of the freedom I was so reckless with, to take my decisions into his hands.

But behind the shadows I sensed him raise an eyebrow, looking for fairness. "Oh, yeah? What's his name?"

"Er. Tom Perce. He... cleans here. At Ultima."

An understanding smirk.

"Right. Gotcha. Mind how you go." He raised a finger and pointed. "I don't want to see you here again."

And as he began to turn, I felt another presence.

"Don't worry mate. I've got this one."

It was a Manc brogue. And it sent a wave of stomach acid into my throat.

A hand touched my shoulder and I saw chewed nails.

He had me.

"Thank you," he said quietly. I turned to face his pale face, illuminated in the light, scars thickened with concealer. He looked painted, normal almost. But his make-up did not conceal his moroseness, and I could see the indentations for his Chelsea smile.

"For what?"

"Coming." His outfit- identical to the man who'd apprehended me- sagged on his tiny shoulders, and the vest and shirt seams hung limply from a quarter-way down his arms.

"Do- you work for them now?"

He laughed; his eyes still sad. "No. *They* gave it to me."

I nestled my head in my hands, hard-hatted fingers pushing their callouses into my forehead. "Ziggy. Who are *they*? Don't play fucking cryptic with me," my wannabe baritone moved up to a falsetto. "You- you come crying to me on the phone, after you left me, saying all this- all this shit-"

Hot tears welled. I bit down hard on my lip. Baby Perce, little boy Perce, don't you cry, now.

"Hey," he said. "Don't make this hard. Please. I'll- I'll show you."

Sixteen

The tables had turned, the turn tables. I was the shrunk one and he seemed so large, big, and boisterous in his boorish outfit. He had a key that he nervously span on one finger as he escorted me down the immaculate streets, about to go through their daily clean by the sub-corporate supply chain, ready to lick the boots of riches. We walked to a fire exit, about fifty metres down the side of Ultima. He walked fast, a quest to manage, a mission to accomplish. He kept tripping and looking up and down and tripping, his trousers and shoes much too big. But he strode with urgency and some sense of pride.

"Are you going to talk to me?" He'd kept up a conspiracy of silence, unmoved by my persecution as I followed his stupid straw-man figurine down the side street.

"Are you going to talk to me? Hey," I ran a little after him. "Don't fucking ignore me-"

He turned one-eighty degrees, holding up a lone, skinny finger to his lips.

"Don't speak to me like that," his voice trembled. "Please don't speak to me like that."

The key, on his other hand, clicked into a fire door on the side of the building, and he swung it open with some difficulty.

"So, er. I don't think you're gonna like this." He did not look at me. "I don't think you're gonna like the job."

We clambered down a ladder into a cellar. It was lit, with green emergency lights and the odd red LED. It was silent apart from the clang of feet on metal.

"After I left, I roughed it for a bit, round here. And then this guy approached me. Said, he wanted to give me a place to stay. So, I went with him."

"Who was it?"

"Well, er," he stuttered. "He was just…this guy. Handsome. And, like, firm. I stayed with him. He looked after me."

The warmth of his voice signalled love. Hate clawed at me.

"And then he said… he said he recognised me from the news. He thought I was the one starting fires. But he said, that… that me and him, we could team up-"

"Wait."

I couldn't move. A thousand storylines. No processing power. Fear had corrupted me, shocked and frozen my components.

"Ziggy. Who was it?"

He laughed. "Well, it was so funny, he didn't even tell me his name for ages. But we started working together. He told me how to…get into buildings. He said if we helped each other out, he'd look after me forever."

"Ziggy. Please. Who the fuck was it?"

"Well, er, actually. He said I shouldn't tell you."

Every fucking cell in my body morphed into a question mark, the mitochondria as the little dots. This was bad.

"Cos, I told him about me and you," he went on, still a little trembly. "And he- went mad. He didn't like it at all. He said all the other fires were you. But they couldn't be, they were all over the city. But he was- adamant."

"WHO was adamant?"

"I'm-" he grasped his ears. "I can't talk anymore."

We kept going and going until the corridor opened out into a clearing. He stopped, breathing heavily. The air was thick and smelt oddly sweet. My head began to hurt like hell.

"So." He sounded final. Defiant. "This is the job."

It was a control room, replete with all kinds of levers and wheels and circuit boards and generators. There was a big, brick-red blob in the middle of the room. Wires stuck out of it.

"Oh, god."

This time, I actually was sick.

My vision went, and hearing went, and everything buzzed, and I hurled on the floor. Kaleidoscope eyes, bang bang bang, it's happening, it's HAPPENING-

"Oh my god," I said. "No, Zig. No. Don't."

"Semtex," he went on, and now there was a glint of glee in his pupil. "Enough to- to blow this place to the ground-"

"What's fucking wrong with you," drops of stomach acid burned my lips. "What's wrong with you?"

"Because it needs to come down. All of it," he heightened, blood rushing blue and green and white through the dark matter behind his eyes, "You and all of this- shit- that comes with it, all this money, all this destruction. It started because of YOU."

And he raised his head, possessed.

I knew where my demon had gone now.

"You- ruined me- you changed everything- and you fucking did it for money,"

He took a step forward, and another.

"You just took, and took and took, and it was all for you."

"No, Zig-"

"You used me for your own needs, to do your dirty work, you wrapped up your fucking toxicity as romance and poisoned me with it, you- you made me touch you, when you wanted me to, you made me want to do anything for you… you manipulated me-"

His hand, shaking like a leaf, went inside his vest. When it came out, it had a knife.

"I'll never fucking unsee the things I've seen," he sobbed, "All the pain, all the damage, hanging over my head- I was wanted for you, and all you had to do was tell the truth, you pinned it on me, you blackmailed me with it, and now I'm fucking ruined-"

The knife quivered, but his arm was tense.

"Ziggy, just listen to me-"

His arm danced, his eyes wide, in joy and agony.

His elbow pulled back to deliver the blow.

But the wound did not come.

"*NO.*"

The voice was not mine.

It was deep, authoritarian, southern.

Familiar.

We froze, knowing damn well who it was.

When the bottle green suit, brogues, and Captain-America jaw loomed from the shadows, I retched again.

"You- you've really got very theatrical timing, Rob." I gasped for air. "I've always thought that."

He smirked. He smirks a lot in this book, doesn't he?

Still writing this down?

"Come here, Zygfryd," he crooned.

Zig did not look round.

"Zygfryd. Come on. Come here."

Like a dog, he slunk to his master. Rob kissed him on the mouth, his eyes open, leering at me over one shoulder. Then he stepped toward me, leaving his new lover cowering in the shadows.

"Well done on getting him down here." Rob's tone was business as usual. "Well done on getting this evil to where we want him."

Ziggy still stared at the ground, lost in his mind.

"You know," he stared down at my hunch, the shadows of his eyes devilish, "it was you who started all this. Your obsession with... fire, and power, destruction. Well, well. It's come full circle, hasn't it?"

"Oh, Jesus Christ," I gagged. "Spare me the bullshit, Rob, what the hell is this, a Michael Bay movie? You've done your dramatic entrance, a fucking soliloquy, you've got an explosion on the way- what's next, guns? Helicopters, fucking rocket launchers?"

I staggered to my feet. My head hurt, it hurt, it hurt.

"Megalomania doesn't suit you, you fuck," I growled. "What- what the hell's this about, Rob?"

"Because, the fires have to stop," he said curtly. "People are beginning to conspire about these things. Police are starting to get intrusive. When they see the sole perpetrator as some crackpot kamizake who blows up one of the most powerful firms in the world- with nothing to gain- it goes under. The case is closed."

"Thanks for the exposition," I spat. "The audience will love that one. Won't you?"

"What- who are you talking to? Hey, Zygfryd, he's talking to himself, did you know he talks to himself?"

Zig was shaking, holding his head with one hand, some hollow look on his eyes. He stared upwards through the roof, past London into the sky, looking for a reason, looking for a saviour. He'd gone.

Rob took one more step forward.

"There can only be one number one," he whispered malevolently. *"There can only be one."*

There was a knuckleduster on his hand.

I didn't expect him to strike me. I never thought he was the type, little Rob, to hit. I thought he'd let his minions do that. But he did strike me, hard, in the temple.

My head spun like a Tony Hawk trick, smelling vodka and bile, my head going into overdrive, my evil self was in the ceiling like a big spider, and the room smelt so sweet it was foul, apple and fucking honey and dribble...

"LeTs GoO," Some warbled, phased conversation was happening near me but I couldn't focus, I was hurt, disorientated, angry... oh, god, I was so angry...

"Let's go, now." I heard him say.

Zig was a ghost. He glowed white, tiny, paper-thin, biro drawing on his eyes as spirals, he was hurt and empty and cold, the scribbles on his hands grew more manic, he had nine fingers, and one knife, one knife, he grew whiter and whiter-

"Let's go, now." Rob, pastel green, thick and lump, dominated my vision. I was so sick, so unwell, so angry, so powerless-

Zig had a parasite growing in him. A big blob of ink. It grew bigger and bigger. His eyes, still a thick scrawl of a squiggle, stared into the distance, he was unresponsive. The knife, stop start in its animation, remained at his side.

"Let's go, now," Rob's tone grew purple and spiked. It brushed Zig, it painted his face a colour he hated.

He doesn't like that. How he doesn't like that.

A scratch and a scream and a tidal wave of red and a scream and a scream and pain, sweet saccharine pain, I'm a human, please, no-

Rob was screaming and gurgling. I didn't know how long he'd been screaming and gurgling for. He was on the floor, writhing, grabbing his neck. Blood covered the floor.

Ziggy remained as paper. His inked eyes stared now at the body.

"Oh," he crinkled, folding into origami, slicing through the air back and forth as he fell. "Oh."

Rob writhed; his pristine suit covered in rainbow blood. He sounded like he was fucking gargling mouthwash.

I moved from the spreading pile of red glitter, backing up against the walls, avoiding it like it was lava-

"Shit," he said quietly. "Shit. I wasn't supposed to do that."

He collapsed to the floor, the blood starting to seep into his trouser leg. Rob had stopped moving.

"Ziggy," I said again. "Ziggy. We need to go. Now."

"I can't," he said, simply. "I can't move."

A whirr came from Rob's corpse. Then another, then another. It emanated from his jacket pocket. There was a light coming from in there.

No, said brain. Enough is enough. Go.

But already my feet were splashing through the blood, my arm outstretched to the pocket. I removed the phone, I looked at the name on the screen. The blood was absorbed into me, all that bile, all that fury. I answered, saying nothing.

"Is it done?" the voice was cool, female, tempered.

I said nothing. Keep quiet, said brain. Enough is enough. Go.

"Is it done?" the voice came again. "I haven't seen anything. I thought there'd be a little smoke."

I said nothing. Enough is enough. Go.

"Well? Is it done?"

"Come down," I spat, "and see for yourself."

A long pause.

Then, a sigh.

"Well," Lola Pink said, "You'd better come up here, then."

Seventeen

Zig huddled, in a ball, on the floor. The knife stayed on the ground. He made a slurred exclamation, his intent to follow. He still looked wrong.

We left bloodstained footprints, as we emerged in the main foyer of Ultima Capital. The streetlights shone in on it, painting them black. And we approached the elevator.

I clocked the desk, again. About a month, maybe, since I'd been here with Rob. The receptionist was depressed. I hope she found her way in life; I really did. It does no good, to be telling yourself all that nonsense about how you're not good enough.

I thought about her for a second.

And one month on from then, Rob was dead, and Lola Pink had plotted to kill me.

In such painfully typical finale fashion, we stepped into the elevator, and pressed floor 48, the very top floor, the director's suite, where we'd met Lola for the first time. The doors clicked shut, and the elevator began to move.

It was floor 18 before I began to speak.

"Did you love him?"

I'd been thinking it since floor 2 and a half, to be fair.

Ziggy was still some kind of paper derivative. He wobbled in the aircon.

"Did you love him, Ziggy?"

He took a breath.

"I do this thing," he said softly, "Where I misconstrue basic fucking human kindness as love."

I looked at him. His cardboard strengthened, reinforced a little.

He turned and looked at me now, not with squiggles. But with his own terrified human eyes.

"I won't be doing that again," he said, firmly, wide-pupilled meaning in his stoic face. "I definitely, definitely won't be doing that again."

We hit floor 48 and the doors slid open. The sound of voices hushed suddenly as we entered. I walked the plush navy carpet, looked up at the segmented glass ceiling.

I had a feeling we might die tonight.

Before we turned the corner into the main room we halted.

"Listen." I kept my voice soft and serious. "You don't have to come with me. Just stay here."

He looked at me again, calm, potent. "I'll wait."

"Chop, chop," her voice trilled from around the corner, high and cold. "Stop the whisper-whisper. We want to see you."

We exchanged one last long look. There was no love there, anymore, just shadows, ruins.

On the huge, semi-circular sofa facing us, sat Lola Pink and Wrighty.

Wrighty clutched the crossbow. Lola had snake eyes, holding her phone in a tentacle.

He looked tired. She had blood in her vision.

"Evening," Lola said. "Come and take a seat." She went back to the receiver. "Honestly, darling, it's the nicest place, walls lined up with Quartz, and the food is just exceptional, you've never tasted anything like it."

"Well," I said, as loudly and drily and theatrically as I could manage. "What a plot twist."

"They use this romano cheese, it just melts in your mouth, and the caviar is so salty, and just plays beautifully with it…"

I cleared my throat again. "Well," I increased the volume. "Quelle fucking surprise, eh?"

"And gosh, the waiter, what a handsome man! A real man's man, you know-"

"OI," I cracked. "What- what the fuck are you-"

"Oh simmer down, kettle," Lola said. "We're talking about Gino's on 12th."

My jaw open like a barn door, I averted my gaze; Wrighty was looking at me. Shivering. His eyes were all- weird, I can't describe it. They scanned around, independently, like a chameleon.

"What-" I lowered my voice. "What are you doing here?"

His gaze could not focus. Green alien eyes darted around, sleep-deprived, mad.

"I just fuckin' love it, don't I," his smile turned sharp. "Just can't stop it."

He glared at the fake fireplace over to the side. It danced in his empty eyes.

"You- it was you?"

Colour me surprised.

"You- tried to kill me, in Guisborough? You-"

I resisted the urge to retch again.

"You killed my stepdad?"

His eyes lolled in his head. "Shit. I haven't slept in fucking weeks," he said. "Yeah. To, erm. Both of those things."

He took the next *why* from me.

"That fire fucked me up," he whispered under Lola's din. "When- after that night. I just started seeing shapes. Like, everything became shapes, when I got stressed. I felt like I wasn't there anymore. But- fire, it's so hot, and- it *dances*-" he grinned again. "Like- when you start the fire, you feel like you're there- really there." He looked at me. In the emptiness there was anger, sorrow. His eyes pleaded. "And fires- they control everything." His speech slowed, slurred. His features swam his face, Picasso style.

"The fire, controlled me," he said again. "It can control everything. I can control everything. If I start the fire."

He pulled the crossbow onto his lap. I took a step back.

"I'm a big boy, now, Perce," he turned reptile, eyes aglow with yellow streaks. "And they said- they said, it was you, who tried to hurt me, you were trying to fuck me over, so you could win, you made this all start, that fucking night where we walked home-" his voice rose and rose- "That was when it started, that was when I started seeing the shapes, I wouldn't be so FUCKED UP if it wasn't for YOU-"

Now Lola turned.

"Tom," Lola said simply. "Where's Rob?"

I gulped. "Dead."

"Wow. Jesus. He did say, he was going to kill you-"

"Listen-" my headache got so worse it nearly split. "Can you please tell me what the fuck is going on before my head explodes, or I have an episode? I feel like I'm about to wake up from a dream-"

Wrighty and Lola exchanged a glance.

"What are you talking about, Tom?" Olyvia said. "This is a pretty necessary set of events. You've been conducting illicit activities. People are dead because of you. You need to be apprehended, and that's exactly what we're about to do." There was some smug smile on her face.

"But- if you knew it was me- why didn't you- argh-"

I was overheating, I was hyperventilating.

"Yeah, not going to lie, Tom," Lola giggled, spilling her drink a bit. "You've made a lot of money for me, in the long run. You chaps played a damn good game, getting every building proprietor in London scared, building insurance at a skyrocketing premium- do you know, how many firms Ultima owns? Jesus, Tom. You thought you were a big wheel, didn't you? Trying to scare me into fucking bending to your will. For every pound you've made in this, I've made a tenner. So thanks, Tom. For doing my dirty work. And thank *you,* Mr Wright, for volunteering to help! Hoorah!"

Wrighty said nothing. He glowed with shame.

"I'll fucking go and do it now," I frothed. "I'll go and do all that Semtex now."

Their polite giggles turned to smiles of sympathy.

"Well, you should have the IED, Tom," Lola said sweetly. "Rob had it. Pop downstairs and find it, give it a shot, why don't you. I mean, it's unlikely you'll get there. There's a police presence round the building. Has been since you went in the fire door at the side." She sipped her drink. "Just be a dear and play along, though, won't you?"

"Fuck you," I breathed. "You can't keep me here."

But as I turned to leave, there was a click. Wrighty had loaded his crossbow.

"Of course, John here isn't best pleased with you," she went on. "And I've said to him, it makes no odds to us if you're caused a little pain. Plans can be so cruel, sometimes, eh, Tom? And remember, it's *you* who started all of this. If you hadn't played your little game, not one of us would be here now."

I engaged Wrighty in eye contact. "No, man, *no,*" I whispered quietly, urgently. My head whirred for a plan, but it was futile. I was done.

"I know what you're thinking," Wrighty slurred. "Why you? Why have we trapped you? Well," red erupted in his bloodshot eyes, "What about *me*? You think I fucking wanted to start those fires? To blow up Rob's car? That's not- me, I'm the fucking *ultimate*, man…" his eyes rolled, then focused in on me again. "But you- you made me burn, you made me hurt, for stupid reasons. And the burns never go away, they're there fucking day and night in your head… you broke me," he said again. "You deserve every fucking thing that comes your way-"

But then he stopped. His eyes looked through me, now. Right to the back of the room.

Zig had peered round the corner. So innocent, like a child, he looked around, baby blue eyes scanning the room, wondering what was going on.

I turned back to Wrighty.

"No, Wrighty, please,"

Everything went black and red and dancey again, a marble abyss-

"Wrighty," I said weakly. "I killed Rob, it wasn't him. I set you on fire, that night, Wrighty, it was me, I set you on fucking fire!"

His eyes did not avert.

"Okay," he said simply, and pulled the trigger.

Eighteen

The arrow went slowly-slowly.

I looked at Ziggy before he died. He was nice to look at, after all.

"Can I keep this?" I said, very softly. The man looked at the money. I could see his face a little better now, soft and kind besides the scars, young looking, dark eyebrows and thick hair and stubble and crazy bright blue eyes. I felt a little nervous. He was handsome.

I remembered telling him to run.

I remembered him walking God-style over the tightrope.

I remembered the week he'd stayed at mine. His stink and the sex and all the rest of it.

I remembered him hiding, running. From the world I'd created.

I remembered him leaving.

And my heart pounding when he touched me on the shoulder, again, a few hours ago.

Then the arrow hit him.

Square in the chest, in the very centre of his torso. He looked surprised, but oh, oh, God, his eyes.

They scarcely reacted to the magnitude of force that'd just hit him.

He just…accepted it.

The arrow's force threw him back to the wall like a ragdoll, some PlayStation like physics throwing his limp limbs here and there and round and everywhere. He wasn't-

Oh, god.

He wasn't a person, now. He was a body.

Bodies don't have souls.

Oh, god, no-

My eyes splintering and my ears shattering and my hands fractured and done, I welped, hitting the deck, dead and done.

And his eyes, his stupid fucking beautiful baby blue eyes, they just looked and looked, not an ounce of understanding in there. He didn't even look sad, just curious-

I remembered how I'd waited in that fucking golf buggy boot, sweating, dying, the thought of him keeping me going.

"Ziggy, fuck, no-" I tried to find eye contact with him, one last time, just to keep a tiny pebble of his soul with me, until mine left this earth-

I remembered looking at him, Rob's car burning, him stood in the kitchen all cool and coy.

"No-"

I remembered his eyes downturned after I got back from work that night,

"NO-"

I remembered what he said. "I'm not really into this."

"NO-"

I remembered everything in that second.

"Oh, FUCK-"

He was really bleeding now, so much of it, spreading over his white shirt and seeping into a murk on his black vest. His eyes still darted around, like a kid, not knowing what was going on. His soul was slipping towards the exit sign. I writhed and writhed on the floor, torn up.

"What the fuck are you doing?" Lola shrieked behind me. "You don't-you don't just shoot someone for no reason, John, what the fuck are you thinking?"

The room was raucous, but I couldn't hear it for the life of me. I pulled my head close, smelling him, I bit his shoulder as the tears welled up and in, desperately trying to look for that last moment of connection and contact with him- one last time, please…

"Fuck him," Wrighty was saying, that god-tone seeping into his maniacal voice again. "He's just a pikey."

His eyes were lolling around. His brain was ceasing to work. Oh, no, please, look at me, please look at me, please look at me, please-

"Please, please please," I muttered, the shadow of my own weird head casting dark over his face. "Pleasepleaseplease."

His breath was warm on my nose, his scars rough under my thumbs. But he would not look.

"You do realise," something was saying behind me, "How much you've jeopardised every single fucking part of this?"

"I don't give a fuck," Wrighty was squalling. "I don't give a fuck-"

He would not look, he would not look.

I remembered his eyes. I'd have to. He would not look.

And then he did look.

His eyes centred on mine. And there was something. Some old affection, some warmth, some recognition. Something. And though it wasn't mine, it was there.

I remembered when he'd fallen asleep at mine, the first time.

I was laid next to him, watching him sleep, his black hair tousled, his scars dimmed. He breathed through his mouth, slowly, deeply. All content and quiet, spooning the pillow, dribbling on it slightly. Radiating heat, and the smell of smoke.

I sat and just looked at him, him looking at me, my mind completely switched off.

He gurgled a little bit.

"In my pocket," he said. "Look in my pocket."

His eyes shut for a while, and my body felt cold and heavy and I thought I'd lost him. But then he opened them for a second, and he smiled a bit.

"Best things in life are bad for you," he said.

And then he was gone. His eyes stared off into space. Nothing. Nothing. Nothing there anymore.

No body, no more, no body, no more-

"Just fucking take care of it," I heard in the back of the room. "Just fucking take care of it, now."

I snapped back. This was my moment of tension. I had to use the nervous energy.

I checked his pocket and pulled out his phone. It was attached to something.

A circuit board covered the front. An ominous black package on the back, gaffa taped on. The IED.

The phone was on. It just needed an impulse.

"John." The voices over my shoulder grew more insistent. "Take care of it. Now."

I was running out of time. My shirt was covered in claret. It ran all over the floor.

I took one last look at Zig, whose life I'd ruined, and ended.

I took one last look at my hands, the doers of the devil.

I shut my eyes one last time, the eyes that had led me astray.

I remembered being sat on that damn windowsill, night after night, playing with fire.

And then I picked up the IED and threw it into the middle of the room, where the triage of destruction was. Wrighty, Lola, me. They looked surprised.

But I was already dialling Ziggy's number. For the very last time.

I heard the phone vibrate and squeezed my eyes shut.

There was a crack, a blinding white light.

And then nothing at all.

ACT FOUR- DISSIPATION

Epilogue

Have you ever lit a match?

I used to play a game as a kid. I don't play that game anymore.

I still light matches, though.

I rake the match down the strike paper, listening to the hiss of the head igniting, watching the smoke billowing out of the end like a head of steam. I watch as the red melted away into grey patches, leaving tiny drops of liquid before they turned into smoke, and the flame-within-flame effect of the different layers of heat dancing with each other.

Then I reach my hand out, the tiny deathbringer in between my thumb and forefinger. I touch the fatal dancer to a wick. It grows for a moment, then falters, passing on its energy, steady, purposeful.

Then I do it again. And again. And again.

Until the whole chapel is lit.

Some of the candles are scented. One is red. That one's pomegranate. Another one is cream, rather than standard white. That one's clean cotton. They're all so pretty. They light up the chapel in the December dark. The floor is cold laminate to prevent any danger. My feet, in my old man slippers, are warm.

The behemoth of crackling light warms me up. It's cold in here. It makes it hard to meditate. But that's the point- accept your surroundings, accept your discomfort. Sit with it. Sit through the feelings. If only I'd been better at this, sooner.

HMP Holme House was not a pretty place, it was not a nice place. My cell was damp and dirty, my clothes were itchy. The people there got into postcode wars, drug wars. The politics of power and intimidation were there. Not so different from the outside world.

I also would be unable to leave for at least the next fifteen years. But the imprisonment was mandatory, rather than self-sustained. This, somehow, made it better.

"They look nice," a voice from the seats. It's Bill- he's on the rehabilitation ward with me. We go to the same, one-size-fits-all classes to deal with our anger issues, our drug problems, our supposed oppositional-defiant behavioural disorders. We have the same psychologist. She's called Hazel. I'd never had a psychologist before.

"Yeah, the way you've, like, arranged 'em an' tha'. Nice, that." Bill's an older fella, from Middlesbrough, same as me. He's a fraudster. Six years, they gave him. He seems nice.

"Thanks," I said. "Yeah. They do look nice."

We sit down, in our group, and meditate. I pick the scruffy mat- it's the comfiest. I focus on the ground pushing up against me, and my breath within my ribcage. Sometimes, I remember what I thought Ziggy's eyes looked like. Or the pain in the hospital for months afterwards. Or my father's tears in court. But then I bring my attention back to the breath.

I had plead guilty to two counts of arson, one count of attempted arson, three counts of attempted murder, one count of grievous bodily harm with intent, four counts of aiding and abetting, ten counts of obstruction of justice, fourteen counts of fraud, one count of breaches of sections 2, 3, and 4 of the 1883 explosives act. One count of false impersonation, two counts of breaking and entering.

I plead not guilty to one count of murder. But I was found guilty.

The judge had sentenced me to a life sentence behind bars, of which I would serve at least fifteen before serving the rest on licence. I'd be almost forty before I got out, Jesus. But that's not to say I don't deserve it.

Almost forty, fuck. That's…awful.

Back to the breath, back to the breath.

We sit in silence, meditating, for about 20 minutes. No one breaks. I was amongst burglars, thugs, drug dealers, gang leaders. They were just trying to find some quiet.

Back to the breath, back to the breath.

Then the chime sounds, and our leader brings the session to a close.

The wing is boring. I have no one to talk to, really. I knew better than to try and fit in with a gang. It was folly. The last time I'd tried to fit in, I'd set someone on fire, which had led to some awful sequence of events that led to me here.

But it's OK, because in about fifteen minutes, I get my visit. I'm looking forward to my visit.

When the guard calls my name, I'm led out, through the dimly lit corridors, out into the open. A maze of huge iron gates and barbed wire and dogs and ugly red brick buildings. The guard doesn't talk to me. He unlocks and locks every door we go through diligently. I am handcuffed, despite being a low-low risk prisoner.

Eventually, we get to the visitors' suite, and I join a line of fellow inmates as we go through the metal detector and are searched. Nobody talks.

"Name?" the guard asks me.

"Thomas Percey."

"Number?"

"HHKJ3292C"

"Search, please."

They check my arms and legs and pockets and torso. They grope between my legs. They shine a torch in my mouth. They ask to look inside my shoes and look under the soles and behind the tongue.

"Straight through, please. Table G12."

I walk through to the visitor suite. Tables are laid out, with one prisoner on one side and their partner on the other. A lot of kids are in here, and some of them are on their father's shoulders, or showing him pictures they'd drawn of them. Some are only here to bring their dad drugs. But hey. Nothing to do with me.

I take my seat at G12. It's a big sports hall-type room, echoey and cool. The floor and walls are a hard green. The windows are frosted. I watch the red door and wait for my Dad to get here.

There are newspapers on the table. I have a flick through, but nothing pressing, Something about a coronavirus, a potential lockdown. Ah, well. I'm already locked down.

Eventually, the red door opens, and Dad walks through, escorted by a guard. He hurriedly picks his way through the mess of tables to me.

"Hello, son." He's overcome with emotion. Poor old Dad. Having to see his prodigal son all locked up.

"Alright, Dad. You're looking trim."

"Oh, this? Yeah, the doctor said I had to go on walks and stuff. And no more parmos."

I suspected the tears in his eyes were at least partly due to that.

"No more parmos? Wow. How on earth will you cope?"

"Well, they do this healthy parmo at this- bloomin- vegan café in town. All soy and oats and all that shite. I'm making do with that."

"Is it nice?"

"Erm, nah, not really. But there's only about ten gram of fat in it. I think the parmo sandwich used to have about four hundred and fifty."

"Well. Good for you."

We shared a moment of awkward silence.

"So," he said. "How's it all going, anyway?"

How's it *all* going. A lot to answer there. I took a breath.

"Yeah, it's alright. I go to my Buddhist thing on a morning and do meditations and stuff. Then I go and help in the education department. It's fine. How are you?"

"Good," he looked down, a sense of relief. "Erm. Yeah, just ticking over. Your mum called, the other day. I'm going to go down and see her, catch up and whatnot. She's very upset."

"Understandably."

Wrighty and Lola had all survived the blast somehow. I'd heard Lola had sold countless assets to pay for their bail after their arrest and investigation. She, however, had still yet to be sentenced.

But Wrighty, well. He wouldn't do well in jail, I feared. But hey. None of my concern.

"So, like," Dad struggled with his words. "Did you- did you do all that stuff?"

"Yes," I said simply. "I did."

"Why?"

"I don't know."

We let that hang in the air for a minute.

"I think," I chose my words carefully. "I think- I felt like I was cursed, or something. I hated everyone, everything. I hated me. I was completely out of control. And then- well. I found a way to create control. So I seized on it."

He looked puffy-eyed again.

"I'm working on it, Dad," I said truthfully. "I want to try. I want to leave all that behind, for good. I swear down, Dad, I don't want to be like that anymore."

He still looked puffy eyed but nodded.

"And...and what about..."

He was tense. A taboo was about to be breached. But he needed closure.

"And what about…Ziggy, do you call him? The lad who you kept talking about in court?"

Static filled my ears once more and my hearing went. I felt very sick in that moment, very confused. But I pulled my attention back to my surroundings.

"Well, I don't really know."

"You don't know what?"

I took a heavy breath, laden with spent fight.

"I don't know if he even existed, Dad."

He laughed, though his eyes were affixed to the table. "What do you mean, you don't know if he existed?"

"As in-" I felt tears prick at my eyes again. "As in, there is no evidence of him ever existing."

I had blamed Ziggy for the murder of Rob. But by every accountable piece of evidence, there was no record of anyone but me entering the building. There was only my fingerprints on the knife found in Rob's body. And only his body was recovered from the scene of the crime. CCTV footage had shown me pacing tersely outside the building, talking to myself.

And as I recounted the entire story- about how he'd scaled a telephone wire to reach my apartment, about how we'd shot flaming arrows from a building, about the existential conversations we'd had. I'd realised how ridiculous it sounded.

"But it all felt so real, Dad," I found myself saying. "It all felt really, really real, every second of it. But I don't know if it was. I don't know if he was ever there, or if he was there some of the time, or what. I'm unwell, Dad," I said simply. "I'm really unwell. I have been for a while. I guess I just hid it very well."

We talked more, about healthy parmos, healthy chips, and TV. It was nice. He told me they'd opened a part of the steelworks again, and that he was going to try for a job.

"That's good," I said. "You liked it there."

"Aye, I did, aye. But when I told Sainsbury's I was leaving, they said they'd promote me again. Store manager. I don't know what to do."

"Fuck Sainsbury's," I said simply. "You hate it there."

He thought again. "Well, that's true," he said.

He asked me about the day to day life in jail, and I told him of the 'distraction books' and the maths lessons I helped with, and the weird staff, and the food, and the itchy beds and the weird people. But I told him I didn't mind it, not really. I told him I was going to be OK.

"You sure about that, son?"

"Yeah. Positive."

I was sure of myself this time.

The hour came and went, and Dad had to leave. He looked sad, and I felt bad for him, going back to that lonely house. But hey, he probably felt bad for me and all.

A few of the lads came up to me when I got back to the wing.

"Tom, mush," one of them- a big lad called Mitty- shouted over. "Mush. Can you help with food, mush? Jetmir's sick."

"Yeah. No worries."

I followed them into the kitchen.

"Do us a favour, yeah?" the kitchen was hot. There were gas hobs everywhere. I felt an itch.

"Chop these onions and celery up, yeah. Fry them in a bit of vegetable oil. Give us a shout when you've done that."

"Okay."

I chopped them up into uniform pieces, drizzled oil in the pan, and then stopped myself.

I could- do something here. Haha.

The itch turned into an ache again.

It wouldn't be hard to just whack on the gas and then leave.

Create some trouble. Control the situation. Establish danger, power.

I turned on the gas, just to test it. It hissed.

"The ignition's, er, not working," I heard myself say, as the colours intensified. "Who's got a match?"

The sound became apocalyptic as the tinnitus worsened, I became... high, again, hahaha- time's weird, right? It just, like, keeps going- I could stop it-

"Here you go," Mitty said. "Bastard thing. Constantly playing up."

I twisted the gas on again and took a match out. Ahh.

I raked the match down the strike paper, listened to the hiss of the head igniting, watched the smoke billowing out of the end like a head of steam. I watched, fascinated, as the red melted away into grey patches, leaving tiny drops of liquid before they turned into smoke, and the flame-within-flame effect of the different layers of heat dancing with each other.

And then I lit the ring, a shockwave of heat next to my hand as it ignited. It burned away steady and hot and constant.

I shook the match til the flame disappeared, and its purpose was black and charred and old and dead, and then ran cold water over it, too, to make damn sure the fire had gone out. And then I threw that match in the bin.

I put the pan of celery and onions on the top. It sizzled. It smelt good.

"You want to stick some salt in that?" came a voice from behind me.

The voice was familiar. When I turned to find who had spoken, I saw a skinny, unkempt man, with scars on his face.

END

Acknowledgements

This book started as a bit of a curiosity project. I'd thought about writing for years and years, but lacked the tenacity to do anything about it. And it seemed so elite and unreachable and beautiful that I just never gave it a go.

So I guess my first thank you goes out to Newcastle's *Writers in the Evening* group for at least giving me the push I needed to do it. I joined as someone who didn't have a clue how to write (and I arguably still don't) but you guys really did help me on the way. Thanks for the advice, and the Zoom coffees.

Second, my awesome Mum and Dad, who helped me out when times got very hard, and who amply feigned interest as I told them I had decided to write a book. They've been unconditionally supportive of their weird and vacuous son throughout this horrible time and I am forever thankful to them. I am actually writing this in my parents spare room, which I guess is my 'creative office' until COVID fucks off and life goes back to normal.

My sister, for the encouragement to keep going, and for the endless supply of high quality memes.

My mates for beer and good times and pretending to read the drafts I sent them. Molto bene.

The residents of 6 The Mill, where I wrote the majority of this book, and who had to deal with the odd temper tantrum and moments of alcoholism. And for being my lockdown familia- thankyou for being lovely.

Sminer33, simodarkthill, for the copyediting and proofreading and pointing out the obvious plot holes.

Daniel Morgan for the awesome cover design, top bloke, thanks man.

And lastly YOU, the reader, well done on making it to the end! Assuming you didn't just skip all the way to the last page. If you did, tut tut tut.

Thanks for picking this up and giving it a go, means a lot.

Printed in Great Britain
by Amazon

55709101R00147